Henry Sutton was born in Norfolk in 1963. He is a journalist and travel writer and the author of four previous novels, *Gorleston*, *Bank Holiday Monday*, *The Househunter*, and *Flying*. In 2002 he won an Arts Council of England Writers' Award. He lives in South London.

Praise for *Kids' Stuff*

'...this intense tale explores family dysfunction and history's nasty habit of repeating itself' *Daily Mirror*

'It is Sutton's greatest achievement here that his narrative keeps us interested in the fate of such a profoundly unpleasant man. This fascination may be unhealthy, even upsetting, but it is expertly managed by acutely observed dialogue and almost forensic description... Countless writers, sociologists and confessional television shows mostly fail to help us to a better understanding of how people can do unspeakable things to each other. Henry Sutton succeeds without even posing the question' *Times Literary Supplement*

'Henry Sutton has taken us into one man's Hell and made it seem frighteningly real' *Sunday Telegraph*

'The points which Sutton wants to convey about modern masculinity seem to benefit from the complete awfulness of the person putting them into practice... *Kids' Stuff* succeeds... through the sheer vigour of its conception' *Guardian*

Kids' Stuff

Henry Sutton

A complete catalogue record for this book can be obtained
from the British Library on request

The right of Henry Sutton to be identified as the author of
this work has been asserted by him in accordance with the
Copyright, Designs and Patents Act 1988

Copyright © 2004 by Henry Sutton

The characters and events in this book are fictitious. Any
similarity to real persons, dead or alive, is coincidental and
not intended by the author.

First published in 2004 by Serpent's Tail
4 Blackstock Mews, London N4 2BT
website: www.serpentstail.com

First published in this 5-star edition in 2005

Printed by Mackays of Chatham, plc

10 9 8 7 6 5 4 3 2 1

APRIL

Words don't come easily to Mark when he's in shock. They don't come easily to him at the best of times. He can read, but doesn't. He's into practical things. Making stuff and repairing stuff, and sometimes taking stuff to bits as well – in his world not everything has to be put back together correctly. Salvage is an important part of what he does, but words definitely aren't. So when Nicole tells him Kim called he can't think of anything to say. Not a word. He thinks he must look guilty too, because when he's speechless like this people have told him he looks guilty – whether he's done anything wrong or not. Beginning to panic, he walks out of the room, without saying a word to his wife, leaving her to think he doesn't know what. He carries on and walks out of the house, not bothering to slam the door behind him, knowing he's only making himself look even more stupid, and in the wrong, but he couldn't have just sat there incapable of saying anything when things obviously needed to be said. After all this time. His mind is swirling with thoughts and emotions, though he isn't able to slow anything down, or make any connections. He feels completely out of sync. He feels disjointed. His house is on one of the few hills in the city, mid-terrace, halfway up, and when he feels angry or frustrated or lonely, or misunderstood – he's never been one for explaining himself, for sharing his thoughts with other people, however close – he heads uphill, fast, hoping the exertion will take his mind off whatever it is that is troubling him and help him to calm down. Yet when he reaches the top this evening, where his street runs square into another road of similar sized terrace houses, which slope away in either direction, though turning left takes you towards the city centre, and right towards more of the same, he is still deeply shocked, and shaking a little too. And scared. Dead scared.

It is a cool, close, early April night, a Friday night – Mark was looking forward to the weekend – and because he walked straight out of the house he hadn't thought to put on a coat and is only wearing a T-shirt and a thin cotton V-neck sweater, and he's already cold despite the exertion needed to get up the hill. Nevertheless he stands for a while at the top, looking back at his road and the warm, homely light seeping round the rows of curtained and blind-covered bay windows. Only half-consciously is he trying to pick out his house and his bay window, behind which he knows Nicole will be sitting, in the hissing blast of heat their new coal-effect gas fire gives off, annoyed and upset at his behaviour. But she's used to his moods and it isn't as if he hasn't left the house like that before, and standing there becoming colder and damper, trying more consciously to pick out his house, his bay window and dark red front door with half the number missing – the 9, so it just says 3 – searching, from the top of the hill, for his home, he thinks, with sudden, almost warming clarity, an electrical charge like a blast of insight, that this is my life. It is where I belong. With Nicole and Gemma. And although he knows he can be difficult and depressed on occasions, that he has something of a violent temper, he understands enough about himself to realise he doesn't want anything to be different. He is happy. He is happy there with his wife and daughter, in his cosy terrace, halfway up the hill.

Despite not having his coat or his wallet, he realises, despite knowing where he belongs and that he doesn't want anything to be different, he decides to turn left and head for the city centre. He doesn't want to bump into any friends or colleagues, but he needs to be among people, to lose himself in a heaving Friday night crowd for a while. He enjoys the feeling of being in the middle of a scene but not being a part of it. Besides, he doesn't have many mates.

None close. Maybe he has started to cry a little, with the shock, with the anger, the powerlessness, all these things that are swirling about his head in such an uncoordinated, complicated, helpless fashion, because the way into town – past more terraces like his and then streets of bigger semis that appear nearer the city centre, along with pockets of cramped, modern housing developments, rows of scruffy, vandalised shops and the odd garage forecourt – is largely a blur. Normally, he would be extra vigilant, peering into property where possible, checking out window locks, well-concealed front gardens, side accesses, the condition of any fences and trellises. He might take some interest in parked cars as well, and whether anything has been left inside them, like the keys. He's always surprised how many people do that. But it would only have been out of habit. He hasn't stolen anything for a long while, not since he married Nicole, and before then he would never have called himself a professional. It was just part of his upbringing, what went on when he was a teenager.

Everyone he knew was involved in some sort of criminal activity, with joyriding at the very least. He only joined in to make some friends. To stop being called a wuss. As it was he developed quite a skill at being able to get into vehicles, smart ones, the supposedly impenetrable ones – BMWs, Volvos, Jags, Audis. They wouldn't drive them far, only occasionally to the sea or to Yarmouth, or to one of the Broads, and usually they didn't trash them, though a couple did end up in the drink. But, he always likes to remind himself, he was never caught. Plus he never hurt anyone. No one died. It was just harmless fun. Kids' stuff.

2

Mark has a problem admitting to things, especially to himself. Part of him would like to make up something about what he did in the city earlier tonight. How, for instance, he wandered through the Castle Mall, and along pedestrianised London Street, looking at the brightly lit shop windows, many with their night-time security grilles pulled down, and on past the packed bars and wine bars and early queues for the clubs in Tombland and Prince of Wales Road, to the south of the city centre, mingling with the noisy, loose crowds but mentally keeping to himself, to his own confusion. Or, perhaps, how he walked across the city to the river which curls around the Cathedral Close and sat on one of the damp benches overlooking the slow-moving water, gently reflecting the yellow street lamps and the swinging headlights of the cars travelling along the nearby inner ring road. And when there were no cars how he watched this slow-moving water, the sluggish River Wensum, become pitted with rain, because it did start to pour later that night.

But he did none of this. He simply slipped into one of the first bars he came to, a place near the market. He had been there a couple of times before, but it had a completely forgettable name and was just like so many of the other recently renovated pubs in the city, being full of wobbly, soft wood furniture, fake metal counters, and these massive chalk boards – covered with unreadable menus and special offers – placed on the wall behind the bar, where they used to keep the spirits upside down, except the spirits were now lined up on a long table, the right way up, getting in the staff's way, so it seemed to him.

Having side-stepped the bouncer and while elbowing his way through the crush, which at least instantly warmed him and made him feel even more anonymous, and slowly skirting the area set aside for tables and chairs and a couple of sofas – for people to sit on and have a quiet chat, maybe even a romantic chat, he imagined, except people were standing there too, and the music was really pumping so they wouldn't have been able to hear one another – while he was squeezing between the queues for the bar and the people trying to keep their footing by the tables and chairs, and the sofas, he happened to see, and he certainly wasn't looking for anything of the sort, someone's puffa jacket hanging on the back of a chair, with the front of the jacket half-folded back and revealing, indeed for the whole world to see, he reckoned, an inside pocket from which the top of a fat, worn, black leather wallet was poking out. He's sure he wouldn't have taken it had it not been quite so easy and tempting, and had he not been in such a state, and without any money of his own. It even occurred to him at the time that the way it was left there so obviously, the way it was almost waiting for someone to steal it, meant it could have been a trap set by a team of plain-clothed. He knew the police had recently been targeting a number of the more popular city-centre bars.

In the toilet he quickly removed the cash, some £85, then threw the wallet out of the window, using all the strength in his fingers to fling it as far as possible between the security bars – he wasn't going to risk hanging on to the credit cards, or the driving licence, which he could have sold to his well-dodgy mate Darren for decent money.

The fact that he decided to stay in the bar, even knowing someone might have seen something and put two and two together, and having contemplated the idea that it might have been a trap in the first place, made him realise just how confused and distraught he was. He didn't care what happened to him – whether he was arrested and taken off for questioning. Or thumped.

He eventually reached the bar, where he made a space for himself up at the zinc-effect counter and drank one lager and black after another, until he went on to vodka and pineapple, trying to ignore the bar staff, who he was sure were chuckling to themselves about him wanting black in his lager and then pineapple with his vodka (they only had this special Swedish variety), rather than straight up, from the freezer, in a shot glass as everyone else seemed to be drinking it. But he's never been much of a drinker and always needs a sweet mixer to go with his alcohol, whether it's beer or spirits. It was a habit he got into when he was in his early teens and first started going to bars and clubs with the kids he used to do his joyriding with.

Looking around him while he was at the bar, trying to stop his mind from reeling but not doing a very good job at it, reminded him of then, with the people in the bar being so young, especially the girls, who were wearing these tiny skirts, with bare legs and tight sleeveless tops which revealed their bra straps – not that he thought many of them needed bras, though a few did, desperately – and masses of make-up, all this lipstick and blusher and eye-shadow, and with their hair carefully stuck in place – swept to the back, or up, or curled forward – by various accessories, and gels, sprays and mousses, judging by the sheen and the smell. He wondered how old they were. With his mind maybe starting to steady at last, despite, or perhaps because of the alcohol, because he couldn't ignore it any longer, he wondered whether they would have been much older than Lily. He wondered what his daughter, his eldest daughter, looked like now, whether she wore such short skirts and tight tops and too much slap. Presuming she was still alive.

It occurred to him then, in this bar with its fake surfaces and badly made furniture, its unreadable chalk boards, snotty staff and gangs of shrieking, under-age drinkers, that he hadn't asked Nicole why Kim, why Lily's mother and his first wife, had called. What exactly she had said on the phone. What she wanted. How, even, she'd got the number. There was so much he didn't know and so much he didn't want to know.

3

Lily. Where does he begin? He hasn't seen her for over ten years. He hasn't spoken to her for over a decade. There have been no letters, no postcards, no photographs. No contact at all. How could there have been? He had no idea where she was. And then her mother suddenly rings. Her lovely mother. Kim. How he hates that woman.

Not bothering to wait for the latest vodka and pineapple he's just ordered – he doesn't know whether it's his third or fourth – and certainly not making any effort to attract the attention of the barman who's in the process of getting it, begrudgingly, mockingly, or for that matter nodding a friendly goodbye to any of the people he's been pressed against for the last couple of hours – mostly this gang of girls with smelly hair and a few blokes intent on downing more than him – he pushes his way out of the bar, aggressively, with his shoulders back and chest out, and elbows held wide and with a deep, sneering scowl on his face, in fact assuming an attitude he thought he'd forgotten all about expressing, he pushes and shoves and elbows his way clear of the absurd place and into the drizzly night. Having been rendered speechless earlier his head is suddenly stuffed with questions he wants to ask. Questions he would like to ask Lily, whether she's dead or alive. Years and years of them. Starting, he thinks, with simple things like, Where have you been living all this time? Where did you go to school? Who did you play with? Who were your friends? What did you do in the holidays? Before moving on to more tricky areas, such as, Did anyone else look after you as well as your mum – a stepdad, say, or at least someone who called himself that? He imagines there were probably a number of men who assumed that role, and that some of them could easily have abused her.

This thought makes him retch as he's walking, half-jogging, back up London Street, past the bright but secure shop windows, with a terrible stitch and a sharp taste of vodka and pineapple in his mouth, now desperate to speak to Nicole at least. He wants to know everything she knows. What exactly Kim said on the phone. He wants to know whether Lily is still alive, for God's sake.

He realises all these other things he can't stop thinking about also will have to wait. Why, for instance, it is that Lily has never attempted to get in touch with him. Whether she just isn't interested in who her father is, or whether her mother has banned her trying to make contact. He wants to ask Lily if her mother warned her against him. If she told Lily about what he once did to her mother – what he did to Kim on a number of occasions, in truth. He wants to ask his daughter whether she hates him. There are so many questions swirling around his brain he thinks his head might burst.

Having run along most of Avenue Road the pain finally becomes too acute and stops him within sight of his street. Propped against a low brick wall, bent almost double, he throws up on the pavement. Violently. Everything he's drunk that night, and eaten, which includes half of Gemma's tea as well as his own. But it isn't enough. He's not sick enough. He wants to completely empty his body. He wants to be free of all these questions which have been accumulating for years, and slowly, quietly torturing him. Until this moment he had no idea quite how much.

4

All the lights are out except for Gemma's toadstool night light, which is plugged into a socket on the landing. Though just enough of an orange glow from the toadstool manages to reach the short way downstairs for Mark to see where he's going, once he's stumbled through the front door and into the lounge – even if he can't co-ordinate himself very well. He bumps into the coffee table and the side of the settee and Gemma's toy box, the one he made for her third birthday, and swears, not trying to be especially quiet, but not wanting to wake Gemma either. When Gemma wakes in the middle of the night, because of a bad dream, or more commonly because he and Nicole have been shouting at each other, she'll come running out of her bedroom and into theirs, clutching one of her Barbies, or a soft toy – she has hundreds – tearful and hot and wanting to get into their bed with them. Mark then usually moves into her bed and she takes his place next to Nicole, because he can't stand her wriggling and thinks the three of them don't fit comfortably together in the king-size. Not by any measure. Mark made Gemma's bed – as well as the toy box, and her dolls' house and chest of drawers, and her Wendy house, which is quietly rotting away in the back garden – big enough for a full-length mattress, thinking at the time that they could always use it for

Nicole's mum, or other guests, when Gemma would simply have to sleep on the camp bed in their room.

He has told Nicole about Lily, of course, and Kim, plus some of the things that went on between him and his first wife. He's been fairly honest with Nicole about all that from the word go, he reckons. But for ages now, he thinks, while navigating further obstacles in the lounge – Gemma's new bean bag from Habitat, Nicole's fat, man-size briefcase – Lily has barely been mentioned. He, or Nicole for that matter, just never says, I wonder where Lily is. I wonder what she's doing now. Wouldn't it be fantastic to see her.

Climbing the steep, narrow stairs, swallowing bits of bile and other bits, a thought comes to him, stunning him for a moment with its shocking nature, the way it's a sort of an about-turn. Maybe, he thinks, he doesn't want to see Lily, or know anything about her, because he doesn't want to be reminded of all those vacant years – those years he didn't have any control over her. Plus he can't face the prospect of trying to build a new relationship with his eldest daughter. He can't see where she'll fit in with his current set-up – something, he realises, his mind must have been circum-navigating all evening. He wonders whether what he actually wants to hear is that Lily is dead, so that he can clear her from his mind and forget about her properly. So that Nicole and Gemma and him can carry on with their lives just the way they have been. With no shocks or surprises, no dramatic changes. They've got enough going for them as it is, he believes.

'Nicole,' he says, moving into the shadowy stillness of the bedroom, trying to work out whether she's asleep or whether she woke up hearing him come in, or hasn't been asleep at all and was lying there worrying and angry, still annoyed with him for walking out earlier. 'Nicole, it's me,' he says louder. She doesn't say anything back, though he quickly knows she's awake, from the way she's breathing and trying not to move, trying to ignore him. 'Nicole, why don't you fucking well speak to me? I know you're awake,' he says, falling on to the bed face first. Heavily. 'I need to know what Kim said,' he continues, but with his voice muffled by the duvet. 'I'm sorry for walking out earlier, but I was in shock. I couldn't handle it.'

'She said she wants to talk to you,' Nicole says, before turning on to her front, clearly, Mark senses, being careful not to move the tiniest bit closer to him.

'So you spoke to her?' he says. 'She didn't just leave a message on the answerphone?'

'No, I spoke to her,' Nicole said.

'What else did she say?'

'Nothing.'

'So that's all she said, that she wanted to speak to me? That's it?'

'Yes.'

'She must have said something else,' he says. 'I mean, she finally decides to contact us after ten fucking years and however many months it is and that's all she said? That she wants to speak to me?'

'Yes.'

'Are you sure? Are you sure she said absolutely nothing else?'

'What do you want her to have said?' Nicole says, becoming cross. 'It was you she wanted to speak to anyway. She was hardly going to talk to me. Now shut up, Mark, you'll wake Gemma.'

He rolls off the bed and once on the floor he gets to his knees, slowly, desperately, and then his feet, using the bedside table to pull himself up. His limbs have gone all stiff and useless and he feels sick again. And his head is pounding. 'What did she sound like?' he says. 'Friendly, aggressive, upset?'

'Sort of normal,' says Nicole. 'In fact more normal than I thought she'd sound.'

'Normal?' he says. 'She's not normal. She's nowhere near fucking normal.'

'Ssshhh. You'll wake Gemma, if you haven't already.'

Mark starts to take off his clothes, not bothering to fold them neatly, or put them away, but letting them fall into a damp heap on the carpet. Usually he takes great care in looking after his clothes. He doesn't have many any more and they probably aren't the most fashionable items around, at least Nicole is always telling him they are not, but he likes to keep what he has got in decent nick, nevertheless. He feels it's good to respect your belongings, your property. To feel proud of your stuff. However, right now he doesn't know what or who he cares about. Part of him doesn't want to know about Lily, and part of him does. A part he can't seem to shake off, despite that blinding thought which came to him on the stairs about wanting Lily dead.

'She didn't mention money at all?' he says, standing by the bed naked and chilly, and incredibly nauseous, and unable to find his pyjamas.

'No, Mark, she didn't,' says Nicole.

'Lily? Did she say anything about Lily?'

'Nothing. I've told you, she just said she wanted to talk to you. She definitely didn't mention Lily. I'm sorry.'

'I'm going to ring her now,' he says.

But he can't because Nicole then tells him that Kim hasn't left a number, and that she forgot to ask her for one because she wasn't thinking straight, being shocked too, and that she also couldn't do 1471 because her mum rang immediately after she put down the phone to Kim.

Mark nearly punches her but just manages to stop himself by punching the wall instead. Hard enough to dent the wall and make a couple of knuckles bleed, badly, because there's not much flesh there. The blood gets all over the duvet cover and the bottom sheet and some gets on the headboard too. He vows to clean everything up in the morning, before Gemma comes in, but he knows he won't be the one who changes the sheets. It'll be Nicole. She'll sort it out. She always does.

5

Dreams confuse Mark because he doesn't know whether he reads too much into them or not enough. He struggles to interpret their meaning, especially recurring dreams, like this one he's been having for years and which he had again one night shortly after Kim's call.

He's on a boat, which he thinks is somewhere on the Broads because the water is a still, dark green and the banks are lined with thick, leafy trees, all squashed together. 'It's just like the jungle,' he hears a girl's voice say, a voice he instantly recognises as Lily's, even though he hasn't heard Lily's voice for many years, and knows she is not on the boat. He has no idea where the voice is coming from.

Harsh sun is striking the water, making the surface metallic, and as his boat calmly ploughs on the intense light catches the crest of the bow wave, which slowly slides towards the banks, making a shifting, V-shaped crease in the still, flat, shiny surface.

'Where are the dolphins, then?' he hears Lily say next. 'I want to see the dolphins.' Her voice echoes from bank to bank, but rather than recede it becomes louder.

Despite there being no one on his boat, not even Nicole or Gemma, he is definitely not steering or in charge. He's just a passenger, the only passenger, on a day-cruiser which is sliding through the dark, green, metallic water, with the bow creating this perfect V-shaped ripple.

Then he hears Lily's voice again. He hears her laughing, and other people talking and laughing too. Plus the putt-putting of another engine. Soon a boat emerges from the dark brilliance, travelling towards him. It's a very old, beaten-up boat, though everyone on it is laughing and having a good time, and as it nears, Mark tries to spot Lily. There are numerous children, all of different ages, clambering about the decks, but Mark suddenly realises he doesn't know how old Lily is and has no idea how he'll identify her. He keeps hearing her voice, her giggling, but he can't match that with a face, a body.

Neither boat slows and they narrowly pass, the V-shaped ripple becoming very churned up for a while. Yet he still can't pick her out from the loud, scruffy crowd clambering around the rotten decks, and as Lily's boat slips further into the blinding, heat-hazy distance Mark attempts, hopelessly, to turn his boat around and chase after the other boat, the boat with Lily on it. However, there is no steering wheel, no tiller. No throttle or reverse. And of course no captain. He gives up and makes for the back of the boat, finding himself balancing on the stern, ready to dive in and swim after it, despite knowing he wouldn't be able to catch up. He can barely swim.

The dream ends here, leaving Mark on the back of the boat, not able to dive in. Afraid to. Realising there'd be no point.

What particularly troubles Mark about this dream is its terrible sense of reality. And it always makes him wonder whether his and Lily's paths could ever have crossed so closely. Whether there might have been an occasion when he could have plucked her out of a crowd, when he could have retrieved her. Or whether he simply brushed past her in the street one day and didn't recognise her.

Mark and Nicole's kitchen is not very big, nothing in their house is, but Mark's pleased with it, plus the fact that it has hardly worn. He knocked it up out of some plywood, beech and a length of American oak, shortly before Gemma was born. This was when he was still working at the factory and could get hold of the materials. Everyone used to help themselves to off-cuts, and the odd piece of quality timber. The management knew it went on but could hardly say anything, Mark has always thought, given what they paid people. Anyway, he never regarded the small amount of helping himself to this and that as having anything to do with his being made redundant. Despite what Nicole thought. As far as he's concerned he just happened to be working in the wrong part of the factory at the time. Half the machine shop were forced to go. Besides, he heard the other day that the factory is now in danger of closing down completely.

He's been self-employed for a couple of years, building people's shelves and cupboards mostly, though occasionally making kitchens and fancier bits of furniture. Work isn't always abundant and he doesn't even have what he could call a proper workshop – he uses a neighbour's garage, mainly to store equipment, though sometimes for cutting and joining as well – but he feels he's doing all right, especially as he's generally paid in cash and doesn't declare much. And since Gemma started school last September, which she loves, Nicole has been back at the marketing agency full-time, earning a packet. (Nicole's sister Louise has Gemma after school mostly, and in the holidays Nicole's mum helps a bit, as does his mum, though more reluctantly even though she lives closer.) In fact their finances are in such good shape he and Nicole have been talking about going on holiday this summer, which will be their first proper holiday for five years. They are thinking about either Greece or Mallorca, because that's where they've been before – to Greece for their honeymoon, and Mallorca for a fortnight the year they met. This wasn't that long after Kim and Lily and the boys disappeared, and at a time when he was trying to forget about his marriage to Kim, and he supposes, by association, his daughter too. He's always found it strange how easy it is to immerse yourself in a new life. To behave as if so much just hasn't happened.

Mark is contemplating all this – the fact that they've obviously turned some sort of corner – while admiring his handiwork, the bevelled edges and dovetail joints, knowing he always makes a tidy job of things, while Nicole is still dressing Gemma upstairs – he can hear Gemma making a fuss about what tights she wants to wear – while he's sipping a mug of extra-sweet tea, and absolutely dreading the phone ringing. Though also desperately wanting it to ring. But, he thinks, probably wanting it not to ring more. Not wanting it to ring ever again. He wishes he wasn't so hopeless at handling his emotions, at dealing with difficult family situations, at talking about things. When he was with Kim he used to become aggressive very quickly during any confrontation. He could never listen to her, let alone see her point of view, however right or wrong she was. He just doesn't think he had the tools, the education or the sensitivity. Certainly not to deal with someone like Kim.

He doesn't know how long he's been standing in the kitchen for, on his own and now with Gemma still whining about wearing the wrong socks and the wrong dress too and Nicole getting the breakfast things out and making more tea and warming Gemma's milk – she still has it warmed. Waiting and yet not waiting. Wanting but not wanting the silence that he's grown used to.

Feeling totally isolated. He knows he's on his own with this one. That Nicole obviously doesn't have the same feelings about Lily as he does, however confused his are. And that Gemma doesn't even know about Lily. They've never told her she has a half-sister, not when she went through a stage where she begged Nicole and him, but Nicole more, to get her a brother or a sister, 'Please, please, please,' she used to say, because all her friends had them. 'I want a sister, and I want a brother. Whitney has a brother and a sister.' Whitney was her best friend at nursery.

Watching the smears of rain sticking to the kitchen window, he finds his focus slowly being drawn outside, to their mossy concrete patio glistening with damp and Gemma's Wendy house. He worries about it being left out in the wet, something he's always worrying about. Finishing is not one of his specialities. He can make most things, solidly and professionally, but applying any varnish or paint defeats him. His brushwork is a complete mess. This has always surprised him because he loves things to look smart. As it is he tries to sell most of his furniture and cabinets unfinished and at home he lets Nicole do the decorating. Well, he does the preparation, the repairing and filling and sanding, and any construction work, while she deals with the paint. She's good at it, too, being dead smooth, and at picking the colours. He likes that about her. How she isn't afraid to get her hands dirty, and how also she instinctively knows what goes with what. She's practical but she has an artistic side too. Unlike Kim, he thinks – unlike Kim in every way.

Eventually, he gives up waiting to hear from Kim again, and they go out later that morning, at his instigation, and are out most of Sunday too, at Nicole's mum's. Next week he starts a new commission and he knows he's not going to sit around at home waiting for Kim to maybe call. Though he does make sure he's left his mobile number clearly on the new Philips answerphone-cum-cordless he recently acquired from Darren, which is who he gets all his electrical goods off. Notable other recent acquisitions include a thirty-two-inch Panasonic wide-screen digital telly and a Sony mini disc player. Nothing comes with any guarantees or paperwork of course, but he's never had any problems. It all works a treat.

And because Kim doesn't try to ring him again immediately he comes to the conclusion that Lily hasn't died, or has had some awful accident. Kim clearly wasn't ringing to tell him that. Though he thinks he knew Lily wasn't dead anyway. Something inside him – running through every nerve of his body, right along his spinal cord, right to the tips of his fingers – had told him so. Although he might not have been in regular, or for that matter irregular contact with his daughter for the last ten years, he thinks he always felt a sort of telepathic connection to her. That he somehow knew she was breathing at least. He wonders whether she felt the same. Whether she was able to sense whether her dad was OK. Whether he was alive. Whether he was thinking of her, even. Maybe, it begins to occur to him later in the week, while he's making, unusually, a kitchen for a friend of Nicole's, that Kim just wants some money – which he's been half-expecting her to get in touch about for years. He supposes she is entitled to something. Though, of course, Kim has never done anything he's ever expected her to do, being totally irrational, so there's no way he can be at all sure.

As the week progresses and the kitchen takes shape – he's building it *in situ*, out of some MDF and maple veneer, which he thinks looks a lot more expensive than it is, certainly it's much cheaper than he's going to bill Nicole's friend for – he can't stop himself from thinking about Lily, and Kim, and quite how irrational and unpredictable Kim was when he knew her, and probably still is, because he doesn't think people can change that much. He thinks people are just born how they are.

All these bad memories keep popping into his head, so he might be scribing a piece of MDF, or fitting a shelf, or happily planing the maple top one moment, and then the next he'll start shaking, trying to make his mind go blank, endlessly repeating to himself a harmless word or phrase like plane, or maple or Black & Decker, repeating it like a mantra, which was how a doctor once told him he could help himself to calm down. But the more he can't stop remembering Kim and her evil ways the more convinced he becomes that she isn't just after some cash, that there has to be more to it. He has no idea what, however, just as he had no idea, all those years ago, that she'd simply disappear with his daughter. The only thing he does know, the only thing that he's prepared to admit to himself, is that she still terrifies him. What she's capable of.

There's an aspect to Kim and Lily's disappearance that Mark doesn't often like to contemplate because he doesn't know where it'll lead – or how much it'll do his head in. It is the fact that when his wife and daughter (and her two boys from previous relationships) did vanish, at first he was relieved. Overwhelmingly so. Indeed, it wasn't just at first. This feeling of relief lasted a while – maybe it hasn't totally subsided. However, he believes he can justify this sense of relief. After all, when they did disappear in many ways it was the end of a nightmare. The end of months, of years, of lying and fighting, of violent confrontation. Of him never being able to say the right thing. Of him becoming almost totally powerless. When he discovered Kim had left, part of him thought he'd been given another chance, and that he hadn't totally fucked up his life after all. But that didn't mean he wasn't furious with Kim for running off with Lily, for not telling him where she was going. He hates people doing things behind his back, ignoring his authority, defying his existence.

Such was her deception he didn't even have much of an idea about when they actually left. They were separated at the time and he'd been staying at his mum's. Kim hadn't been answering the phone for well over a week, which wasn't entirely surprising, he later realised, as she probably knew it was him calling as stupidly he did often call at roughly the same time – like shortly after the pubs shut – and then the phone went dead.

It wasn't until this happened that he decided he'd have to go to the house, the house he regarded as his, the house he used to share with his family, with his little Lil. He would have gone sooner had he not been banned from going there, or more specifically had there not been an exclusion order on him. This still enrages him. At least, what he'll never understand is how he could have been excluded from seeing his own daughter, this part of him, except that his wife was a more competent liar than him. Except, he reckons, women are more readily believed than men. Except, as he sees it, the system is heavily weighted in their favour.

Of course he cared for Lily. He wouldn't have risked going round there if he hadn't. He remembers it so clearly. It was an early evening in July, still warm and light, with the sun pouring across the road, swarming round the lampposts and hedges and the concrete pillars of the empty chain-link fences, making it hard for him to see clearly – this aching sunlight and shade. So he drove slowly and cautiously down their road, a cul-de-sac, which ended in a sort of narrow crescent rather than a simple dead end, afraid a young child might run out, afraid Lily might run out. Not wanting to draw attention to himself, either. There were times when he used to screech up that road and spin the car around the crescent-shaped end, leaving everyone in little doubt as to who was behind the wheel, even if they'd been watching TV full blast, as most of the residents did, all the time. Though there were a couple of blokes living nearby who drove in a not too dissimilar fashion, and maybe Mark had a bit of a competition going with them – to see who would pull the handbrake last, with their vehicles often careering up on to the pavement, across bits of verge, lawn and flower-bed. But he always won. He had the edge on them when it came to experience. He'd put in the hours.

Lily didn't come running out, and neither did her half-brothers (who were themselves half-brothers) and he drew up a little way past the house, casually getting out and locking his car. He wasn't sure whether the neighbours knew about his exclusion order or not, but they weren't the type to interfere in other people's domestic problems anyway. They knew when to keep their distance. So he wasn't exactly trying to be invisible but neither was he trying to make a show of himself. He was too fired up for that. Too proud.

It is possible he wasn't only going round to check Lily was OK. Knowing himself then, he has since reflected, it's possible he was looking to even things up a bit with Kim. It's also possible, he would like to think, he was planning to take his daughter away from her deceiving, dishonest mother, despite knowing he couldn't have coped with looking after a small child on his own. Still, being concerned about Lily running on to the road and into the path of his car, and perhaps being observed by someone who did know there was an exclusion order on him, he hadn't noticed anything unusual about the house when he'd driven slowly past to park. It wasn't until he was walking up to the front door, on the short, scruffy garden path, with its missing paving slabs so there was just a hard dirt trail embedded with shredded sweet wrappers and old crisp packets, squashed cans and fag ends – he and Kim never looked after the place – that he could see into the lounge and see how glaringly empty it was.

8

It's been a week and a half since Kim's call, including of course another whole weekend when Mark took Nicole and Gemma to the Broadland go-kart track for the day, not far from where he used to live with Kim and Lily, and Kim's boys Sean and Jake. He's still working at Nicole's friend's house, but has moved on to doing some lounge shelves. He often finds that once he starts a particular job, once he's working in a house with all his gear, and there's dust and chippings everywhere, and the smell of scorched wood and PVA, people ask him to do one or two other small jobs as well, possibly something they've been meaning to get around to themselves for ages. Because they've put up with so much disruption, they say, they don't think a little more will make much difference. In Nicole's friend's case it's these alcove shelves, complete with a fitted cupboard underneath, where Lorraine wants to put her TV and ITV Digital box. What might initially be a one-week job can easily stretch to two or three weeks' work. However, Mark always lets the client suggest the extra commissions and never hassles people into giving him more work, unlike a lot of chippies he knows. He doesn't want people to think he's taking advantage of them, especially friends and family.

Ignoring what he's meant to be doing for a moment, which is

fixing a batten to the rear of the alcove, a series of them, ignoring his stuffy surroundings, he wonders how much of their old home, of that whole set-up, Lily might remember herself now. He tries to remember something about his own life when he was three to see how much people remember from that age, but he quickly decides Lily would have been too small to remember much.

They were lucky to get the house, though Kim knew how to work the system, and was always brilliant at screwing more benefit and allowances out of the social services – just as she proved so effective at getting this exclusion order on him. What she did manage to secure, in rapid time too, was a three-bedroom, 1950s ex-council, then housing association semi, in that scruffy cul-de-sac, on the edge of a small town near one of the larger Broads, a few miles from the city. Mark remembers Kim wanted this particular house because it backed on to a field and she thought it would be like living in the country. At the time she had decided she wanted to live right in the middle of nowhere – 'Well away from everyone,' as she used to say – though, typically, this would have been completely impractical of her because she had two young kids and was pregnant with Lily and she couldn't even drive.

She liked to go out at night, too, Mark recalls – she would have hated real isolation. He doesn't think he's ever met anyone who was so into the city bars and clubs, and picking up men – before he started going out with her for sure, he'd been observing her, and he's pretty certain during the time they were married as well. He's more than pretty certain, he had proof.

With his tape measure and pencil to hand he finds himself contemplating what, if anything, Kim has told Lily about the house. Whether she has told her that she had the smallest bedroom, which wasn't much more than a cupboard. Though it was the warmest room in the house, being so small and incorporating the hot-water tank, and also, Mark thinks, Lily did have it to herself whereas Kim's boys had to share. Plus it had carpet and the window looked out over the front garden and the road and the front gardens of the houses opposite, houses just the same as theirs, but mostly with better-kept gardens and front paths. It was a friendlier view than the fields you could see from the back, which Mark regarded as bleak and depressing and endless. And there was nothing like the draught in the front of the house that you got in the back, either. All that wind blowing off the fields. He hated that house. He loathed it. He found it intolerable. But he made sure Lily was as comfortable and secure there as possible. He felt he did his best for her.

9

Lily was an ugly baby, everyone thought so. With her tight little chin and large pointy nose, large for a baby anyway, and tufts of red hair, her green eyes and eczema, her big ears, especially her big ears, people said she looked like a garden gnome. Mark, and Kim, laughed about her appearance too. They made fun of her, plonking her in ridiculous places, putting silly clothes on her, generally encouraging the jokes. Kim's boys weren't too kind either, thinking Mark and their mum meant it. Thinking, Mark understood only too clearly, that their little sister was some kind of a freak. And they laughed with everyone else. They laughed with extra-loud, extra-cruel effort.

Having been largely responsible for instigating the whole gnome thing, Mark then found it hard to change people's perceptions of his daughter, his own included. So for a while Lily became even more gnome-like, even more laughable. He and Kim took photos of her by the duck pond on the way into the town, holding this stick they'd rigged up with a bit of string and a weight to look like a fishing rod – having already stuffed a bobble hat on her head but making sure her ears still stuck out. They thought about sending the snaps to the local paper to try to make some money out of her at least.

Thinking about this now, Mark wonders whether the situation arose because it was the only way he and Kim could relate to each other in a civil, light-hearted manner. That they had this one thing in common they could laugh about, and yet which they could also maintain a distance from. Because this child was so odd-looking, so alien, so unlike them, they clearly couldn't have produced her themselves. She wasn't a product of some passionate coupling, some fantastic session in bed, as that just didn't happen, at least it hadn't for a long while. No. Lily had come from Mars. It was easier to think that way.

Nicole says, almost two weeks to the day after Kim's brief call, when Mark has completely given up thinking he'll be hearing from Kim, for another ten years at least, when, indeed, he thought Nicole and he had stopped talking about Lily again too, when they are in the car, just him and Nicole, on their way to pick up Gemma from swimming, having already been to the supermarket together so the back seat is crammed with the shopping because his tools are in the boot, his second wife says, while they are stuck in crawling rush-hour traffic, 'Who do you think she looks like now? You or her?'

'She never looked like either of us,' Mark quickly says, knowing immediately who Nicole's talking about, before looking out of the side window – his eyes focusing on the lights stretching and distorting in the wet dark, on the shine from the street lamps pooling over the pavements and slipping on to the road, on the people waiting for buses, and those dodging cars, searching for cover, out in the weather, as well as, for a brief moment, a faint, colourless reflection of his face in the misting, rain-splattered glass.

'I always thought she looked like her,' Nicole says. 'From that photo of Lily you once showed me.'

'Just because you thought she didn't look like me?' he says.

'I suppose. But I've never seen her, have I? You've never shown me a picture of Kim.'

'I don't have any. I threw them all away years ago. Everything to do with her. You knew that. What would I want a picture of Kim for?' But as the traffic starts to shift Mark decides that Lily did have a few of his features, what he remembers of her. And he suddenly feels ashamed that he's always convinced himself otherwise, especially after he and Kim had separated. When he obviously didn't need to invent some weird scenario about where she came from. He decides Lily had his chin, which is tight, but strong. She was also getting his slightly hooked nose, though she had more fat on her face than he reckons he's ever had and which helped soften her features. Which stopped her from scowling like him and made her look, really, rather sweet and cuddly. She wasn't funny-looking, no more so than any toddler. Of course she wasn't. She was cherubic, not gnome-like. Though she had Kim's ears all right. And Kim's red hair. But the green eyes were all her own – he has blue-grey eyes and Kim's, if he remembers correctly, were light brown. 'She did take after me,' he says, pulling into the packed swimming pool car park. 'More so than Kim.'

'Oh,' says Nicole. 'I haven't heard you say that before. What's brought this confession on?'

'Just thinking about her. And trying to remember. I've been doing a lot of that recently.'

'Do you think she'll ring again?'

'Who?' Mark says distractedly, trying to find a parking space with a bit of room in it. He hates leaving the car too close to someone else's, especially at the swimming pool, or the supermarket, where there are likely to be a lot of women drivers on the loose. They are forever scratching his car, trying to get into or out of the next-door spot. Or if they manage that manoeuvre successfully, he thinks, they'll fling open their door, or a passenger door for the kids, having no idea how tightly they've parked. Or if they don't do that then they're almost certain to let their supermarket trolley roll against his car while they are loading their shopping because they haven't realised the ground is on the wonk. He always tries to go to the supermarket with Nicole to protect his car. And swimming, of course. And the park. She's as bad as the rest of them.

'Kim,' Nicole says. 'Who else?'

'I don't know. I doubt it,' he says, having found a nice wide spot for the car. 'But you never know with her. Who knows what goes through her mind?'

'Suppose she wants us to have Lily,' Nicole says, flinging open her door, Mark sees, not having checked the clearance first, not having even thought about it, and quickly climbing out, making a big effort not to catch his eye.

'No chance of that,' he says, getting out too. Though as he follows Nicole across the car park, skirting the larger puddles, he starts thinking for the first time whether this could be the case. That maybe Kim has finally decided to let him have Lily. For whatever reason. And that this could also explain why she hasn't rung back, because although she's decided this, and having made one attempt to get hold of him, she's now having second thoughts and can't quite bring herself to pick up the phone again.

'How do you know?' says Nicole, as they reach the sports complex entrance. 'You just said you never knew what was going on in her mind.'

'All right,' says Mark, 'so what if she does want us to have Lily?'

'It wouldn't be fair on Gemma,' she says. 'We don't have the room anyway. Besides, we don't know what she's like. She might be, you know, completely out of control. Maybe that's why Kim doesn't want her any more. Because she can't handle her. You hear about these kids. With this disorder or that disorder. All screwed up.'

By the snack machines and pay kiosks, the place where they always wait for Gemma, Mark says angrily, 'You're talking about my daughter.' Though he recognises there might be some truth in what Nicole has just said, despite doubting whether he could ever express similar concerns himself.

'Your other daughter,' Kim says. 'The one you just so happened to have lost contact with. Here comes your proper daughter. The one you live with. The one who calls you Daddy every day. Hi, sweetie.' Mark watches Nicole waving at Gemma, beckoning to her, as she shuffles up the squeaky corridor with a couple of school friends, all of them with wet, straggly hair. 'Just remember that,' Nicole whispers. 'I won't have you fucking up her life too.'

II

Mark looks at Gemma, her long, wet hair, hair that turns blonde when dry, shockingly blonde, and evenly so, and with thick, loose curls in it – hair she gets from her mother, though her mother's hair isn't now a totally natural colour – and he thinks of Lily's hair, which, when he last saw her, was short and tufty and a gingery red, and had barely stopped being baby hair. They couldn't get it to grow, but she was only three and a bit.

Gemma has always wanted to look like Barbie and Nicole is forever helping her, patiently styling her hair and dressing her up, and he thinks how lucky it is that Gemma has such blonde curly hair, hair that can easily accommodate her Barbie aspirations. He worries how Lily would have felt had she wanted to look like Barbie when she was a little older, when she was Gemma's age. He doesn't remember her being aware of Barbie when he lived with her. She had toys, but he doesn't think any Barbies, or Shellys, or Kens. Or a box full of their sparkly clothes and tiny high-heeled shoes and mini hair-bands and necklaces, and combs and mirrors and handbags, this huge assortment of accessories that Gemma's dolls seem to have. Or Barbie's handsome horse, Blue Diamond. Or Shelly's pink and white plastic fairy-tale castle, which keeps breaking and he has to keep mending, once he's retrieved all the bits from under Gemma's bed. From all over the house. And he thinks that Gemma was never soft and podgy in the way Lily was. Even as a small baby she was bony and angular – his build exactly. She also has his nose – like Lily – and eyes. Though she has Nicole's hair, of course, and Nicole's skin, which is eczema-free and able to cope with the sun. It often occurs to him how much more like her mum Gemma is than him. Temperamentally, they're the same person. They're both confident and determined, and they don't get anything like as moody or angry as he does. However, Gemma does still have the odd tantrum, especially when she's lost one of her Barbies, but he reckons she'll totally grow out of that.

Watching her tell Nicole all about swimming, her sharp face turning round every so often to see whether he, or probably more likely any of her friends are listening as well – she enjoys having an audience, being so confident and determined, and happy with her appearance, even if she doesn't quite recognise that feeling yet, but she will, he thinks, if she continues to be so like her mum – watching this clearly happy, secure little child, he doesn't believe there's much chance of him fucking her up. Not seriously. Not lastingly. Besides, it's not as if he should blame himself for what's happened to Lily. Whatever Nicole sometimes says. And he also knows that however he behaves Gemma has a mostly reasonable mum. Nicole couldn't behave in the way Kim did if she tried. She would never become hysterical in front of Gemma, or make fun of her, or shake her until she cried. Gemma will always be fine as long as Nicole is around. He didn't marry Nicole just because she was gorgeous-looking – with her hair and her figure and her year-round, all-over tan (artificially enhanced or not) – and because she had a bit of cash and a steady job in a rapidly expanding marketing agency, in something that had a future, unlike cabinet-making. It was because of her strong, rational nature too, her reasonableness. The very obvious fact that she was so unlike Kim. That was what clinched it for him. And as everybody said, including his mum, especially his mum, again and again, behaving as though she couldn't quite believe it, he was lucky to get her. Considering.

Although the kitchen looks out over the back garden – which is floodlit, for decoration as much as security, Mark's paranoid about security – and Gemma's quietly rotting Wendy house, and despite there being plenty of room in the kitchen for all of them to fit comfortably around the table, he and Nicole still usually eat their tea in the lounge, on the settee, in front of the box. If they're eating after Gemma's gone to bed, that is. Mark makes sure Gemma always eats in the kitchen, however, where there's no carpet so it doesn't matter if she spills anything. But tonight, a Friday night, Gemma has already been taken to bed and Mark and Nicole are tucking into a Sainsbury's chicken korma, in front of *Casualty*, as a treat, Mark believing they needed a treat after all the confusion and anxiety Kim's one call caused, and the fact that they seem to have come through it and are letting the whole topic drop. While the food was warming they were considering their holiday options once more, coming down in favour of Mallorca, because it is not as far as Greece, and not as hot, and should be cheaper.

Nicole has her feet tucked under her with her skirt bunched up, revealing her bare thighs, having balanced her plate on the arm rest. Mark can tell she's completely absorbed by the telly, forking in the curry on automatic, while he has his feet firmly on the floor with his food on a tray on his lap, and with a can of Sainsbury's shandy wedged into the corner – he's not going to spill anything. He is not as absorbed by *Casualty* as Nicole, it's not his favourite programme, but he's trying to follow the story line anyway, though wishful-thinking a bit also about suddenly removing the food from his lap and slipping his hand between Nicole's legs to find she's not wearing any knickers and that she is already wet and excited, which is how it sometimes was, too long ago.

Because his mind is drifting it takes him a few seconds to realise the phone is ringing. He's not sure whether it's his moby, or the new cordless, but for some reason he just knows it's Kim. He looks at Nicole but she's so into the TV he doesn't think she's aware of the ringing, realising she isn't going to get up to answer it. For a short while he's unable to get up himself, finding he's frozen to the settee, with his heart feeling like it's going to burst out of his skinny chest. When he does finally move, and once he's carefully put his tray on the floor out of anyone's way, he starts panicking about not getting to the phone in time, still not sure which phone it is, or even where the cordless is. He knows his mobile is on the window-sill in the kitchen, where he always leaves it, so he rushes in there but immediately discovers it's not the mobile which is ringing, knowing it has to be the cordless. 'Nicole,' he shouts, 'where's the phone? Where's the fucking phone?' He leaps back into the lounge to see Nicole has stood up, perhaps having some idea of what's going through his mind, of why he's so panicked, and is looking behind the cushions on the settee – all these frilly, patterned cushions her mum makes for them. They get a new one every Christmas.

'It's here,' she says, retrieving the handset by its aerial from under the cushion she'd been leaning against, her favourite cushion in fact, made from this purple satin fabric and with a black fringe of dangly bits around the edges. 'It's here, Mark. Calm down, for God's sake.'

He grabs it from her, pushing the green answer button, says all breathless and warbling, 'Hello?'

'Mark?' this voice says. This voice he immediately recognises. This voice that used to give him so much grief. 'Is that you, Mark?'

'No, Kim,' he says, catching his breath, 'it's fucking Santa Claus. Who the fuck do you think it is?'

I

So much happens so quickly the next thing Mark knows he's driving to Newbury to see Lily. It's the first weekend in May, the bank holiday weekend. The Saturday. And the weather is terrible. As is the traffic. Though he minds about the traffic a lot more than the weather. Bad drivers infuriate him. They drive him crazy. What really gets him are the people who sit in the fast lane for no reason, overtaking nothing, completely unaware there's someone behind them who wants to get past. He knows there have been occasions when he's probably driven too close behind these head cases, flicking his lights, indicating, hooting, shaking his fist out of the window, doing anything to get them to budge over, but he's certain he's only ever done this when they could physically get out of his way. Not when they themselves were being held up by traffic. Because what also really gets him are people who drive right up his arse, flashing and tooting when he clearly can't go anywhere anyway. When he's in just as much of a hurry as they are, probably more so. Few people get to overtake him. And if this happens, at night say, he normally sticks on his fog lights and starts tapping the brake pedal, trying to get them to back off. During daylight he has just slammed on the brakes, not caring if they smash into his boot, knowing it will be all their fault anyway. That they can buy him a new car. Hoping they seriously damage themselves while they're at it, too.

They haven't even reached the Thetford roundabout, when stuck on the bypass in thick traffic doing forty, forty-five max. – surprise, surprise, he thinks – a guy in a Jeep Cherokee comes zooming up from nowhere, lights on full beam, outside indicator going berserk, expecting Mark to simply move over to the inside lane. Expecting everyone to simply move over. Except of course there is an equally long, slow-moving queue in the inside lane, preventing him or anyone else from shifting over, let alone do any undertaking of their own. So naturally he doesn't get out of the Jeep's way, despite the fact that the driver, he can clearly see from his rear-view mirror, has a large shaven head and a fat neck. What Mark does do is brake sharply, and then accelerate. Again and again, but varying the time between the two manoeuvres, as well as how hard he brakes and accelerates, so as to completely confuse him. A couple of times, when he's particularly heavy on the brake pedal, the Jeep manages to slip into the inside lane, though, Mark's happy to notice, the driver isn't quick enough to get past him that way. His Astra might only have a 1.6-litre fuel-injected engine, plus well over 90,000 on the clock, but he's pretty useful with the odd spanner and ratchet and keeps the vehicle well tuned. And well polished, too – at the very least it always looks mean. He's sure it's nonsense but he's always felt the way something looks affects its performance. That it can make the difference between a tenth of a second 0–60, for example.

'Pack it in, Mark,' Nicole shouts. 'You'll kill us.'

'He started it,' Mark says. 'It's his fucking fault. He came zooming out of nowhere, right up my arse.'

'Why do men always have to behave like this?' she says. 'You're all animals.'

Nicole's intervention winds him up further – her wanting him to back off when it's obviously the other guy's fault. He hates that about women, how they are always so willing to let things go for the sake of a peaceful life – except Kim, of course, he thinks. She never let anything go, not if it didn't suit her. 'Bollocks,' he says, to himself mostly, though so Nicole can also hear, and he continues to try to shake off the Jeep, now completely wound up. Given where they are heading he was edgy enough as it was.

Shortly the traffic comes to a complete standstill, both lanes, and Nicole says, 'Oh shit. Now you've done it.'

He's pleased Gemma isn't in the car, he'll admit that. They've left her with Nicole's sister Louise, thinking it was too long a drive there and back in one day for her, plus they still haven't told her about Lily. Mark had tried to get Nicole to say something to her, because he knew he wouldn't be able to say all the things that needed to be said, in a coherent, sensitive manner. He knew Nicole would be able to word it right, on Gemma's level. But Nicole didn't want to tell Gemma about Lily until she had a better idea of what Lily is like now and exactly what the situation with Kim is. Nicole kept saying, 'I'm sorry to say this again, Mark, but what if Lily's, you know, completely out of control? What if she's got a screw loose? I don't want Gemma coming into contact with someone like that. At least not until she's been properly prepared.'

Mark supposes he should have gone on his own anyway, and not made Nicole come too. Though he knew he couldn't have faced that. He needed support. He still has no idea how he's going to react when he actually sees Lily in just a few hours' time. Whether he'll lose it, or remain calm and perhaps a bit distant. However, he realises, had Nicole not come, and especially had she not made those comments about men and his driving, he wouldn't be quite so heated and ready to smack the fat, shaven-headed driver of the metallic-blue Jeep Cherokee in the face – nice vehicle, idiot driver, he thinks. As it is, Mark leaps out of his car first – he'd learned a long while ago that attack is the best form of defence, that there's no use waiting for someone to just come up and hit you, you have to get in there before they've even taken aim – and by the time he reaches the Jeep he can see the driver is still undoing his seat belt. He's not sure, but Mark quickly gets this idea that he must look a lot more capable than he really is, because he can see the guy is clearly fumbling in the comfort of his leather-clad, air-conditioned interior, making sure the doors are locked as well, he's certain of it. When he tries the handle it doesn't give.

But by now Nicole has reached him and is trying to pull him away, grabbing his arms, his waist, screaming, 'Don't be a fucking jerk, Mark. Leave him alone. He hasn't touched you. Mark, leave him alone.'

No one else, he sees, has got out of their car. He isn't even aware of anyone else watching what's going on. However, he begins to realise that the guy with the shaven head and fat neck isn't quite so large as he imagined, and that his seat must be pumped right up or something. He is still locked inside, now trying to wave Mark away, to dismiss the situation, obviously having decided not to get out and confront him, and the traffic has started to move on and a couple of people are hooting, so Mark simply slaps the offside window with both his hands, hard though, shouting, 'Fucking arsehole,' before returning to his car, with Nicole in tears collapsing into the passenger seat, and it beginning to drizzle, but only slightly so he doesn't have to turn on his wipers for a minute or so. Until the rain has completely smothered the windscreen, the drops all squashed and trailing. With nothing but a flat grey sky ahead. And with him no longer bothering to look in his rear-view mirror, and turning up the volume on the Blaupunkt, hoping to knock out the silence and the distance.

'I love this tune,' he eventually says. 'I fucking love it.'

2

Nicole is always telling Mark that he is never straight with her. That he never comes right out with what's on his mind. That he's afraid of saying exactly what he means. Of being specific. Half the time, he says in return, he doesn't know what's on his mind. But he'll accept that he is easily distracted and can lose the plot, and then spend hours day-dreaming, letting his mind idle around stuff that is not important – though that's how people cope with life, he thinks, isn't it? When he's working he often finds he suddenly can't remember what it is he's meant to be doing, so he wastes even more time trying to get back into it. Though as he sees it there are some things which are too difficult to be specific about. Issues that are best avoided. Especially if you are as uncertain of yourself as he is. If you don't quite trust who you are. And if you suffer a little from paranoia. Otherwise, he thinks, you might create even more damage.

He's contemplating all this stuff as they approach the M25, still not chatting to Nicole, though he can tell she's cheered up a bit and isn't nearly so cross with him. The weather has brightened, too. The sun is flashing on the wet asphalt and verge, glinting on windscreens and wing mirrors, finding a way through the mass of suddenly cracked and shifting clouds.

However, it occurs to him that while he was just thinking about how he never gets to the point, how he's always trying to avoid certain issues, he was of course trying not to think about Lily and what it'll be like seeing her for the first time in over ten years, and seeing Kim also, and possibly the new bloke she said on the phone she's recently set up home with – the man whose idea it was she got in touch with him, for Lily's sake, so Kim said anyway – and what this place is like, whether it's warm and comfy and secure enough for his precious daughter. It also occurs to him that perhaps he's simply thinking and worrying about these things he's trying not to think about, out of guilt, out of some tremendous guilt – for really not having thought that much about Lily, and her security and comfort, her well-being, for years and years. For forgetting her. For abandoning her. After all, he's survived happily enough, hasn't he? He's built a new home and family. He wonders whether he's trying to cram almost a decade's worth of concern over his missing daughter into a car journey. That in a way he's trying to change the past, to reinvent himself, to reinvent his feelings retrospectively. Deep down he wonders whether he'd be feeling any different if he and Nicole were simply heading for Ikea in Chelmsford, rather than to Newbury and Lily. With him not saying much, except to swear at the odd other driver, and Nicole curled in the passenger seat, her shoes off and her feet tucked under her, yawning, fiddling with the radio, mucking up his pre-set choices, talking about Gemma's school, and her sister, and her mum and when her mum will be coming to stay next. Talking about her job also. About how she's now in charge of a team of six. That she's the big boss.

3

Mark and Kim had arranged to leave Jake and Sean with a neighbour, but Lily came two weeks early and the neighbour was away so Mark had to look after Kim's boys while his daughter was being born. He took them to the cafeteria, which was on the ground floor of the hospital and which stank of fat and stewed coffee, and cigarettes – just like the services he and Nicole have stopped at, on the A34, a few minutes from Newbury. The cafeteria was meant to be non-smoking, he was sure of that seeing as it was in a hospital, but everyone seemed to be dragging away. He's always hated smokers, thinking they're totally anti-social. Why should he have to breathe someone else's poisonous fumes? But he and the boys couldn't get away from them, nor the glare of the strip lighting, nor the stuffy heat coming from the hot food-warming lamps, which made the faces of the obese kitchen staff shine a sickly yellow and the peas in a tray on the counter look purple.

Until then, he'd never been with just Jake and Sean on his own, not when they were both awake, and he knew they were finding the situation as hard to cope with as he was. They were seven and four and didn't like each other much. Jake had this habit of suddenly smacking Sean on the head, then laughing like a hyena while he skipped around the room, smacking the air, re-enacting his moment of glory. Sean would usually burst into tears, though sometimes he would just sit there, still and silent, with maybe his bottom lip quivering slightly. That boy freaked him out. They both did.

The cafeteria didn't have a kiddies' play area, unlike the services – pointing out the Barbie-pink Wendy house to Mark, Nicole says, 'Gemma would have enjoyed that' – and in the hurry and panic to get to the hospital he'd forgotten to bring anything for the boys to play with. The baby was the wrong way up and Kim had been booked in for a caesarean. He wasn't expecting her waters to break, not a fortnight early, not when she was making tea – she hadn't told him it could happen. He wasn't prepared mentally, and was probably half-pissed, having then been in the habit of spending lunchtimes in the pub with some lads from work, playing pool, drinking lager tops, always too many for his light head.

Stuck in the glaring, smoke-filled hospital cafeteria, he soon developed a massive headache, which he thought was being made a million times worse by Jake and Sean, who were fighting and crying, knocking over chairs, knocking over these big, artificial palms – cracking the pots they were in, too. He was getting snarly looks from the sickly-faced staff, and quite a few of the customers when they weren't dragging on their fags as well, but he couldn't control the boys. They never listened to him. The only way he got them to remain reasonably calm was to keep feeding them crisps and sweets and cans of Coke. It cost him a fortune. And then the place shut and they were turfed out and into a corridor-cum-waiting area, which was OK for a bit because Jake and Sean used the space as a giant skid pan, pelting from one end to the other. Their shoes squeaking wildly on the waxy floor.

He probably should have taken them home and let Kim get on with it on her own, but he wanted to be there when his first child was born, regardless of what his feelings were for Kim at that time. He doesn't believe he's ever been one to shirk responsibility. No, not him. He definitely had had every intention of being present at the actual birth. That's what they'd agreed upon, and arranged, but then Lily came early, didn't she, when their neighbour was away, and so he was stuck looking after the boys.

Not knowing how long it would take having a caesarean – Kim

had dismissed the idea of them going to a prenatal class together, saying she had had two kids already and could tell him everything he needed to know, but she never told him anything – half-expecting someone to come down to get him when it was over, and more than sick of the boys squeaking about, getting on everyone else's nerves as well, he eventually decided they'd better go up to the maternity ward themselves, which was on the seventh floor, through a maze of corridors, in a different block. But Jake and Sean didn't want to leave their skid pan and both were screaming at him and Jake was swearing too, shouting, 'Get off me, you're not my fucking dad.' He was always saying that. So Mark had to drag them by their arms, grabbing them hard, not caring if he was pinching them, if his nails were digging into their thin flesh, and not caring what anyone thought of him treating them in that way either. He was being authoritative for once. Parental.

By the time they eventually got to the seventh floor and were reluctantly – as it was out of normal visiting hours, despite him being the new father, though for some reason they didn't want to believe that – shown to the post-operative maternity ward, Lily was already born. She was fast asleep, tucked under a tiny blue cotton blanket, in a clear plastic cot, next to Kim who had zonked out also. He told the boys to shut up, making them stand back, while he leant over the cot to stroke his daughter's red cheeks, and her warm, wrinkly forehead, and the top of her head, which was smothered with strands of slimy ginger hair. Leaning closer, he caught her breathing, which was not smooth and even but crackly, as if she had a snotty nose already, and he smelt an earthy, bloody smell mingled with the smell of clean laundry and disinfectant. He was unable to read what they'd written on the tag attached to her tiny wrist, which was out of the blanket up by her head, though he did notice her fingers were tightly curled before all of her turned into a big watery blur.

4

Nicole says, as Mark emerges from the toilet, 'Are you feeling all right?'

'No, I'm fucking not,' he says. He has diarrhoea. 'How would you be feeling?'

She's paid and has been waiting for him outside the toilets, which were by the entrance to the services, this bright orange and lime green everywhere, along with all these giant posters advertising breakfast specials and ice cream sundaes. Great big stomach-churning photos of the shiny dishes. She ignores his question, which he didn't expect to be answered anyway, saying instead, saying calmly, as if they are just off to the supermarket, or to pick Gemma up from swimming, 'We should get a move on, love.'

He wants to say, Wait a minute, can't we have another coffee, another burger, another sundae? Not that he could eat the food he'd ordered. He wants to say, Can't we just sit in the car for a bit, in the car park? And watch, he thinks, the people pile in and out of the services, and the traffic crawling by on the main road, and the clouds still going mental, letting the sun through one minute, in big, misty shafts, and then becoming fused and heavy and dark the next, threatening a downpour. He feels the clouds are as unsure about what they're meant to do next as he is. Operating under all this conflicting pressure. And his stomach is not helping matters. He's not sure how far from a toilet he should stray.

'It'll be fine,' says Nicole.

'How do you know?'

'I can just tell.'

He gets into the car, feeling he isn't really in control of his limbs, which have gone all weak and shuddery.

'She is your daughter,' Nicole says, as he accelerates on to the main road, managing to nip in before a car towing a caravan – but only just and he's hooted at – realising his legs, his arms still do what he wants them to do, more or less.

'Imagine what she's feeling now. It's going to be much harder for her. She's only thirteen.'

'Oh yeah?' he says.

5

Nevertheless, he does try to imagine what she's feeling, as he negotiates Newbury, the high street with all these cars either parking or waiting for a parking space, taking forever over it, and then a complicated one-way system full of mini roundabouts, pedestrian crossings and dawdling, lost, bank-holiday traffic, with Nicole shouting out the directions, many clearly wrong – though he knows this could be Kim's fault because they were her directions originally – and with him snapping back, slapping the steering wheel, slamming to a halt every so often, on the verge of losing it again. He tries to imagine what it would be like to be a kid, a teenager, and to see your father for the first time in a decade. But all he can think about is suddenly seeing his father again, who he hasn't seen for something like twenty-five years. Since, it occurs to him, he was thirteen, roughly Lily's age, when his dad left his mum for this other woman, taking his younger brother Robbie with him. How they decided upon that he'll never know. Though he quickly realised it was pretty final because they went to live in Canada – his dad and his brother and this woman Sue, and her daughter from her first marriage. A brand-new family unit, except it didn't last very long, he later found out.

Meanwhile, Mark was left in Norfolk with his mum, just him

and his mum and his mum's new lease of life. She was forever going out, leaving him at home on his own, forgetting to make his tea, forgetting to check he had any emergency pocket money. Until anyway this wimpy-looking, silver-haired bloke called Lawrence appeared on the scene. She married him within months and they went to live with him in his executive home on the outskirts of the city. Mark wasn't given the choice as to whether he wanted to go or not. His mum never even asked him what he thought of Lawrence, though he reckons she probably knew the answer to that. He loathed the man, from the beginning. He loathed his silver hair and flat, expressionless face, and weedy build. And he loathed him also for being such a prissy snob and having three equally prissy, privately educated kids from his first marriage – a girl and two boys – but they only came to stay occasionally in the holidays, and he did fuck the girl once. When she was fourteen and clearly a virgin. She cried as he slowly managed to stick it in and she cried again when the Durex came off inside her and she had to pull it out loaded with his come.

But mostly it was just his mum and Lawrence and him, though he spent as little time in his sumptuous new home as possible, sneaking off at night when they thought he was in bed – staying with friends, sleeping rough. His mother is still with Lawrence and consequently he doesn't have an exactly brilliant relationship with her. He doubts whether he's ever forgiven her for marrying him. Though she was helpful when he was splitting up with Kim, he has to give her that, and he supposes his dad is the person he should really be angry with.

When he thinks of his family, when he tries to picture it, say in terms of a family tree, as he was once asked to do at school – a big, leafy beech tree perhaps – he just sees all these broken squiggles, no healthy, leafy branches. Though he's sure his family structure is no worse than millions of others, and at least when he was a bit older, when he thought he could step away, when he thought he had stepped away, he remembers he made a commitment to himself that if he ever had children he wouldn't put them through anything similar. He'd see they were all right. He'd stick with them. He'd keep everybody together.

Nearing his daughter's house, which he discovers is on the edge of Newbury, in an old council estate full of semis, of exactly the same period, with similar metal window frames and pale yellow bricks and mossy roofs, as where he and Kim used to live, it's even in a sort of cul-de-sac, at least there is a fence at the end of the road (rather than a crescent-shaped turning), with a scruffy front garden, the scruffiest on the street too, and with his stomach almost going into spasm, and heart thumping wildly, like he's OD'ing on speed, he realises, way too late of course – though he'd obviously, conveniently managed to forget that particular pledge to himself for a very long while – that he's failed. Spectacularly. Crawling along this dead end, past Lily's dilapidated house, looking for a place to park, but not wanting to draw attention to his car – he doesn't want it vandalised – he suddenly can't bear to imagine what his daughter must have gone through growing up, sure she's experienced many worse things than he ever did. How can he possibly know what she'll be feeling, waiting for him to arrive? This man who's meant to be her father, but who she hasn't seen for so long. Who she probably can't even remember. But who, he imagines – maybe he does have an inkling of what she might be feeling – she hates.

Except this is where he hopes it will all start to go differently, where history won't repeat itself, where generations begin to diverge, where his dad and he differ, because he does care for this child he was forced to abandon. He never stopped loving her. He just wasn't able to show it. He can promise her that, whatever she thinks of him. Whatever she's like. He's positive of this now he's finally here.

6

Nicole grabs his hand as he walks up the wet path, trying to stick to the drier patches and the patches free from sweet wrappers and squashed drinks cans, fag ends, old fag packets and what looks to him like cat shit, some sort of shit anyway. She did suggest she should stay in the car but he wanted her by his side. Though he doesn't want to be seen holding her hand necessarily, not by Lily or Kim – he's not sure why, he can't stop to think about it, but he doesn't – and he pulls his hand back and stuffs it in his jeans pocket, which is not that easy because he's wearing his smartest pair, which are very tight (he knows he's still got a great arse), but at least it's firmly out of Nicole's way, wedged in there, as is his other hand in the other pocket, and she quickly gets the point, he thinks, seeing her bite her bottom lip and suck in her cheeks and then smack her lips, the way she does when he's upset her.

They don't have to knock. The door, which is covered with dark, hardened dribbles of a tar-like substance, and flaky light green paint, opens before they reach it, as if it's on automatic, Mark can't help thinking, like the doors you get at the supermarket, and there, standing behind it, totally motionless, totally expressionless, is this skinny girl wearing a clingy, but much too long in the arms, faded purple top and flared jeans, heavily frayed at the bottom. She's almost Nicole's height and has a deathly pale face, except for a number of big spots on her forehead, and maybe there are a couple on her chin as well, though she's looking at the ground, and she has straight, limp, clearly dyed, almost scarlet-coloured hair hanging to just below her shoulders. Her feet are bare, Mark notices, seeing her toes sticking out from under the dirty frayed denim, and her toenails are painted purple, a shade or two darker than her top. Mark can't understand why she's bothered to paint her toenails with everything else about her being so unwashed and unkempt, so grungy, though he supposes the colour is pretty weird. She is wearing a Discman and he can hear she has the volume on high, though he has no idea what she's listening to.

'Hi,' Nicole says loudly, but the girl says nothing back, careful not to look up. Mark smiles nervously, scanning the dim front room behind her, for any sign of someone recognisable, for a sign that they've got the right house.

He's still looking, still not drawing any conclusions, still not even attempting to contemplate the obvious, when Nicole shouts, 'Lily?' And the girl finally lifts her pale face, putting on this scowly, half-sarcastic smile, his smile, spot-on, and he can see she almost has his eyes, that they are no longer really a green but have somehow become more a bluey grey, and despite the nose ring he can see she has his large, slightly hooked nose. And trying to dismiss the frayed, ill-fitting hippy clothes, he can tell she almost has his figure as well – all hard angles. Though he's never been quite so skinny, not even when he was a teenager and stopped eating for a bit so he could fit into a pair of twenty-six-inch waist Wranglers. However, what shocks him the most is how much older she appears to be than he imagined, and how much less girl-like. How scruffily androgynous. He's seen her type before, hanging around the pedestrianised streets in the city centre back home, selling the *Big Issue*, begging, harassing shoppers, drinking from two-litre plastic bottles of cider. Letting their flea-ridden dogs piss all over the pavement. And because it is so obvious that she is his daughter, his long-lost daughter, with exactly his scowly smile, all he can think is that she doesn't belong in those clothes, with that hair and that bloody nose ring. With all that attitude. At her age. And being his daughter too. He's suddenly filled with a burning, violent urge to rip it all off her. To strip her of being someone she's not. To strip her naked.

What's making it worse for him is the fact that he's wearing his best jeans, and blue Burton shirt with a button-down collar, and his cream and fawn chequered V-neck sweater which Nicole bought him for Christmas, and Nicole is wearing her light pink, satin skirt and jacket, the suit she wears for weddings and christenings and other special occasions, and that he's feeling embarrassed about their outfits, for them having made the effort to dress up. He's not just embarrassed about it, he's annoyed. He's annoyed for bothering to come, also, already. He wants to turn around and leave, without saying anything, without complicating the matter further. Wanting, if anything, to go back to the beginning, to when he was twenty-three so he doesn't have to make that terrible mistake with Kim.

However, Lily suddenly removes her headphones and, smiling more sarcastically still, just like he can, with her head tilted to one side, which somehow makes her clingy faded purple top fall off her right shoulder to reveal a tattoo on her upper arm, a tattoo of some kind of flower, but without the flower bit, without the petals, so there is just a stalk with green, spiky edged leaves, and says, 'Hi, Mark. Hi, Mark's wife,' in a totally deadpan voice.

Nicole says, 'Hello, Lily. Wow. Here we all are. Then.'

Mark looks at Nicole and she mouths, at least he's pretty sure she mouths, Say hello to her, Mark. She's your daughter. Grumpily he says, 'Hello.' Though he doesn't move any nearer to her. He doesn't rush forward with his arms open. He doesn't make any effort to hug her. To pull her close and tight. To pull her into him. Her bony, tattooed body and pierced face and stinking, limp hair. All of her. As if, he once imagined, he'd never let go again. He makes no physical contact whatsoever.

'Mum says you're not allowed in the house,' she says in return, in this voice that is not so deadpan this time, but has a hint of nervousness, a distinct shaky unevenness in the pitch, along with a slight West Country accent. 'Mum,' she shouts, shrilly, and much more nervously, quickly looking behind her, 'Mum, they're here.'

Not attempting to move further into the house, or any closer to his daughter, Mark looks at Nicole and he can tell she's concerned about the situation. That she's concerned for him, because she's put on her, what he calls, cheer-up-lovey smile, her, well, things could be a lot worse look-cum-shrug – with her eyebrows raised and her nostrils flared slightly and her mouth forced into a wide, toothy smile.

He doesn't think things could be much worse, though when Kim appears he feels it's like another blow. Like he's had the air knocked out of him again and that his chest could cave in for good. And he honestly wouldn't mind if that happened. If he was wiped out. Despite the time that has elapsed since he last saw Kim, or perhaps because of it, the sight of her instantly fills him with a sickening dread. Though he thinks this feeling of dread, and of anger and fear also, must be being made worse because he knows she's obviously let Lily become the way she has. That Kim's responsible for this mess which is standing directly in front of him. Who else can he blame for Lily's tattoo and pierced nose and dyed hair, her sad, scruffy, ill-fitting clothes? Kim looks no better herself, having made her own hair scarlet, except she's closely cropped all of hers apart from a long thin, platted ponytail, which hangs not from the back of her head, but from one side. She's also had her nose pierced, and various other bits of her face, and is wearing numerous studs and earrings, her ears being weighed down by them – stretched like some tribal African woman's, he thinks – and is clothed in baggy, hippy garments – an orange tie-dyed ankle-length, wrap-around skirt-thing and a loose, also orange woolly top with holes and tears in it that might have been put there on purpose, or not – how's he meant to know?

When he was with Kim she was into neat, fitted items – short skirts and tight tops – things that showed off her bum and her tits to the best of their advantage. She wasn't pretty in the way Nicole is, not all the way up and down, not proportionally, not conventionally as his mum has said, and she didn't have anything like Nicole's complexion, Nicole's smooth, tan skin, but she made the most of what she had. Enough people certainly thought so. Enough of them regarded her as a top tease.

7

This woman, who on the first night he met her had given him a blow job in the ladies' toilet of Henry's Nitespot, and who had then sat on the toilet and changed her Tampax while he was zipping himself up, this woman who he'd married some four months later and who, two months after that had had a miscarriage, though who a year on had given birth to his daughter, by caesarean section, this woman who'd then disappeared, with his daughter, when his daughter was not quite three and a half, for a decade, for a few months over a decade, this woman who called herself Kim, but who was in fact christened Kimberley, said on the phone, after he'd told her he was fucking Santa Claus, and after they'd asked each other a few simple but strained questions – things like, 'So how are you then?' and, 'Where the hell have you been exactly?', in between these long stretches of tense silence, when he hoped she wouldn't be able to hear his heart beating, and after both of them had kept clearing their throats, obviously trying to breathe and speak more calmly, and with neither of them, he noted at the time, saying anything like, It's nice to hear from you, nothing like that – Kim said on the phone, after no prompting from him, 'I'm obviously getting in touch because of Lily. Surprise, surprise.' She was always saying surprise, surprise, he remembered. 'We think it's about time she got to know her dad.'

'Who's we?' he said.

'Me and Dave, the man I'm living with – we're getting married soon.'

'I don't get it,' Mark said. 'Why now? Why not ten fucking years ago?'

'I'm not going into all that, not on the phone,' she said, 'but Lily has been asking about you, and we're settling down. Somewhere permanent. We've been travelling.'

'So that's it?' he said. 'You've decided it's time Lily got to know me? You and this bloke Dave have decided this?'

'Yeah,' she said. 'I don't have to explain any more to you than that.'

'Yes, you do,' he said. 'You owe me an awful lot of explaining.'

'Look, Mark, I'm not going to get into an argument with you now. I can easily just put the phone down and never call you again. If you want to see your daughter I suggest you be a little more cooperative about it and keep cool.'

'Keep cool? Yeah, right,' he said. 'That's easy with you blackmailing me. I can't win, can I? I never could with you.'

'Mark, I'm running out of patience, I'm warning you.'

'OK, whatever you say. It was always like that, wasn't it?'

'When do you want to see her then?' she said.

'Today,' he replied. 'Now.'

'Well, that's not going to happen, is it?' she said, before going on to tell him where it was she was now living, with this guy Dave, and when it might be possible for him to come to see Lily, because she said, in this first instance, she was going to insist he came to them. He could take Lily out for a few hours, for lunch or whatever, but it would have to be in Newbury. She didn't want him upsetting Lily too much. She's a shy, sensitive kid and obviously wasn't used to him.

'Whose fault is that?' he said.

'Mark,' she said, 'I'm warning you.'

So he felt he had no option and he went through some dates with her, feeling totally powerless and used, again, this familiar feeling sweeping through him, in fact choking him up, while he held the phone to one side and shouted at Nicole to look at the calendar they keep in the kitchen, next to the fridge, and heard Kim saying something to someone in the background also, either this Dave character or possibly his daughter, though he didn't get to talk to Lily during that phone call, and eventually they settled on the Saturday of the May Day bank holiday weekend. At least that's when Kim made out it was the earliest date he could possibly see Lily, but he wouldn't have put it past her for picking that day because she knew the traffic would be bad then and wanted to inconvenience him as much as possible – it was the sort of calculated thing that she was entirely capable of and used to initiate. Just as he suspected, having listened to the tone of her voice – it was as clipped as ever, as snidely, though with this slight West Country accent she never had before – that there was another agenda for her getting in touch with him, anyway, like money, of course.

Certainly Nicole went on about this to him, saying how obviously the new bloke in Kim's life was pushing her to get some money out of Lily's proper father. Maybe, she said, he wanted to get rid of Lily altogether and was urging Kim to hand the girl over to her dad. Especially as they were about to get married. Mark tried to assure Nicole that that wouldn't be the case, that Kim wouldn't do that, knowing how uncomfortable she was with this idea, not just because of Gemma, but because she was worried that Lily might be out of control or something, and besides she thought they didn't have anything like enough room. Though he didn't really know what this man might be up to.

But when he does see Kim and Lily, and the dismal condition of the council house his daughter is living in, with cardboard plugging up the front door, and this overwhelming smell of damp, and cigarettes and cats, and the fact that there is no furniture fit to sit on, not in his mind anyway, not in anyone's mind, he reckons – just these old bean bags and a hammock in the lounge as far as he can see – and with there being no sign of Dave or Kim's other kids, who he can't think how old they must be by now, and understanding that this is supposedly where they have decided to settle down – after years of travelling, as Kim intimated, God knows where or how – he's even more convinced there is another agenda for Kim getting in touch. If she doesn't want to offload Lily on to him it has to be cash at the very least. He's not that naive. Not any more.

He actually thinks all this before she has the audacity to ask him out right. Before she says, in front of Lily, 'I would let you in but the place is a total mess, we're still trying to get things together, aren't we, Lil? She's just started school, Mark. Haven't you, Lily? Except we can't afford the uniform, or these books she needs, and all this other stuff. I suppose you can't help us out a bit, can you? I wasn't planning to ask you, not now, but I didn't want to miss my chance and I'm sure you can spare it. You've got an expensive car, I saw you drive up, and looking at you in your smart, neat clothes, and your pretty woman in her lovely pink suit, you're obviously not short of any cash. And it's not as if you've been paying maintenance or anything, is it? I've fed and clothed your daughter all by myself for the last ten years. I've done everything on my own, Mark.'

He wants to say, well that was your choice, darling, you're the one who fucked off, but he doesn't. Standing on her doorstep, with Lily next to him, having come this far, and being only too aware of how unpredictable Kim can be, how wily and conniving – he hasn't forgotten everything – and realising that he hardly looks as if he doesn't have any money, he knows he'll have to give her some, if he wants to see Lily again. If, at least, he wants to have the chance to see her again, which, for some extraordinary reason, he seems to want to do – despite hardly having spoken a word to her and his initial shock at her appearance, despite all her attitude, her frayed, ill-fitting clothes and nose ring, her tattoo and dyed hair, and purple toenails. Perhaps he thinks, reaching for his wallet, there's just this natural bond between them, stronger than any prejudice he might have. A bit like a gut reaction, but more so.

It's only after he's opened his wallet, fumbled through it and has handed Kim £45, saying, 'That's all the cash I've got on me. Sorry,' after which, Kim says, 'You could always send us some more, in the post. Or set up one of those standing order things. I've got a new bank account. Let me give you the details,' and after he then says, 'Sure,' but before they head off for lunch, Nicole, Lily and himself, just the three of them, that it occurs to him Kim has managed to get some money out of him before he's even had a chance to talk to his daughter without her mum around, as if she's afraid that once he's spent a few hours with Lily he'll not want anything more to do with her. That he won't want to see her again, even on his territory, and that he'll forget the whole idea, and disappear himself. What does she know about his natural bond with Lily, his growing urge to give her a chance?

He glances Lily's way to see she's sort of jigging on the spot, shaking her head from side to side, stuffed inside her headphones, with her eyes virtually shut and the music blaring.

8

The last time Mark took Lily to the pub on his own, he thinks she couldn't have been more than two and a half, three at the most. She was no trouble then, he recalls, looking away from her now, nor a joke. She was a dream. Of course she was. A bright, loveable, little bubble. His funny features. His child through and through. Not a gnome. Not some sick joke.

He took her to The Swan, which was on the other side of town from where they lived, by a slipway used by one of the smaller pleasure-cruiser hire firms. It was a cold day because he remembers making sure Lily was well wrapped up, in her blue padded anorak, which used to be Sean's, and her green bobble hat. They sat outside because children weren't allowed in the pub and fed Hula Hoops to the ducks which waddled slowly and shyly up the slipway, with Lily giggling hysterically as the ducks came closer to her pushchair, and as they fought amongst themselves for the food. He must have had a couple of pints of lager and black while she had plenty of Hula Hoops and a few sips from her bottle, though the milk soon became too cold for her and she wouldn't drink a Pepsi he bought for her either, and then her nose started to run badly, though she still seemed to be enjoying feeding the ducks. They got through five packets of Hula Hoops, and a packet of crisps before he eventually decided to take her to the amusement arcade – he couldn't think of anywhere else that would be warm and inside.

Luckily, he found she enjoyed the flashing lights and the noise of the machines – the bursts of electronic rock music and machine-gun fire and mini-explosions, and sounds of screeching cars and motorbikes and runaway trucks, and occasionally the clatter of money – almost as much as she'd enjoyed feeding the ducks. She was happy to observe it all from her pushchair for a while, though when he started to play a few of the machines himself, particularly this one that involved shooting cowboys in a saloon with a laser gun, where the cowboys would emit a strange yelp whenever they were hit, and where he could shoot the bottles behind the bar as well, making them turn into fountains of pixilated glass, she wanted to have a go too, and started struggling to get out of her pushchair. Eventually, he had to unstrap her and pick her up, which was when he discovered her trainer pants were heavy-feeling and her tights were already damp with pee. He hadn't thought to bring any spare pants or clothes, having left the house in a rush – after yet another argument with Kim. Now out of the pushchair, Lily definitely didn't want to go back into it, though he wasn't going to carry her anywhere in that state, with the risk of pee, and he didn't want to even think about what else, getting on his jacket. With a bit of force and bribery he did manage to get her back in and strapped up, knowing he couldn't stay out any longer and that he'd have to take her home and to her mum to be cleaned up. But the thing Mark remembers most about taking Lily out on his own is how happy she always was, and how she wanted to be a part of everything, to get involved. And how she never ever seemed to be affected by his arguments with Kim, by all the screaming and shouting that went on between them – they went for each other regardless of whether the kids were present or not, it wasn't something they could control. Though his mother thought differently. She was concerned about Lily not being toilet-trained by the age of three. She said the girl was clearly disturbed. That this was a classic sign. He had no idea. He left all that stuff to Kim, anyway.

9

As soon as Mark has pulled out of the cul-de-sac, with Nicole next to him and Lily in the back, with Lily having ignored her mum, who'd tried to wave at her from her doorstep, Lily produces a packet of cigarettes from her tatty, faded, drawstring bag – so he observes from his rear-view mirror – and calmly lights up. Without saying a word.

'Not in my car,' he says. Although Lily's still wearing her head-phones he knows she's heard him because he sees her avoiding his eyes in the mirror, staring out of the passenger window instead, blasting her smoke against the glass so it bounces back, enveloping her face, polluting his space. 'I said not in my car,' he shouts, turning round ready to swipe the cigarette from her mouth, but he has to turn back quickly because the road is particularly narrow, being lined with parked cars, and another car is coming his way, not making any effort to slow down or move over, which it could and should have a moment or two ago, so he gives the driver the finger.

'Mark, she's all right,' Nicole says. 'If she wants to smoke let her.'

'Let her?' Mark says. 'In my car? You've got to be joking.'

'Come on,' Nicole says. 'It can't be easy for her.'

'Apart from gumming up my windows and poisoning us all,' he says, 'she's only thirteen. It's not even legal.'

'Since when have you ever bothered about the law?' Nicole says.

'That's beside the point, she's my daughter. She does what I say.'

'No, I don't,' says Lily, removing her headphones, but still, Mark sees, looking directly out of the window, smoking furiously. 'You're not my dad. I've never seen you before. You're just some wanker who thinks he can tell people what to do because he's got a smart car. You're nothing to do with me. You can fuck off.'

Mark stops the car in the middle of the road, completely blocking it. He doesn't get out or turn round to face his daughter or say anything further. He just stares ahead, at the drying, patchy road, at the pollarded trees, at these stumps pointing hopelessly towards the heavy sky. He thinks it must be about to rain again.

'Mark,' Nicole says, 'don't create a scene.' She turns to Lily in the back. 'I'm sorry about this. We've driven a long way. Where was it your mum said we should go for lunch?'

'I'm not hungry,' Lily says.

'I'm not going anywhere anyway,' Mark says. 'Not until that girl puts that cigarette out.'

'It's finished,' Lily says, holding up the butt. 'See.'

'Where did you put the ash?' Mark says. 'Where did you stub it out? Not on my fucking floor, I hope.'

'On my jeans, if you really want to know. Don't worry, I haven't messed up your precious car. I wouldn't waste so much as my breath in here if I could help it.'

'Mark, have I got to drive?' says Nicole. 'Or are you going to grow up and take us to the nearest pub or something?'

'I'm not having you drive,' he says. 'In a town you don't know. Forget it. You'll massacre the car.' He puts the car into gear, pleased Nicole has given him an excuse to drive on, which he does extra slowly for him, and with what he thinks is extreme care, as if this will somehow appease the car for it being soiled by Lily. And by Nicole for even thinking about driving it. His precious car – yeah, he thinks, Lily's definitely right there. Turning into a one-way system which seems to take them around the centre of town, he observes shop after shop – some chains he's heard of but most he hasn't – and pavements packed with people and kids, and muscular, short-haired dogs, yet he doesn't see any sign of a pub or a café.

'What sort of town is this?' he says.

'A dump,' Lily says.

He smiles, he laughs, he can't help himself, suddenly feeling an enormous sense of relief. Realising that maybe he will be able to connect with his daughter. That she and he might be able to find a bit of mutual ground. That she's his kid. And that sometimes, admittedly, he does behave like an arsehole. But not without provocation. Never without provocation.

10

Once they are all seated at the table, and despite her headphones hanging round her neck, nowhere near her ears, Lily immediately starts moving, as if to some furious beat. Jerking her shoulders up and down, waving her hands about, clasping and unclasping them, snapping her fingers, constantly crossing and uncrossing her legs. She quickly turns to the cutlery – tapping the handle of the knife on the spoon, trying to bend the fork – and when she's seemingly bored with this she begins rolling the salt and pepper pots across the table, seeing how close to the edge she can get them before they fall off, which they mostly do, and which Nicole obligingly, happily, picks up, as if, Mark thinks, she's in league with Lily. That the two of them are well on the way to forming a close relationship. The thought makes him feel surprisingly jealous.

It was Nicole who spotted the pub, with its own, large car park. Inside they found a couple of bright bars and a conservatory-style eating area, where they quickly plonked themselves.

Mark had suggested, having driven through most of Newbury, that they might as well go back to the services where they had stopped on their way into the town, as there appeared to be nowhere else to eat and it had started to spit and he didn't see the point in just parking, if they could, and then wandering around in the drizzle for hours. He was half-joking about eating in the services, but Lily had said, seriously he thinks, too, 'No fucking way, Mark, I'm not eating in a Happy Eater.' This endeared her to him further, the sudden confidence, the belligerence – just how he was at her age – so he turned round and smiled at her. One of his genuine, non-scowly smiles. The first proper smile he's given her, in fact. But he only got back a brief, sarcastic version.

And it was Nicole who made them get a table immediately, by the window, overlooking the car park, regardless of Mark saying he wanted to have a drink at the bar first – though he was quite happy with the position, knowing he'd be able to keep an eye on his car, and he didn't want to lose the table once Nicole had located it – and regardless of Lily saying she wasn't hungry and didn't want to sit down anyway.

'Well, I am,' Nicole said determinedly. 'And I'm dead tired. We can have a drink at the table. Please?' Mark noticed that Lily appeared to listen to Nicole, making no more fuss about not being hungry or not wanting to sit down while she followed Nicole and himself to the table.

While Lily's building a structure with the table mats, a sort of pitched-roofed hut, perhaps it's a wigwam, and after no one has come to take their order, or to tell them how the salad bar and buffet works, after none of them have said very much, Mark pushes his chair back and stands up. He can't bear Lily's fiddling any longer. And he needs a drink, a double vodka and pineapple, he reckons.

'I'm going to get some drinks,' he says. 'Who wants what, then?'

'White wine spritzer, please,' Nicole says.

'Bacardi Breezer,' Lily says.

'I don't think you should be getting her that,' Nicole says.

'Why not?' he says. 'She looks old enough.'

'Cool, Mark,' Lily says.

'Get her a soft drink,' Nicole says. 'She's only thirteen. Get her a Coke.'

'I don't drink Coke,' Lily says. 'It rots your teeth.'

Mark walks across the bright, hot restaurant bit of the pub, which has filled up considerably since they sat down, aiming for the bar, hoping they don't stock Bacardi Breezer. As much as he's finding he wants Lily to bond with him, by bribery if it takes that, he nevertheless agrees with Nicole. He definitely doesn't think his thirteen-year-old daughter should have a Bacardi Breezer, regardless of the fact that he used to drink spirits when he was her age. He doesn't think she should smoke, either. But at least he doesn't feel responsible for her having developed these habits. He knows whose fault that is, all right.

However, the bar does stock Bacardi Breezer. It stocks four or five different flavours. There's a whole dedicated fridge of the stuff, which is clearly labelled, with posters and stickers and neon. He assumes it's a Bacardi Breezer promotion and if Lily was to walk anywhere near here, on the way to the toilet perhaps, she wouldn't be able to miss it. He orders his and Nicole's drinks and a lemon and lime Bacardi Breezer for Lily, having no idea whether she'll like the flavour but picking it because that's the flavour he'd go for. Wondering, indeed, how similar her taste is to his – what exactly she's inherited from him, and how much of that her mother has tried to destroy.

Walking back to the table he can't help thinking about Kim and what she's done to his daughter over the last decade. How she's let her become quite so thin and scruffy, so tramp-like. He can't imagine Gemma ever wearing those sorts of clothes, or having a tattoo, or a nose ring, or smoking, or drinking so blatantly. At thirteen. He'd never let her. Anyway, he knows Gemma's being brought up properly. That she just wouldn't do it. His precious little Gem would never call him Mark. Not with such sarcasm. Such aggression.

'So where have you been?' he says, before he's even sat down. Before he's handed Lily her lemon and lime Bacardi Breezer, noticing she's smoking another cigarette, in the non-smoking section of the restaurant, and that Nicole has probably said nothing to her about it, nor, seemingly, have any of the people on the nearby tables, nor any waiting staff, if there happen to be any in the place. He thinks it's as if everyone is too afraid to approach this weird-looking, maniacally fidgeting teenager, because they are afraid she might erupt in their face if they do. But he's not scared of his elder daughter. 'Where have you been for the last ten years?' he says.

'Are you talking to me, Mark?' Lily says.

'No, that woman over there, actually.' He tries to laugh.

'She says she's been travelling,' says Nicole. 'You know, in a sort of convoy. In caravans and old buses. With travellers.'

'With travellers?' he says, addressing neither Lily nor Nicole specifically, letting them reach for their drinks. 'Kim with a load of travellers? What, New Age travellers? Going where, exactly?'

'All over the country, apparently,' Nicole says. 'In Ireland too.'

'What about school?' he says.

'We didn't go to school,' Lily says. 'Never. It was wicked.'

'Well, how did your mum pay for everything, like petrol?' he says. 'You must have needed that. And food. Did your mum work?'

'There are always people who give you what you need on the road,' she says. 'You share things. It's a way of life. Though Mum did work occasionally. Making things for festivals. Bits of jewellery and clothes. She did fruit-picking and stuff as well.'

'Fruit-picking?' Mark says. 'Kim fruit-picking? I can't see that for a second. And, like, was she seeing anyone in all this time? You know, a bloke? She must have been. Quite a few, I should think. And how did they treat you, Lily?' He knows he's becoming agitated, but he's not sure whether he's specifically concerned at the prospect of Lily having been badly treated by these men, being sexually abused by them, even, or out of some jealous hangover regarding Kim. The fact that she obviously fucked her way around the country. Just because she's become a hippy traveller he doesn't think should mean she's lost her appetite for sex, for casual sex. In pub toilets. In caravans and the backs of old trucks and dilapidated buses. Old library buses, probably – he's seen them. In fields too, he wouldn't be surprised, while out strawberry-picking. 'Did any of them get, you know, funny with you?' he says.

'You mean did any of them stick their fingers up me, Mark?' Lily says. 'Did any of them fuck me?'

'I don't think we need to go into that now, Mark,' Nicole says.

'Yes, we do,' he says. 'If it concerns the welfare of my daughter. We need to go into everything. We need to get to the bottom of all of this. I want to know what she's been doing every single day for the last ten years.'

'Going skitzy,' Lily says, clasping and unclasping her hands again. 'Skitzy, ditzy, witzy,' she laughs, suddenly looking very unsure of herself. Suddenly looking very much like a child, Mark thinks, his child, with her bony shoulders, her small, sunken greeny-blue grey eyes, and not an adolescent. Not a fucking New Age traveller. 'Yuk,' she says, sipping her Bacardi Breezer through a straw straight from the bottle. 'What did you have to get the lemon and lime for? I hate that. The best is water melon. Water melon is cool.'

Nicole says, leaning forward, 'The waitress came. She's given us a ticket. We have to just go up to the buffet. You can have a small salad bowl with the hot food, as a starter or on the side. Or you can have a large salad as a main. They're two different prices.'

'What if I just want the hot food?' Mark says.

'You get the salad anyway.'

'I don't want salad,' he says.

'I don't want anything,' Lily says.

'You two can do what you want,' Nicole says, 'but I'm going to get mine. I'm starving.'

Mark watches Nicole set off for the buffet, his eyes inadvertently following her bottom as she threads her way through the crowded tables, carefully dodging stray children. Her pink suit is badly crumpled at the back, though her trim figure is clearly definable through the material nonetheless – a figure which can still excite him. A very supple figure. Occasionally Nicole used to pretend to act out what she thought were porn-mag poses for him, with her legs all over the place, with her bum stuck right up in the air, but she hasn't done that since Gemma was born.

Turning back to Lily, he finds she's still doing this clasping unclasping thing with her hands, and looking straight at the floor, obviously not wanting to talk to him. It's the first time they've been alone together for over a decade and he feels awkward and shy too, certain that whatever he tries to say next will come out wrong, so after a couple of minutes when neither of them say anything, with her fidgeting making him even more uneasy – he's sure she's doing it to annoy him – and with no sign of Nicole coming back yet, not a sign of her bright, wavy, blonde hair, he decides to get some food himself, leaving Lily on her own.

At the hot-food counter, where the food is being kept warm by a series of lamps, which are making the chicken pieces glow orange and the broccoli florets purple, and the faces of the fat staff, as he looks up, yellow and ill, and because someone's smoking in the queue, and the fact that there are a number of pretend palm trees in big pots scattered around the room – all these stiff, shiny green leaves – and the floor's been laid with a municipal-looking cream tile-effect lino, he's suddenly, overwhelmingly reminded of the hospital cafeteria he took Lily's half-brothers to on the evening Lily was born. He wonders what's happened to them. But not for long. Something else occurs to him, something much more crucial. He wonders if he'd been present the moment she was pulled from her mother's stomach, if she'd been placed in his arms then and there, all bloody and screaming, taking her very first breaths, whether things would have somehow turned out differently. That there wouldn't be this awkwardness between them, this gulf. That, regardless of any great periods of separation, there would be more respect and understanding between them, a true bond. Not just a flicker of one. Some slight recognition.

'Excuse me, are you going to take all day?' the man just behind Mark in the queue says, nudging Mark in the back with the corner of a tray as well, attempting to push him forward. 'I'm getting hungry, mate.'

'Do you want me to stub that cigarette out in your fucking eye?' says Mark.

JULY/AUGUST

I

Nicole made him go alone. Nicole said he was the one who had to tell his mother. She wasn't going to do it for him this time. She said his mum was Lily's grandmother, after all. At the very least, Nicole said, he had to tell her he'd seen Lily and that she was alive, and living in Newbury, and that she will be coming to stay with them shortly. It was only fair, Nicole said, seeing as how much his mother had loved Lily and how supportive of him she had been when Kim had disappeared. Or so he's always maintained to her, anyway, hasn't he?

The one decent thing his mum's done, Mark thinks. Though he's never been sure how much of it was fuelled by her love for Lily or her guilt over all the shit she put him through when he was growing up – by marrying Lawrence. By letting his father and brother just slip off to Canada in the first place. And keeping him here to herself. Keeping him and not his brother. Just keeping her eldest son. He has no idea what Robbie thinks of all this. How he feels about having been abandoned by his mother when he was ten. He hasn't spoken to him since, he has had no direct communication with him whatsoever. The only bits of information he gets to hear about Robbie, and his father, come from Sue, the woman his father originally ran off to Canada with. She is still in contact with his dad and very occasionally sends letters to his mum – perhaps out of her own guilt at helping so dramatically to wrench apart his family, Mark has thought. But what does he know? However, from this very indirect and occasional source Mark has found out that Robbie went to university and has become an architect, of all things, and now runs a successful business in Toronto, apparently specialising in urban regeneration projects. His mum is always saying how proud of Robbie she is, though she rarely mentions the fact that Robbie obviously doesn't feel quite so proud of his mum. At least, as far as Mark knows, his brother has never made any effort to contact her directly, let alone come and see her.

Which is something Mark has become rather thankful for. He doesn't want Robbie turning up, looking and sounding so successful, so clued up, being this fancy architect and nearly American, and therefore making everyone, especially his mum, his adoring, proud mum, think even less of him. Poor, ignorant, fucked-up Mark, he can just see them thinking in comparison. What's more, he presumes that his mum would readily transfer, but probably with twice the conviction, twice the eagerness and energy, so as to make up for lost time, for her betrayal, all her affection away from him, her waste of space of an eldest son, and shift it over to her once lost youngest son. This affection, this love Mark might have taken for granted over the years, that he might have tried his hardest to ignore on occasions too, and distort and abuse as well – like the time he slashed her car tyres, or the time he set fire to her bedroom – but which he nevertheless realises (he probably realised this even when he was trying to hurt her) he very much needs. He surely needs more than his super-successful brother needs anyway. Not that he'll ever admit this. Not to his mum. Not to Nicole. Not to anyone.

It's a short drive to his mum and Lawrence's house, just a mile or so beyond the outer ring road, but still within the southern bypass. He doesn't come this way very often any more, yet when he does, and despite the fact that it all looks so different now, with the main road having been widened and many of the big detached houses lining it having been expanded and renovated, in the boom, with the gardens having been fancied up too and stuffed with exotic trees and shrubs – palms and monkey puzzles and yuccas, so

Nicole's always pointing out – he finds it still fills him with the same sense of dread and claustrophobia, and of boredom also, that afflicted him when he lived there as a teenager, with his mum and Lawrence. The three of them, just the three of them, except when his marvellous stepbrothers and stepsister came to stay.

He especially remembers this feeling coming on when he used to take the bus home from school – that is, when he went to school. Sitting in the back with his mates, with all of them taking the piss out of each other, or out of the girls down the front, pelting them with empty Coke cans, or chewing gum, or showering them with handfuls of crisps, or sometimes crunching crisps into their hair, he would always have this suffocating tightening in his chest. Which, he supposes, only made him behave more boisterously, more mean, as he fought for air, for space. Those girls really hated him.

Mark turns off the main trunk road which has taken him out of the city, just before it becomes a dual carriageway, and on to a winding, but smooth B road. He has a couple of small, executive housing estates to drive through before he hits his mum and Lawrence's estate, which, like the other two, is made up of detached, four- and five-bedroom homes built in the late 1960s and early 1970s. The whole area has become increasingly sought-after, now finding itself located near the southern bypass, the new hospital and the city's high-tech industrial park. Though it's always been quiet and affluent, friendly and trusting. Certainly Mark found it remarkably easy to lift items straight from people's gardens – everything from portable barbecues to garden furniture to koi carp. He took a few cars from here as well, though he always preferred taking cars from the streets around where he used to live, with his mum and dad and brother, which was closer to the city centre and made up of badly lit Victorian terraces. Where people left their cars on the street, and where many of the streets were cut off and others were one way, maze-like, so you could easily get stuck, though he knew his way round every inch of it and could easily outrun the fuzz. He could outrun anyone, in a strange car loaded with his mates all screaming and yelling with laughter.

The funny thing is, he thinks, approaching his mum and step-dad's house, which is set back from the road and perched slightly up a hill, with its sloping front garden filled with neat, blooming flower-beds, and its timber porch thick with climbers, and its frosted-glass front door and large lounge windows, its double garage and steep pitched roof complete with a thick chimney stack clad in crazy stone, that despite all these feelings of dread and bitterness, of an aching boredom, just driving to the place seems to inspire in him, he actually likes the house. He likes it more and more, he thinks, seeing it now. The fact that it's so comfortable and private, and obviously worth a packet. He'd love for Nicole and Gemma and him to be able to live in such a house. Though probably it would have to be in a different part of the city, without quite so many memories.

Somewhere off the old Yarmouth road perhaps. Just the three of them, but this time it would be a complete, unbroken family unit, wouldn't it – with Lily not in the picture. With Lily nowhere near. With life plain and simple, and super-comfortable. The height of his ambition, he thinks. His ultimate goal. He doesn't want to lose sight of it.

2

'Nicole wanted me to tell you myself, Mum,' he says, before taking another sip of tea, while keeping the cup attached to its dainty saucer, relieved Lawrence is out playing golf. 'She would have come too,' he says, swallowing, 'but said if she came then I wouldn't have said anything. You know how I am. Not very good with words.'

'How is she?' Mark's mother Anne says.

'Who?' Mark says.

'Nicole. And Gemma. How's my darling little Gemma? Still playing with her Barbies? Still drawing those lovely pictures?'

'They're fine. They're all right,' he says.

'And your house? Built anything new recently?' she says.

'No, not really.'

'How's the kitchen?'

'It's fantastic, Mum. Standing up brilliantly.'

'When are you going to do one for me?'

'You know I don't like working for family or friends,' he says. 'In case anything goes wrong or I break something, or whatever. It's just too tricky.'

'You could make an exception for your mum, surely?'

They are sitting in the conservatory at the back of the house and it's baking, despite the door to the garden having been slid wide open. His mum's old dog, a small brown terrier, is lying across the entrance, panting and stinking. His mum has always had small brown terriers which stink. He used to kick them when she wasn't looking, hard in their sides, sometimes getting them airborne. Particularly this one called Mini. 'No, Mum,' he says. 'I don't make exceptions for anyone.'

'I bet you would for Nicole's mother,' she says. 'You'd do anything for her.'

'I said, Mum, I don't make exceptions for anyone. Even if it was Nicole's best friend I wouldn't do it.'

'Just come and have a look at the space. You might change your mind, or at least you could give me some advice. Lawrence is itching to get it done.'

His mum never lets him say what he wants to say. She's always butting in, talking about what she wants to talk about. She does this with him, she does it with Lawrence, he's observed. As soon as he sat down he tried to bring up the topic of Lily, having thought that that was the only way he'd be able to do it – to get it out immediately. Now he's already finished his tea and is starting to sweat badly, knowing he can't go home without telling her about Lily because Nicole would kill him – how he wishes his wife was with him. It's always so much easier in situations like this with her around. He sometimes thinks of her as his brains, his mouthpiece.

'Mum,' he says, the heat, and the stinking dog making him determined not to let her side-track him further, to lose his place – he wants to leave like ten minutes ago – 'I haven't come here to talk about bloody kitchens. There's something I have to tell you.' He sees that his hands are shaking, so he puts his empty cup and saucer on the windowsill, between two pot plants, and sits on his hands, looking straight at her, noticing how old she suddenly seems, how much older than the last time he saw her. Her face is so lined and the skin on her neck so droopy. She has his build, being thin and angular – Lily's build – though her hair was always darker than his, almost a chestnut, but for a while she's been having it highlighted in a bid to hide the grey and to make herself look younger, though he thinks it's only doing the opposite. 'Mum,' he says, 'I've seen Lily. Kim got in touch and we went to see her. She's all right. Well, she's not all right. She's all screwed-up, if you ask me. But she's alive.'

'I know,' says Anne, nodding, the folds of skin on her neck visibly moving too – not quite flapping but moving independently of her neck and head, moving with her hooped earrings.

'What do you mean, you know?' he says, jumping up – something just stopping him from kicking the dog out of his way.

'Kim rang me a few weeks ago wanting your number. Didn't she say that's how she got your number?'

'I suppose I forgot to ask,' he says. 'But why didn't you tell me she rang? Why didn't you tell me that you had heard from her? I can't believe you kept quiet about this. I can't fucking believe it. Who do you think you are?' He steps over the dog and into the garden, into direct swooping sunlight – feeling a blast of sun on his face and forehead, and an intense heat boring straight through his clothes too and on to his bare chest and legs – before he quickly steps back into the conservatory.

'I was only thinking of you,' Anne says. 'I didn't want you getting worked up, in case she decided not to ring you. In case it didn't work out. She sounded very uncertain about it all on the phone. Very nervous.'

'That's hardly surprising,' he says. 'And what else did you two talk about?'

'Nothing much then. She just told me how Lily was, and that they had been travelling but were now settling down. And I told her a bit about you. How things have been going well for you, that you're married to Nicole and have Gemma. She's rung back since. We've spoken again.'

'So what, you and her are like that, are you?' he says, crossing his fingers and shaking them at his mother. He could slap her. He really could. 'Best mates all of a sudden?'

'I always could talk to her,' says Anne, standing up, but backing away from him. 'You know that. I obviously didn't agree with her about everything, but I could talk to her at least and try to understand her point of view. I always thought that that was the best way forward. After all, Lily is my granddaughter. It's her interests I have at heart.'

'What about me? Who's got my interests at heart?'

'Come on, Mark, we're talking about a young girl. A vulnerable young girl from a broken home. You can stand up for yourself. You're quite tough enough.'

'She's not that young. You haven't seen her. Or have you? You probably have. You've probably been there to stay already. Being Lily's posh gran all over again. Like nothing's changed. Maybe you've secretly been in touch with Kim for the last ten fucking years. I wouldn't put it past you.'

'No, Mark, of course I haven't. But I'm longing to see Lily. Kim's told me all about her. She sounds so pretty and clever. I can't wait until she's here next week.'

'I don't fucking believe all this, you even know when she's coming to stay. I don't fucking believe it,' he says, making his way through the house, the house he covets so much, his ideal home, through the hall on a plush new cream carpet – his mother is always buying new carpet – towards the bright glow of the frosted-glass front door.

'Kim just wanted to make sure that Lily will be properly looked after when she's here,' Anne says. 'That I'd be around to keep an eye on her.'

'It gets worse,' he says. 'I hate things going on behind my back. You're as bad as Kim. You're as bad as each other. Fucking conspiring against me. What the fuck have I done to deserve this?'

'Mark, I'm only doing it for Lily's sake, and yours. Surely you can see that. And please, don't talk to me like that, I am your mother. You should show me a little more respect.'

'You're lucky I'm talking to you at all,' he says, struggling with the latch – Lawrence and his mum are as paranoid about security as he is.

Eventually getting the door open and stepping on to the drive, which gently slopes away from the house between a low box hedge on one side and a bed of yellow chrysanthemums on the other, he turns towards his mother, who has followed him outside but is clearly still keeping her distance, and he says, absorbing her aged features again, the wrinkles and spare folds of skin, the grey-brown hair absolutely failing to make her look any younger, the tired, bloodshot eyes, he says, 'Don't tell me, you've heard from Robbie too. Well, has he got AIDS yet?' He surprises himself by saying this. He hasn't associated AIDS with Robbie before but in his boiling anger, because Robbie is this fancy architect in Toronto, because, as far as he knows, he has never been married or has any children, and has never bothered to contact them, it suddenly seems to make perfect sense – that his brother is bent and ashamed of it. It's also something else to attack his mother with, he thinks – not just mentioning Robbie but suggesting he's a homosexual, and has AIDS. He can't let the idea go.

'Is that why he hasn't come to see us? Because he's covered in sores and cancerous growths. Because he's bedridden and unable to walk – I've seen those homo AIDS victims on telly.'

He gets to his car and unlocks it and climbs in but before driving off, before flicking the car into reverse and flooring the Astra's tightly sprung accelerator, he opens the window and shouts, 'Who's got his interests at heart? Not fucking you. You didn't just abandon him, did you? You kicked him out. Your youngest son. Now look what's happened to him. You heartless cunt.'

3

Seeing his mother turn away from him but hesitate for a moment or two before going back into her home, makes him think of Lily standing by the front door of her house, with him and Nicole having just dropped her off after the pub lunch, where she didn't eat a thing, though she did manage to drink three Bacardi Breezers, the lemon and lime one and then two water melon-flavoured bottles Nicole bought her, all through a straw. He thinks of Lily standing there with her headphones firmly back on, facing the door, determined not to turn round to wave at him and Nicole as they drove off – waiting for her mum to let her in. Not wanting him to see she'd been crying.

He'd noticed the tears welling as she got out of his car. When he said, 'You shouldn't drink so much at your age.' And Nicole then said, 'She's all right. I'm sure it's only once in a while. We've all done it.' With Nicole being so calm and understanding made him feel foolish for admonishing Lily. And he suddenly felt desperately sorry for his daughter too, for having to go back to Kim and that dilapidated house. As he watched her get out of the car, with part of him somehow still wanting to hang on to her, to protect her – he was so confused – he couldn't help saying, 'Perhaps next time you might like to come up to our place. You know, to come and stay for a few days. With your old dad. With Nicole and Gemma. I'll talk to your mum about it, I promise.' She nodded at him, with her eyes watering up, but she didn't say anything, not even a, Sure, Mark, and once out of the car she didn't look back either. Her skinny, awkward body just shuffled up the grubby path, with the frayed ends of her jeans already as dirty as they could be.

Nicole said, as they drove off, 'It's not surprising she's upset. It can't have been easy for her. And you weren't exactly very charitable, Mark. You could have been a bit more sympathetic. You are her dad, after all.'

'What do you mean, I've just asked her to stay, haven't I?' he said.

'Yeah, but you didn't talk to her much at lunch. Except to ask her those stupid questions about whether she was interfered with by Kim's boyfriends. You didn't have to do that. Not then.'

'Look, I've asked her to stay,' he said, feeling even more foolish and guilty. 'She knows I care about her. I even gave Kim some money for her. What more could I do?'

After a long pause Nicole said, 'I'm not sure I want her to come to stay. Not just yet. We haven't even told Gemma she exists. Besides, I'd worry about having her in the house. She might drop a cigarette and cause a fire or something.'

'Now who's being charitable?' Mark said. 'I thought you and her really hit it off – at my expense.'

'I felt sorry for her with you being so difficult,' Nicole said. 'Someone had to talk to her. But that doesn't mean I want her invading our lives. Mucking everything up. She's completely nuts.'

'Kim probably won't let her come and stay anyway. I wouldn't worry about it. Or Lily won't want to come. One or the other,' he said, agreeing in his mind with Nicole about Lily being nuts. About not wanting her invading his space, mucking up their lives. Causing a fire. At least part of him not wanting this – he wished he understood himself better.

However, he thinks, returning to the city from his mum's, along the newly widened main road, past the big, smart, detached houses – properties he might once have checked over for a security lapse, an unlatched window, say, or a loose door, a faulty alarm – Kim did want Lily to come and stay. He didn't even have to ask her. She rang him about it, three weeks or so after their visit to Newbury, saying Lily had been particularly upset after that day, and consequently hadn't been getting on at all well at her new school, but she had been a lot better recently and had mentioned that he had asked her to stay, and that they had both discussed it and decided it would be all right, as long as he and Nicole promised to keep a good eye on her – she was a sensitive kid and not used to them, after all.

Kim told Mark it wouldn't be possible for her to come and stay until the summer holidays because she didn't want Lily being distracted from her school work again, but sometime towards the end of July would be about right. Lily could even come down by train, but he'd have to send her the money for the ticket, and while he was at it, could he send her a bit of extra money as Lily desperately needed some new clothes, some summer clothes, and she wanted a mobile phone as well, just a Pay As You Go, because all her friends at school had one. Kim told Mark that their daughter was sick of being the only person she knew who didn't have a mobile. 'She's under a lot of pressure about it,' Kim said. And anyway she thought it would be a good idea if Lily had one because then she'd always know where she was, and of course Lily could always ring her or the police if she were in trouble. It would make things a lot easier and safer for everyone.

4

He sent the money, just as he feels he's always done exactly what Kim's asked him to do. Like marry her, for instance. She came up with the idea one evening shortly after they had had an argument, it was probably their first proper argument, when they'd screamed at each other and she had cried and he had thumped the wall, in frustration. The argument was about the night before, how they were in a club, Henry's again, it mostly always was Henry's, and he had wanted to go home and she hadn't, so he left, returning to her flat rather than his, paying for her baby-sitter too, and how she then didn't appear until the morning, saying she had gone to a girlfriend's for a chat after the club shut and fell asleep on her friend's settee, and he hadn't believed her for a moment, of course. She said, when they'd both calmed down a little, when the pain in his hand was subsiding and she was sitting on the sheepskin on the floor, with only a towel wrapped around her, with her pink legs spread out on the white wool and her hair still dripping, because she'd had an early bath, she said that what she really wanted was a man to make her feel secure. She was fed up with men who just wanted to screw her. Men who screwed her and got her pregnant and then fucked off. She wanted someone she could rely on. She wanted someone who was prepared to make a proper commitment to her. Someone permanent. A husband. And for that she'd do anything. She'd suck their knob twice a day. She'd wank off in front of them. She'd get out her Mandy's Magic Wand – had she showed him that yet? – and demonstrate how it should be done with a dildo. She'd make sure she fucked them senseless, every night – frontwards, backwards, sideways, on top, underneath, inside out – every which way. She'd fuck the wind out of them. She'd smother herself in baby oil and let them fuck her up the bum also, if that's what they wanted. She'd be up for it all the fucking time. Like a rabbit. Like a wild rabbit. A wild nympho rabbit. Quickies in the back of the car, behind buildings, in public conveniences. Out in the open. What's more, she said, they'd be the only one. She would never sneak off with anyone else. She would guarantee them that. An exclusive contract. On paper. Something she'd never promised anyone before. 'Come here, you,' she said, letting the towel fall open, 'and fucking say you'll marry me.'

5

They arrive half an hour early only to find, once they've located an arrivals screen which works, the only one that does seem to work – tucked into the far corner of the entrance hall, just by Costa Coffee – that Lily's train is running twenty minutes late and hasn't yet been given a platform. Mark and Nicole walk out on to the small concourse to find it's completely packed, and raucous, with holiday-makers and foreign-language students (the city's always full of them), with shoppers and commuters. Judging by the noise and the way people are milling about restlessly, Mark reckons no one knows anything. Plus there are no guards about. No Anglian Railways staff. No British Transport police. And not a single train in sight.

Nicole suggests they go to the café for a cappuccino and perhaps a nibble, seeing as it's nearly four, but Mark doesn't feel like sitting down, nor drinking anything, and he says as much. Apart from the fact that his stomach is incredibly unsettled – he's had the squits all day – he's worried that he won't be able to get a good position on the platform when they do announce which one the London train will be arriving at. He's worried that maybe the train might suddenly come in on time, or early even, and that the screen is showing inaccurate information, or hasn't been updated quickly enough. Whenever he gets trains, or uses any form of public transport, which isn't often, he's always being given wrong information. He would ask at the information counter to check that the one working screen in the station, over by Costa Coffee, is showing the correct information, but the queue is huge, and from what he can see there is only one person in attendance, and he thinks he could miss the train arriving just by waiting to get the information, stuck in the ticket hall.

He's also worried about his car. The only space he could find in the car park was between two estate cars, one of which he noticed, a 200-series Merc, already had a number of dents and scratches on one side, the side in fact which he had to park next to. He reckons that people who drive around in cars full of dents don't usually give a monkey's whether they accidentally happen to add a few more while they're parking, or leaving a parking spot, and are therefore that much more careless than other drivers. Besides, he also hates parking in the station because people never look what they are doing with their luggage, especially those big cases on wheels. He thinks he should have written down the Merc's registration number in case he finds some scratches on the Astra later – he's been caught out by people doing a runner before. For a moment he contemplates sending Nicole back to wait in the car, to help protect it, to go bloody berserk if someone dares touch it, but he needs her with him more, on the platform, ready for the moment Lily steps off the train – whenever that'll be – in her ridiculously frayed jeans and saggy top, with her nose stud sparkling for half the city to see, and her Discman clamped about her head. Not paying attention, not looking where's she's going, completely lost to the world. He can just see it.

'Fucking typical,' he says. 'Why isn't the train on time? Why do none of these information screens work? Why does nothing ever work in this fucking country? I'm going to look at the magazines.'

'What do you want me to do?' Nicole says. 'Stand here?'

'You can come if you want,' he says, setting off in the direction of Smiths, or where Smiths used to be the last time he came to the station. Except, having pushed through a large group of foreign-language students, all wearing huge, floppy black and red jester hats with bells at the end of the dangly bits, and fat, multi-coloured rucksacks, he doesn't see it this time. It has gone. Or rather it has been boarded up, he slowly realises, and there's a sign explaining that the store has closed for refurbishment, but will re-open shortly and that a temporary news-stand is located by Costa Coffee. He didn't want to buy a paper, he just wanted to flick through some car magazines, and perhaps *Playboy* or *Penthouse*, or *Razzle* – if no one was standing too close. He looks over his shoulder to see Nicole has followed him through the jostling crowd of jesters. 'Look what they've done here,' he says. 'They've shut Smiths.'

'Mark,' says Nicole, 'get a grip. They're just refurbishing it. Why should it bother you anyway? You never come to the station.'

'I just wanted to look at some magazines,' he says, 'and take my mind off things.'

'Well, you can talk to me instead. I haven't left work early just to be ignored by you. I'm extremely busy at the moment – a lot of people depend on me now. You know it wasn't easy for me to get the time off, especially as we are going on holiday soon. Anyway, I could be picking up Gemma from Mum's, rather than putting up with you, you moody git.' She pushes him on his arm, but play-fully, affectionately, how she only ever pushes or punches him. 'At least Gemma appreciates me.'

'Sorry. Sorry, sweetheart,' Mark says. 'It's this Lily stuff. It makes me all edgy. Thanks for coming. You know I couldn't do it without you.' He grabs hold of Nicole's bare shoulders – she's wearing a short black top with straps and a lace trim, having taken her work blouse off in the car – and pulls her to him so he feels her breasts squash against his chest. Her head falls on to his shoulder and nestles against his neck, making space for itself. Holding her, unconsciously pressing his fingers into the flesh on her shoulders, picking up her inner warmth, her body glow, he thinks, smelling her fragrant hairspray, he peers through her hair, trying to get it out of his eyes with his nose and his mouth by gently blowing, and sees, thickly spread across the whole of the concourse, the hundreds of people still clueless as to where they should be standing, as to what is happening regarding arrivals and depar-tures. There are still no trains in sight but despite the general air of chaos and frustration Mark begins to feel much calmer – holding on to his wife, his rock. The one person who keeps him together.

The one person who is definitely all his. As he is all hers. And has always been. He knows she likes that about him – his focus, the strength of his commitment, his passion. When Nicole initially said she thought she might not be able to get off work early, he actually contemplated ringing his mum to ask her to come with him to the station to meet Lily, which would have meant having to apologise for losing it with her when he last saw her – but he knows he'll apologise for that eventually. He always says sorry to her. Not that he always forgives her, there's too much anger and pain deep down for that. However, he does like to know that she'll be around and willing to talk to him if he happens to need her – when he needs her next.

Apart from Nicole, he has no one else he can turn to, no brother, no father, no close friends. He's been in enough trouble in the past to know you can't shut everyone out, that there should always be someone you can rely on. Just as, he thinks, when he used to nick cars there were always at least two of them. And the few burglaries he was involved in usually consisted of a team of people. Safety in numbers, he thinks. Strength in numbers. He gets scared on his own. He's a complete wuss – they were right at school all those years ago. They could see through him even then.

'Thanks for getting off work specially and coming,' he says, loosening his grip on Nicole. 'You know I'm hopeless without you. And thanks for telling Gem about Lily so brilliantly. I couldn't have done it. Not after my attempt at telling Mum. That really knocked the shit out of me.'

'You've got to learn to face up to things on your own. I can't be with you all the time,' she says. 'I can't say everything for you.'

'Why not?' he says. 'Women are much better at saying things than men. They don't get stuck, not like I do, anyway. That's why I always lose arguments.'

'No, you don't,' says Nicole.

'Not when I start hitting people,' he says, laughing, standing on tiptoes and pretending to head-butt her. 'But that's different. That doesn't count.'

6

Because the train is delayed another five minutes Mark realises they will have to get a new Pay and Display ticket for the car. He only bought a one-hour ticket and there is no way he is going to risk his car being clamped by some idiot who'll wreck his alloy hubs and six-month-old low-profile Contis. But before he has time to tell Nicole he's going to get the new ticket she's snatched the keys from his hand, saying she'll do it, leaving him by the platform, the number of which they eventually announced, along with news of the further delay, as if it was some consolation. He would chase after her but he doesn't want to lose his place right by the platform barrier which he pushed and shoved so hard to get, and so he finds himself at the head of a crowd of foreign-language students, with their massive hats bobbing about behind him, when the train slowly appears out of the distant tangle of glinting track and railway workings.

The train seems to take forever to pull into the station and come to a juddering stop, and by the time it does the foreign-language students, along with just about everyone else, have flooded past him, ignoring the pleas of an official – who appeared from nowhere at the last moment – and broken through the barrier and made their way right up the platform so as to be sure of a seat once the arriving passengers have disembarked. Mark walks a little way along the platform but he doesn't want to miss Lily and he stops, trying to pick out exactly who's getting off and who's getting on from where he is, not sure how the hell he's meant to locate this skinny girl with lank, shoulder-length hair and scruffy clothes. Though he doesn't want to appear over-anxious and attempts to remain calm and rooted to the spot, while looking over his shoulder every so often for Nicole. He can't imagine it can take that long to get to the car park and back. What the fuck is she doing? he says to himself.

It is not until the platform begins to really thin out, with fewer and fewer people disembarking and with the students and their silly hats mostly loaded on, with there now being virtually no chance of him missing her, that he begins to worry that she wasn't on the train. That either she never got on it, or something happened to her on the way. He did express considerable concern about Lily travelling all this way on her own to Kim, given her age and her drinking habits – he came right out with it, telling Kim about Lily's problem with Bacardi Breezers, and fags, and probably drugs too – but Kim just dismissed him, saying she was perfectly sensible and quite streetwise and not a child any more. And that she was used to travelling long distances on her own.

Mark starts imagining what could have happened to her. How she might have got drunk and been picked up by a stranger, who then forced her off the train at say Ipswich, and who is now raping her in some squalid bedsit – holding a knife to her throat, ripping her frayed trousers off, spreading her skinny legs, muffling her screams. He knows who to blame if that's happened, all right – Kim. He doesn't know how she could have been so stupid as to have suggested Lily took the train in the first place, and then supposedly put her on the bloody thing – his thirteen-year-old daughter. She's still only a kid, he thinks, whatever Kim says. A vulnerable, innocent kid. His kid. Nothing can change that.

Lily's almost bang in front of him before he realises she isn't being raped in a squalid bedsit in Ipswich and that she did make the journey in one piece after all. He simply didn't recognise her as she walked up the platform. He didn't recognise this girl, this child, his kid, who's now smiling at him, that same old scowly smile, just inches away, because of her clothes, because she's wearing a shiny tight black skirt and short pink T-shirt with 'Babe' written on the front in sequins. Because she's got short, bright blonde hair too. And because she tottered and zig-zagged down the platform on a pair of white stilettos, dragging a large bag. Oh, he noticed her all right, he couldn't not have noticed her, perhaps she even reminded him of someone, however, it didn't occur to him for a second it could be Lily.

'Hi, Mark,' she says, loudly, confidently, dropping her bag at his feet. 'Aren't you going to kiss me, then?'

Not knowing what else to do, completely shocked by her appearance, he leans across and kisses her on the cheek, smelling a very pungent perfume, a perfume he couldn't possibly name – he only knows the smell of what Nicole wears, which is *Romance* by Ralph Lauren, and it's definitely not that – and cigarette smoke, and also alcohol. Possibly Bacardi. 'Have you been drinking?' he says.

'What me?' she says, pointing to herself with both hands, pointing to the word 'Babe' on her T-shirt.

'Yeah, you,' he says, noticing the small ring in her belly button, and, looking up, the matching nose ring, plus the layers of make-up, the lip gloss and light blue eye shadow, the mascara and thick foundation she has applied, though which hasn't quite hidden all her spots – her adolescence, her youth, he thinks. The fact she's still a kid.

'I don't drink,' she says. 'Alcohol's bad for you. Where's Nicole? And where's this Gemma? Where's my little sister? It's not just you, is it? Boring old Mark.'

'Nicole went to get another ticket for the car,' he says, surveying the rest of the platform and the now largely empty concourse, but he can't see his wife.

'Gemma's with Nicole's mum. You'll meet her at home later, don't worry about that.' He looks at Lily again, her dramatic change, wondering if this is where the money he'd sent to Kim has gone, the money supposedly for her new summer clothes – sensible, practical gear, he'd imagined, for a girl her age – and her mobile, which no one has yet given him the number for. 'You've had your hair cut and got some new clothes, then,' he says.

'So what if I have?' she says.

'Just noticing,' he says. 'They must have been expensive – that skirt and those shoes.'

'They're not all new, if you have to know. Some of them are a friend's.'

'Where did you get your hair done?'

'At a friend's.'

'The same one?'

'Yeah, the same one.'

'Good friend.'

'Yeah,' she says. 'Are we going to stand here all day, talking about my clothes? I'm thirsty. I need a Diet Coke.'

'The car's this way,' he says, starting to move towards the concourse, looking behind him every so often to check she's following, hearing her dragging and clunking her bag along the ground. It occurs to him that he should at least offer to carry her bag for her, but he decides she is thirteen and quite capable of carrying it herself. Or would be if she wasn't wearing such ridiculously high heels, which is her problem. Catching her from the corner of his eye again, wobbling along, bent forward with the strain of the bag, and with her breasts in her short, tight Babe T-shirt seemingly thrust out, so she appears to have a cleavage even – at her age – he realises who she reminded him of when he first saw her (though hadn't yet recognised her) tottering up the platform. She reminded him of Kim, of course. At least how Kim was all those years ago when he first knew her – before she became a hippy. It's Lily's pushed-out tits and tight, tarty clothes – remembering when he last saw his daughter in Newbury, when she was wearing the droopy purple top with too-long sleeves, that she didn't appear to have breasts, or anything touching a womanly figure, that she appeared more like a scruffy boy then. But now there's no mistaking her sex, and, he reckons, what she's up for. Being Kim's daughter. Despite her age.

Reaching the concourse with Lily still behind him, dragging and clunking her bag, he can't decide what version of her he prefers, what version he finds less troubling, less offensive. In a way he thinks Lily's new look is probably more how he originally imagined his daughter would be, before he saw her in Newbury – knowing Kim, knowing himself. But he also finds it more disturbing somehow, more worrying. He can easily imagine the sort of trouble she could get herself into wearing that tiny Babe T-shirt. Coupled with her cocky attitude – which doesn't seem to have changed much.

As he'd been frantically trying to finish a job before Lily arrived – these shelves and a bathroom cupboard for a friend of Nicole's sister's – and had been troubling himself over Gemma's reaction to the news that not only did she have a sister after all, but that this long-lost big sister was about to come and stay, and the fact that he'd fallen out with his mother and wasn't quite sure how to make peace, he hasn't had time to think about what they would actually do with Lily when she arrived – how exactly they would entertain her, how they would cope with her. The only thing he decided was that he was not going to let her smoke anywhere near his house, inside or outside – he doesn't want a load of fag ends littering the patio – whatever Nicole says about it. And now she's here looking like her mum did fifteen years ago, like some hot tease, his own daughter – what's he meant to call her now? Babe? – he starts to worry seriously about what the hell they are going do with her for the next few days. If indeed they'll even be able to keep a proper eye on her (which is definitely his and Nicole's job, not his mother's).

For a moment he contemplates putting her back on the train and returning her to Kim. He doesn't see why he should be responsible for Lily's welfare, for keeping her out of harm's way, not with her looking like this. That has to be Kim's job, as she clearly encouraged this transformation. He's furious with Kim, and with himself for saying Lily can come and stay. He's absolutely furious. But if anyone can knock some sense into the girl, he decides, it'll be him. It'll have to be him. He'll teach her some manners all right. He'll teach her how to behave. And how to dress like a proper thirteen-year-old. Who does she think she is?

7

'Hey,' says Nicole, appearing in the grand station entrance hall, below the newly cleaned Victorian clock, which is telling the wrong time, just as Mark is convincing himself that something awful must have happened to his car – to really make his day.

'What's happened to it?' he says.

'What?' says Nicole.

'The car. The fucking car,' he says.

'Nothing,' she says. 'Nothing's happened to it.'

'What have you been doing, then?' he says.

'I don't know. Looking at the river. Sitting in the sun. I suppose I thought you didn't need me there after all. That it would be better if I wasn't.' She turns to Lily. 'Look at you, miss. You look great. I love your hair.'

'Fuck this,' says Mark. He feels that far from Nicole thinking she didn't need to be there, he's the one who shouldn't have bothered to come. That he's the one who's not necessary – the complete outsider. He looks at his wife and elder daughter together, in their tight tops and skimpy skirts, high heels and bright, highlighted hair, with both of them a little flushed, Lily more so, and wonders whether in fact Lily's trying to style herself on Nicole, and not on her mum, seeing as she probably has no idea what her mum used to look like before she became a scummy hippy traveller.

Mark can hear Nicole say, as they head across the car park, with him leading the way, eager to get on with the next diabolical part of today, he hears Nicole say to Lily, in the car park, above the hum of rush-hour traffic on the nearby inner ring road, and the piercing squawks of a flock of gulls swooping over the River Wensum, 'So how was the train?' And he hears Lily reply, in her squeaky, nervous, West Country accent, without any of that earlier confidence with which she presented herself to him, 'Wicked. I met a man who kept buying me drinks. He wanted to snog me but I wouldn't let him, so he held my hand instead.'

8

The night before Lily arrived, when Gemma had finally gone to sleep – after dressing and undressing and dressing again her Barbies, after doing some colouring in, after looking at a couple of books, after pretending to read a few short sentences, after Nicole had told her that she did in fact have a sister – Mark went into her warm, soft room. He had been too scared and ashamed to go in while she was awake. Scared because he didn't know how she would react to him, he couldn't have coped with any sign of rejection or hostility, not from his little princess, and ashamed because he hadn't told her himself, and hadn't told her sooner. He'd only ever said that she was his precious princess, his one and only sweetheart. His flower. His petal. His beautiful curly wurly, who he would always protect. She could count on him. He'd be right there, just for her, his only child, forever. He'd whispered this stuff to her for years, while stroking her hot forehead as she tried to go to sleep, and as she slept too, all well out of earshot of Nicole.

He knew he shouldn't have been scared or ashamed, particularly after Nicole came downstairs to tell him that Gemma seemed fine about it. 'She wasn't fazed at all,' Nicole said. 'I don't know why we worried so much. Gemma even said she's really looking forward to showing Lily her Barbies, and her Wendy house, to having someone to play with for once. I tried to tell her Lily was much older and probably wasn't interested in Barbies, or playing with little girls, but I'm not sure she took that bit in. She also asked whether she had a secret brother as well. I said I didn't think so. Unless Daddy's been up to no good behind my back. No, I didn't really say that last bit. I know you'd never do anything like that to me.'

Nevertheless, he still couldn't go into Gemma's room until he was certain she was asleep, until he heard her snotty, congested, hay fever-induced snoring. Normally, Gemma insists on keeping her sidelight on, but Nicole had obviously turned it off when she was going to sleep so only dim light from the landing was drifting into the room, and he felt a few bits of Shelly's house or Playmobil crunch under his shoes as he stepped over to her bed, the bed he'd made specially for her. Removing a few cuddly toys, her tiger and rabbit and dog – the Andrex dog they got free after buying all this toilet paper – he sat on the edge of her bed, careful, too, not to sit on a stray arm or leg, as he'd done that before. He pulled the duvet away from her face and felt her cheek, the intense warmth, before running his hand over her hair, her mother's thick, curly blonde hair, lightly brushing it off her forehead. Feeling how sweaty and damp she was. And as he sat there loving her, idolising her, worshipping her, trying to make up for the fact he was useless at saying important, even necessary things, by way of kinetic energy, or telepathy, or whatever it was called – like this connection he'd always felt he had with Lily – he thought of how much he hadn't wanted Gemma in the first place.

He remembered just how much he hadn't wanted another child after his experience with Kim. How he'd said to himself shortly after Kim had disappeared, never again, no more kids. No more shit like that ever again. Kim had made him realise quite how much he distrusted women. As far as he could see, women didn't stop at anything to make a point. Kim had taken his child away, to get at him, hadn't she? She had lied to the social services. She had lied to the police. She had lied to him, continually. And then there was his mother, also, who had happily waved goodbye to her youngest son when he was only ten. She had let him go off to Canada, with her ex-husband, her violent ex-husband if she was to be believed, and his new girlfriend, a woman Robbie barely knew, fully understanding there would be no contact in the future, no contact whatsoever, that that was part of the deal. Mark didn't know how women could be so cruel, so spiteful. He thought men were meant to be the shits when it came to kids and families and responsibility, but in his experience it was the women. They were like a completely different species. They were inhuman.

Despite meeting Nicole, despite falling for her sensibleness, her rationality, her easy-going but caring nature, despite realising she was the best thing that could have happened to him, despite eventually marrying her – oh, she went for his looks all right, his swagger, his strength, and strength of purpose – and them setting up home together in the cosy terrace, halfway up the hill, he still felt uneasy about having a child with her. He kept thinking she might suddenly turn, that his luck wouldn't hold out and that she wasn't being honest with him, that she was just another Kim. For Nicole longed to have a child, she begged him. She said there wasn't much point in them being married if they didn't at least try to have children. It was what being married was all about. Why she stupidly married him. He said she had to understand things from his point of view – why he was being weird about doing it without a Durex.

But she got pregnant soon enough after they were married anyway – he couldn't resist her, her gorgeous body, her uncomplicated eagerness in bed, the way she was always so undemanding yet always willing to satisfy him. She couldn't resist him, could she – her bit of rough, as she used to say, her Jack the lad, her main man, the first real man she'd been with. The first man she'd felt secure with. Her protector. Her saviour. And he found himself surprisingly happy about her being pregnant. Overjoyed, really. It was as if a gap had been filled, as if his life had suddenly come together and he felt complete again. And he realised that he had just been being paranoid. He told Nicole as much. He said he'd do anything to make it up to her. So she said, right, he could redo the kitchen at last. And re-lay the patio. And build the brick barbecue in the corner he'd been talking about. He did get round to doing the kitchen and the patio but he hasn't had time to build the barbecue yet. If he's not working there is now always Gemma to play with. His little Gem. His curly wurly. The centre of his universe until very recently. He certainly made sure he was right there the moment she was born. Holding Nicole's hand, flinching as she screamed and whimpered, and fought for breath, he watched this bloody, dark head slowly emerge from between Nicole's legs, and then the rest of her tiny, slimy body quickly slip out on to the mucky white plastic sheet. It was in the same hospital as where his first daughter was born, in the same block, on the very same floor, nearly seven years later, but how different it all was this time round, how natural. Both he and Nicole were soon crying, with Nicole having been given the baby. With the baby on Nicole's chest, nestling between her enlarged breasts, leaving these smears of blood and mucus on her smooth, tanned skin. Making her mark, he thought at the time. Claiming her territory. A bit like a giant red slug, he couldn't help thinking. He didn't pick the baby up until a nurse had cleaned her first and weighed her and wrapped her in a blanket. Then he held her in his arms, knowing there was no danger of her messing up his shirt, and said, 'Hello, gorgeous.'

In Gemma's warm, dim bedroom he stopped brushing the hair away from her forehead, and standing up, he leaned over her and kissed her on her cheek. A big, wet kiss. A kiss he wanted to make sure contained everything he felt for her. Everything, in fact, he felt about his life with his wife and daughter, in one big, sloppy kiss, the summation of his feeling. As if by expressing it like this it wouldn't just reconfirm his feelings, to his family, to himself, but would also somehow seal them forever. In case they ever came under threat. In case any doubt crept in. For whatever reason.

9

Mark thinks he's the first up, he thinks he's the first up by miles, and he comes thundering down the stairs in his pyjamas, and goes straight to the kitchen sink, desperate for a glass of water. Because he's operating on automatic, knowing where everything is so well, expecting everything to be as it always is, barely thinking because of the hour, because he's slept so badly, it takes him a few moments to register he's not alone. Lily is sitting at the kitchen table, staring at him, looking perplexed, beginning to smile, that smile of hers, of his – perhaps it's really not quite so mocking, so sarcastic, he thinks, but how you start to look when everything is waged against you – with her headphones rammed on. And with tinny rap music just audible.

'Put it away, Mark,' she says.

Instantly knowing exactly what has happened – his cock is always falling out of his loose pyjamas' flies, especially in the morning when he needs a pee and it's swollen and heavy – he turns away from her, trying to get the material to overlap. He continues to stare out of the kitchen window, at the weak sunlight just beginning to reach the corner of the patio, the corner where he's meant to have built the barbecue, while feeling himself blush, the skin on the back of his neck burn, and thinking that there is nowhere he can go to be alone, to have any peace without being spied on, to have a moment or two to himself without having some teenager taking the piss out of him, even at this time in the morning, thinking his house has been taken over. That it has been invaded. Lily's only been there two days but already he's finding her presence suffocating. The way he never knows what she's going to do next, where she'll pop up – with her amazingly irrational, restless habits. Yesterday, for instance, she didn't appear until almost lunchtime – though they heard her moving about Gemma's room, where she's sleeping, much earlier – and now today she's downstairs at 6.30 in the morning, fully dressed, listening to her Discman.

Plus yesterday she was wearing her Babe T-shirt and skimpy black skirt again, and had lavishly reapplied her make-up, whereas today, he sees, she's wearing a pair of baggy, frayed jeans, probably the pair he saw her in in Newbury, and a tatty, camouflage-print T-shirt, and although her hair is still bright blonde, perhaps because it is so clearly fake, and not neatly brushed or moussed, he reckons she looks more like a hippy New Age traveller than ever. Like she should be out on the street, huddled in some doorway, under a piss-stained sleeping-bag, and not in his kitchen, being cheeky, embarrassing him.

'What are you doing down here at this time?' he says, loudly.

'Nothing,' she says, not looking at him. 'Where's Nicole?'

'In bed, asleep,' he says.

'What time does she get up?' she says.

'In a bit. It's not even seven,' he says. 'Why? Why do you want her?'

'I want to go home,' Lily says, still not looking at him. 'I want to see my mum.'

'Oh, right,' he says. 'But you're meant to be here for a week. You're not meant to go home until next Thursday.' He can't think why she'd want to see her mum. He can't think why anyone would ever want to see Kim.

'So,' she says. 'I want to go home now. I'm bored.'

'Watch TV,' he says.

'It gives you square eyes,' she says.

'Read a book,' he says.

'Books are boring,' she says.

'You better go home, then,' he says, helping himself to another glass of water while looking for the kettle.

'See, I knew you didn't want me here,' she says.

'No, that's not true,' he says. 'I asked you. I am your dad. Of course I want to see you.' He feels funny saying this, as if he still hasn't acknowledged to himself that he is her father. Since she arrived he's been avoiding thinking about that. He's been trying to avoid her too, letting Nicole and Gemma entertain her, with Gemma proving to be surprisingly good at it – his little angel, his precious Gem.

'Yeah, well, now I'm here you don't like it much,' she says.

'Yeah, I do,' he says. 'But we all have to get used to each other, don't we? It's going to take a bit of time. Besides, this house isn't huge, is it?'

'You mean you don't like me in it – in case I mess it up or something. In case I make it dirty,' she says. 'Like your stupid car.'

As much as he'd love her to go home right now and leave him in peace, leave him to have a quiet cup of tea on his own, to have a quiet life, he knows that he can't let her do that. It is not just that he feels he's totally failed so far to impress on her the fact that he is her father, to get her to respect him as such, but that he doesn't like the idea of her running back to Kim already. He doesn't see why Kim should be so important to her. He wants to be the person Lily would run to when she's unhappy, or in difficulty. In a way, he realises, he wants to take Lily away from Kim. He wants to punish Kim. It's his turn to be in control of their daughter. To have the last say.

'Look,' he says, 'I'm sorry. Treat this house like your own. Do whatever you want.' And he gets this idea, standing in the kitchen in his loose pyjamas, as the sun sweeps into the small yard, high-lighting Gemma's Wendy house – which only reminds him that he's never built Lily anything, he's never made her a Wendy house, or a bed, or taken her to swimming – that he'll show Lily where they used to live. He'll prove to her that he's her dad. He'll show her the pub he used to take her to as well, The Swan by the slipway, where she fed the ducks Hula Hoops, and he'll show her the arcade she loved – all this mutual history. This shared past. Then they can hire a day-cruiser and spend the afternoon on the Broads. She'll love that, he thinks. Everyone loves that. 'Don't go yet,' he says, suddenly desperate. 'I'll make it up to you, honest. I've got some plans.'

'Your cock's sticking out again,' Lily says, still with her headphones on, though Mark can't hear any noise coming from them now. 'Do you want me to touch it? Do you want me to suck it? Is that what you're after, like all men? Like all mum's boyfriends?' She pulls half a cigarette, a long, charred stub, from a front pocket of her jeans, pops it between her lips, produces some matches from the same pocket and lights up, immediately sending a cloud of thick, stale-smelling smoke directly towards him.

Kim said to Mark, it comes straight back to him, 'Why shouldn't I? It's a free world. You don't own me. How else will we earn enough money? I don't want you nicking stuff on the side forever. I know what you get up to at work, Mark. Who's going to help me with Lily, with all the kids, when you get put away? I've been through that one before. Why shouldn't I get a job? So what if it's in a nightclub? I'm only going to be working behind the bar. For three nights a week. That's it. And so what if I once slept with the owner? He's been decent enough to offer me a job. The only person who has.'

'Of course he fucking has,' said Mark. 'So you and him can carry on behind my back. In his office, or wherever else it is you do it.'

'I'm not fucking him now, Mark. I've told you that that was ages ago, and only a couple of times anyway.'

'Don't fucking lie to me,' he said.

'I'm getting sick of this attitude of yours, Mark. I can't fucking breathe without asking your permission first. I can't fucking do anything.'

'Whose fault's that?' he said. 'If you were honest with me there wouldn't be a problem.'

'I am being honest,' she said.

'No, you're not,' he said. 'I can tell.'

'All right then, yeah, so what, I have been fucking Chris behind your back. Of course I have. For fucking ages. Yes, old mumsie, with my saggy tits and three young kids. He fancies me like mad. And do you want to know something? Do you want to know something else, Mark? He's really good at it. In fact he's fucking brilliant in bed. He's got a lovely cock. I love sucking his cock, and licking his balls, and letting him come all over my face.'

That was when Mark hit her for the first time. He pushed her against the living-room wall and took a swipe at her with the back of his hand. It wasn't a punch – as she later claimed – he would never have punched her, but he swiped her, catching her on the side of her head. Maybe it was hard enough to make her ear buzz a bit. Though he's always suspected she fell to the floor on purpose, overreacting as usual. He remembers her slumped there, unwilling to get up, shrieking and crying and telling him to get the fuck out of the house. Nobody hits her and gets away with it.

'We're going to need that holiday. I can't wait for next Saturday. Driving to Gatwick and getting on the plane. That's when I'll know we're really on our way,' Nicole says, turning on to her back, pulling her arm from under Mark, in the fuggy darkness of their bedroom, with just the sound of Gemma asleep on the fold-out in the corner – her heavy, blocked-up, but strangely comforting breathing. Comforting, Mark decides, simply because she's there, in the room with them, quite safe.

'Yeah,' he says, physically tired but his mind still restless, unable not to think about yesterday evening, about Lily's sudden screaming fit, in front of him, and Nicole and Gemma. He only wanted to know what she ate at home, what her mother fed her on. Whether she fed her at all. And Lily starts screaming at him, saying he should leave her mother out of it. Her mother has had enough shit from him to last a lifetime. She said she knew what he used to do to her. How he used to beat her up. She said there was nothing wrong with her mother. Her mum was great. She never gave her any hassle, and always let her do whatever she wanted to do, without questioning her about it, without interrogating her. Exactly, he said, or said as much. And continued – the problem with her was that she had never been disciplined, by her mother, by anyone. She had been allowed to get away with murder. Well, life was going to be different from now on. Now her mother had other things to occupy herself with, such as this Dave bloke, and their young boy – he couldn't believe it when Lily told them yesterday that Kim had had another child, the fourth with four different men – and that she obviously didn't have much time for her any more, despite Jake and Sean apparently no longer living with Kim. Not that he reckoned she had ever given Lily much of her time and attention. Yes, she did, Lily said, more than you ever did, before she rushed out of the room and upstairs to the bathroom where she locked herself in and wouldn't stop screaming and sobbing until they heard her being sick, this tremendous retching. Nicole said she was making herself sick on purpose because she had eaten loads for tea compared with what she'd been eating for the last few days, and had even had a plate of ice cream – she'd been watching Lily, worried about her eating habits, whether she was anorexic or bulimic, knowing all about it as they'd recently been running a series on eating disorders in the *Mail*.

'I know they seem to play nicely but I bet Gemma will have had enough of Lily by then,' Nicole says. 'Besides, I don't think it's a good thing for Gemma to be exposed to too much of her, all that hysterical behaviour. OK, she's only six but children Gemma's age are very impressionable, Mark.'

'Come on,' says Mark, still thinking about Lily's screaming and vomiting fit, about her telling him that he'd never given her as much time and attention as Kim had – he couldn't argue with that, he supposes, however slack he thinks Kim's been – 'Gemma's fine. You can't protect her from everything. Lily is her sister.'

'Half-sister,' Nicole says. 'There's a big difference. I dread to think what her mother's really like.'

'Please, I don't want to think about her mother,' he says, turning on to his side, away from Nicole. 'Not now. I'm knackered.'

'That skirt Lily was wearing,' she says, 'used to be Kim's, apparently. And the shoes. She put them on specially for you. She thought you'd be pleased. That you'd notice her this time. When she told me this I thought that's sweet, that's really touching, but I don't know now, she's beginning to seriously freak me out.'

'Give her time,' he says – he's not going to mention the fact that he recognised the look at least. 'It must be really hard for her, being in a strange house, with a load of strangers. She's probably missing her mum, too.'

'Christ, you've changed your tune,' she says.

'So have you,' he says.

'I just don't think I can handle her for much longer. I'll lose it if she has another screaming fit in front of Gemma. Or if I have to listen to another one of her stupid conversations with her mum on that blinking mobile. She's on it all the bloody time. Whoever bought her that? She must spend a fortune on phonecards.'

Nicole pulls more of the duvet on to her, heaping some of it between them – it's her way, Mark knows, of saying don't touch me tonight, don't even think about coming anywhere near, how it's been for ages. 'She looks at you oddly sometimes, too.'

'I don't know what you mean,' he says, though he has an idea, thinking of the morning he came across her in the kitchen. 'Anyway, she's not here for much longer already. A couple of days, that's all. And tomorrow's sorted out, going to the Broads. She might enjoy that.'

'I doubt it,' Nicole says.

12

It's another hot, sunny day, part of the mini-heatwave the news has been talking about but which is turning out to be not so mini, and which is starting to annoy Mark because they are going to Mallorca in three days' time, to somewhere that is always meant to be hot and sunny – which is the only reason why they're going, their first holiday abroad for over five years, to sit by the pool in the sun – and he reckons they'll be wasting their money, that they might as well have stayed in England.

Plus the traffic is bad. It was solid between the inner and outer ring roads, a molten line of glass and metal, with everyone heading for the coast or the Broads, with the city smog turning a cloying, dirty orange, with the heat haze rising off the asphalt and quickly dissolving into the murky air, with people desperate to get out of the city, so he can just see that by the time they get there all the day-cruisers will have been hired out, or at the very least there will be pandemonium with thousands of people, half of them drunk no doubt – he remembers there were always gangs of drunks wandering about that place – trying to secure the few remaining boats, the crappiest, most unreliable boats at that, boats with mouldy seats and leaky hulls, with the newest and best, the sleek all-fibreglass models equipped with powerful diesel engines, with snug-fitting canopies, with all sorts of on-board gadgets, long having disappeared downriver.

Gemma will be wanting to have a strawberry ice cream, no doubt. In fact, she'll be going berserk about it because Nicole will be saying not before lunch, while Lily will have probably wandered off somewhere, her headphones clamped to her head, or her mobile, a cigarette between her lips, puffing and sulking at the same time, not paying attention to where she's going, deliberately wanting to get lost and for them to have to come looking for her – presuming she's not going berserk herself in the middle of a crowded pavement because he's said the wrong thing again, because he's asked her why she has to phone her mother all the time, or whether she thinks it's clever to have a pierced belly button, along with the nose ring. Whether she's going to feel quite so happy about that tattoo on her shoulder when she's his age, a tattoo of a cannabis leaf, Nicole's pointed out to him. And his mother, his mother will be wanting to go to the toilet. She'll be asking strangers where the nearest toilet is, not bothering to look for herself. Unable to grasp any sense of the local geography. Repeatedly asking for directions. He can just imagine it.

Mark takes his eyes off the sticky road for a moment and glances over his shoulder, at his mother squashed in the back of the Astra, with Gemma in the middle, and Lily on the other side. He takes in the fact that he's looking at his family, as much of his family as he could ever hope to assemble in one place, and that he's the only man and thus the head of this family group – as he sees it. It fills him with a sense of purpose. It makes him feel conciliatory, calm – despite the traffic. He's pleased his mother is here, that Nicole suggested at the last moment that he invite her – his wife realising that if they didn't bring her along today she probably wouldn't be able to see Lily before she went back. This gave Mark a good opportunity to make it up to his mum, without having obviously to apologise, without having to grovel. He just asked her to join them and Lily on a day out to the Broads. He knew that that would be enough.

And as it has transpired he's also pleased she's with them because he thinks she will be able to help with Lily, to ease the pressure on him and Nicole by helping to keep Lily entertained, and ensuring that no harm comes to her. Following a few comments from Nicole yesterday, he's not sure how much he can rely on his wife to do that any more.

'Shit. Look at this,' he says, as the traffic slows to a standstill again shortly before the old railway bridge, just outside the small Broads town where he used to live with Kim. 'It's solid. I've never seen a jam quite this far back. We should have left earlier. I kept saying we should leave before ten.'

'We weren't ready then, were we?' Nicole says. 'Lily was still in the bathroom.'

'Yeah, well, we were still waiting for someone to turn up. Weren't we, Mum?' Mark says.

'I did my best,' Anne says. 'You know what I'm like in the mornings.'

The traffic eases forward and as they reach the top of the railway bridge Mark sees there is no on-coming traffic and pulls out. Accelerating hard, he steers the car down the bridge on the wrong side of the road, where he keeps it for a further 150 yards or so before he brakes at the last moment to take a right-hand turn – the hot tyres screeching on the soft road. He's done this before. He knew exactly where the turning was, the fact that he had plenty of time even if an on-coming car had suddenly appeared on the horizon.

'Did you have to do that?' Nicole says, still gripping her seat.

'Cool,' Lily says. It's about the first thing she's said since they got into the car, having totally ignored her grandmother. Having just sat in the back in her Babe T-shirt today, with her headphones on, and stared out of the side window. But she hasn't lit up yet, which surprises Mark. She hasn't had a screaming fit either.

13

Because of the traffic and the lateness and the likelihood that there'll be few boats left to hire, if any, Mark decided, before they'd even hit the place, that if he was going to show Lily where they used to live, in the bleak semi that backed on to fields, in this domestic war zone, but at least it was where they lived together – wasn't it? – as father and daughter, as a family – the proof, if any were still needed, of the fact that he is her dad, of their brief shared past, that they do indeed have a history – he'd do it on the way home, when they had some time, but he finds, having decided to skip the queue and take a back route, that they are on the road which just so happens to pass the cul-de-sac, and because Lily clearly appreciated his skill behind the wheel – that 'cool' still rings in his ears – and is thus endearing herself to him today, he decides to drive via the house now.

For a long time he wouldn't have shown Nicole where he used to live with Kim. He wouldn't have gone anywhere near it with her, or on his own for that matter, but lately he's found he's not so afraid of the past – of thinking about it, of trying to make sense of it. Catching Lily's blue-grey eyes in his rear-view mirror, realising that she's been looking at him, studying him, and not just staring straight out of the window, he thinks that perhaps some good did come of his time with Kim. That it wasn't a complete mistake.

'Isn't this where you used to live?' his mother says.

'Well done, Mum,' he says, turning into the cul-de-sac. 'I thought I'd show Lily.'

'I thought we were so late,' Nicole says.

Not answering her, he slows the car to a crawl, taking in the old chain-link fences, with most of the chains still missing, leaving bare, concrete bollards, and the small front lawns, many now, he sees, having been crazy-paved, or turned into drives, and the houses in varying states of repair, though most now seem to have been refashioned with glassed-in porches and diamond-patterned windows, with window boxes and frilly venetian blinds, but nothing new seems to have happened to his and Kim's house. It's the grottiest on the street by far and he wonders for a moment whether some houses can't help but be neglected – no matter what you do to them, or who lives in them, even if they've been sold off by the housing association. This was always an uncared-for house, an unloved house, he thinks. A miserable place. He starts to regret bringing them here, letting Lily see it. 'Here we are then,' he says, embarrassed, now definitely not wanting to point out the particular house. Reaching the crescent-shaped end, he swiftly turns the car round, thinking that actually he is still afraid of the past. That it does contain too many bad memories.

Passing the house again, which, in its dilapidated state, he thinks so obviously looks like it used to be his and Kim's house, that there could be no mistake about that, and that he doesn't even have to point it out, Lily says, 'Which was my bedroom? Where did I sleep?'

'In the front,' he says, resignedly. 'That window on the right. You had a bedroom all to yourself. The warmest in the house. Fully carpeted.'

'Mum says you made me sleep in a cupboard. That you shut me in a cupboard without a light,' Lily says.

'No, I bloody didn't,' he says. 'It was a small room, fair enough, but it wasn't a cupboard. It was a proper bedroom, all to yourself. Jake and Sean had to share theirs.'

'Mum said you didn't want me to share with them, so you shut me in a cupboard on my own. She said you never even let me play with them. And that I wasn't allowed to have any dolls, or any toys.'

'That's not true,' he says.

'She said you made out I was like this big joke to everybody,' Lily says, her voice rising. 'Like I looked like a garden gnome or something. That people called me Noddy, or Big Ears or whatever. I've seen that photograph you took of me, by the pond, in that stupid hat, trying to catch a fish.'

'Your mum's a liar,' he says. 'She's a fucking liar. She's –'

'Gemma's in the car, Mark. Watch your language,' Nicole says.

'I am looking forward to getting on the river,' Anne says. 'What a treat.'

Shortly passing the duck pond, where Mark and Kim had rigged up Lily with the baby fishing rod all those years ago – with the idea of trying to make some cash from the local paper and not accepting Lily could be a product of their union, that she was their beautiful daughter, a large bit of each of them, linking them for ever – he stays silent. He stays silent until they've rejoined the traffic and heatwave mayhem nearer the river, nearer where they need to be to hire a day-cruiser.

14

Where were they, he thinks? In Boots. Yes, it was Boots. Boots on London Street. Kim was heaping all this stuff into a basket, new bottles and tins of powdered milk, sealed packets of teats and dummies, nappies and wipes, then some shampoo and conditioner for herself, plus a couple of lipsticks, a thing of mascara, a compact, some purple nail vanish – she loved purple, he suddenly remembers – a tube of fake tan, and numerous women's make-up things Mark had never come across before. He was pushing Lily, trying to keep an eye on Jake and Sean. When Kim added a bottle of Calvin Klein perfume, or perhaps it was a fancy bottle of Chanel something or other, either way it looked expensive to him. It looked completely over the top. So he said, 'Who's going to pay for all that? I thought we were just meant to be getting stuff for Lily.'

'Don't worry,' she said, 'I'm paying for it. I know you're Lily's father, and my husband, but I wouldn't dream of asking you to pay for anything. I'm quite capable of paying for it all by myself.'

'How?' he said.

'Chris gave me a bonus, didn't he,' she said.

'What for?' he said. 'Fucking him on the side?'

'Yeah, that's right,' she said. 'Fucking him on the side.'

She threw the nappies at him first, then proceeded to chuck all the unbreakable contents of the basket at him, so he was cowering in the aisle, trying to hide behind Lily's pushchair as these smartly wrapped toiletries rained down on him, as lipsticks and mascara and tubes and tubs of this and that bounced off him and clattered to the floor. As other shoppers and the shop assistants stopped what they were doing and started to stare – though no one intervened. As Kim began crying, saying between great breathless sobs, 'I only wanted to make myself look pretty – for you, Mark. Yes, you. What's wrong with that? You were never going to buy me anything. You were never going to surprise me. Chris doesn't want me, Mark. How many times have I told you that? He's just kind, he just knows how to treat a woman, which is more than I can say for you, you miserable wanker. You don't deserve me. You don't deserve anyone. Come here, boys, Sean, Jake, and give your mum a cuddle.'

Mark bent down and began picking up the stuff and putting it back in the shopping basket, moving out of the way so Sean and then Jake could get round him. 'Sorry,' he said. 'Sorry, love. I'll pay for it all. Of course I want you to look pretty for me. For just me. Love.'

He found that Kim had this real talent for making him feel sorry for her. And making him feel guilty also – guilty for ever having doubted her, her conviction, her word, her very being. He wonders quite how much of this talent Lily has inherited. And thinking of Lily wearing Kim's old skirt and shoes, of the way she looks at him sometimes, also, he wonders quite how wary he should be of her. Of his own daughter.

15

They get a boat surprisingly quickly. And it's not a clapped-out sieve, but a modern, fibreglass vessel, with an electric engine. Pushing the little bulb of a throttle as far as it will go, hearing this whiny hum, like a Flymo, and feeling the boat begin to float gently forward, Mark says, 'It's pathetic. It's completely crap. It's going to take us all day to get anywhere.'

'That's the point, isn't it?' says Nicole, sitting up front next to him, relaxing into the padded seat. 'So we can admire the scenery. Come on, Mark, it'll be good for you.'

'It would be quicker to paddle,' he says. 'I feel like I'm in Toytown. It's a fucking Noddy boat.' He looks behind him – realising what he's just said – at Lily, and his mother and Gemma, all sitting in a neat row on the back seat of the open rear of the boat, and beyond them at the growing expanse of shiny smooth water as the quayside from where they hired the boat slowly, almost imperceptibly shrinks.

On either side of the waterway are newly built holiday home developments – big, triangular, wooden-clad chalets, each appearing to incorporate numerous apartments with balconies, some of which are already occupied. It's boiling in the front of the boat behind the large windscreen and canopy. There is no breeze whatsoever. Mark looks over his shoulder again to see Gemma wave at people on the banks – his little Gem swamped in her bright orange life jacket, the only one of them wearing one, and the only one of them open to the world, he thinks, willing to engage. Too young to scowl. He could cuddle her. He decides to cuddle her, and get some air while he's at it, and leaves his seat and the controls, leaving the boat to slip gently forward on its own.

Pulling his jeans away from the backs of his legs, where they are sticking to him, and half-crouching, so as not to bump his head on the canopy, he makes his way to the rear of the boat, feeling particularly clever with himself for having abandoned the controls, knowing they are going so slowly no harm could possibly come to them, and that the boat will simply stay on course. 'Look, no hands,' he says, holding his hands up to the sky.

Gemma smiles, she laughs. 'You look stupid, Dad.'

'You can say that again,' says Lily.

'Who's driving?' says his mother. 'Shouldn't you be driving, Mark?'

'It's on autopilot,' he says, deciding not to cuddle Gemma because she's sitting next to Lily and he's worried that if he cuddles Gemma he'll then have to cuddle Lily. He wouldn't know what to do with his arms, presuming she'd let him anywhere near her.

'Mark,' Nicole says, 'we're coming to a junction. Get back here, you cretin. Get back here now. I don't know what to do. I've never driven a boat before.'

'Just steer it like a car,' he says.

'But where are the brakes?' she says. 'Mark?'

'OK,' he says, 'I'm coming. We all know what your driving is like.' He clambers back to the front, his hard shoes making a hollow, echoey sound on the clean white fibreglass floor – realising just how much his family relies on him. He's in charge, isn't he, the head of the family? And he can't even swim. He'd be hopeless in an emergency out on the river. He's the one who should be wearing a life jacket, not Gemma. Gemma can swim.

He steers them on to the main river, slotting between a small day-boat like theirs and a much larger cruiser. The traffic on the river is almost as congested as it was on the road leaving the city, with two seemingly endless streams of boats, all going at the same ludicrous, comical, Toytown pace. With people crowded on the decks, waving and shouting and a few zonked out in the sun. He looks behind him again, he keeps looking behind, not certain whether to be proud or ashamed – at Gemma still waving at people and Lily still sitting hunched in her Babe T-shirt and skimpy skirt, looking dead bored next to her, and beside his mum, who's on her other side. He can tell she is trying to talk to Lily, but he can't hear what they are saying above the whine of the electric engine, in the boiling, close heat of the cockpit. Whether, amazingly, Lily's opened her mouth for more than a couple of seconds yet. Whether she's managed to put a sentence together without being rude.

And it goes on like this for a considerable while, with them sitting in this formation, as the houses and chalets and prim, river-fronted gardens die out and the banks become dense with lush scrub and trees, a jungly wilderness – just as in his dream about Lily – as the river, with its endless Dinky traffic, curls and snakes its way to Horning. As Mark does his look-no-hands routine a couple more times, clambering around the boat, playing the fool, trying to get a few laughs, a bit bored with the river too, already. Not sure why he suggested the trip, which was meant to be the highlight of Lily's visit. Nothing ever turns out how it is meant to, he thinks. Not in his life.

For a time Nicole goes to sit at the back in the sun and the breeze with Gemma and Lily, who have both been pulling faces at other boats and giggling, while his mum – who's been much quieter herself than usual, who he can tell still hasn't quite forgiven him for his latest outburst, despite him asking her along today, or perhaps, it occurs to him, she's just freaked out by Lily, by her eldest granddaughter, what's become of her – moves up to sit next to him. Her presence at the hemmed-in front of the boat immediately disconcerts him, making him sweaty and defensive.

'Lily's a bit too thin, Mark,' Anne says.

'She doesn't like food,' he says. 'She prefers drinking and smoking. And drugs too, probably.'

'I don't know about that,' she says, 'but I've sent Kim a bit of money recently. I hope she's spending some of it on feeding Lily properly. We don't want her developing any of those problems at her age.' They both avoid looking at each other and stare ahead, at the glassy river, the hot, steamy river banks. 'I'm not too happy about her school situation either,' Anne continues. 'She tells me she's been asked not to come back after the summer. I don't think she's been expelled, but they don't want her there any more. She just said she didn't get on with the teachers. She doesn't know where she's going to go in September. There's a shortage of schools in her area, apparently. Though there's a special school not too far away which might be able to take her. It's a school for kids with learning disabilities. She can't read, you know.'

'I haven't heard about any of this,' says Mark. 'For fuck's sake. I thought she'd only just started this school. I've been giving Kim money for Lily's uniform and books and stuff, and now you're telling me she's not even going there?'

'I think you'll have to have a proper chat with Kim about it,' Anne says.

'I thought you were the one who spoke to her all the time,' he says.

'Mark,' says Lily, putting her hands on the back of his seat, having crept up behind them so Mark doesn't know what Lily's heard of the conversation, whether indeed she wants them to stop talking about her and her eating and schooling problems, 'this is boring. I've done this before. I want to get off.'

'I can't just stop here,' he says, looking at the impenetrable mass of reeds and foliage lining the banks, remembering his recurring dream again, wondering whether it wasn't just a dream, whether he did pass her on the river one day – he did take a boat out with Nicole once, shortly after he'd met her and when he was still trying to impress her, when he hadn't yet told her he'd once been married and had a kid (when, had he spotted that very child, quite out of context, he probably wouldn't have said anything about it) – or whether Lily's just saying she's done this before. Even if he asks her for details he knows she won't necessarily tell him the truth. He can't get a straight answer out of her. 'You're going to have to wait until we get to Horning,' he says.

'Well, I need to go to the toilet,' she says. 'I've just come on.'

'Oh dear,' says Anne. 'What are we going to do?'

16

The first Mark knows of it, the first his mum and Nicole know of it too, is when they hear the splash and Gemma shouting, 'Mummy.'

He had been attempting to get to Horning as quickly as possible, but there was little he could do. They'd been going flat out as it was. He cut a few corners, forcing on-coming boats to pull out of his way – a couple he had to yell at – but they didn't even manage to overtake the day-cruiser in front of them. So he shortly gave up trying to go any quicker, thinking Lily would just have to hang on until they got to Horning, there was nothing more he could do.

Nicole joined him and his mum up front, saying she didn't have any Tampax with her, not that Lily would have been able to sort herself out on the boat anyway. Nicole started having a conversation with Mark's mum about how good Lily was with Gemma, though what a shame it was she obviously didn't feel comfortable around them all yet, and seemed so shy and sensitive, despite trying to be the opposite all the time. Anne talked about Lily's skinniness again and the fact that she couldn't read, though she wasn't too surprised about that because Mark had had problems learning to read. She said he'd had all sorts of problems at school, which was when they heard the splash and Gemma shouting, 'Mummy.'

For a moment, Mark feels that everything freezes, even sound. Then time speeds up. Time goes twice as fast as normal. Nicole's at the back of the boat first, snatching hold of Gemma. Mark climbs over his seat, not waiting to let his mother get out of his way, but forgetting to put the engine into neutral, forgetting to stop the boat. 'Where is she?' he says, peering into the glistening wake of their boat, kneeling on the back seat, clasping the transom, making sure he's got a good hold, watching them sail away from the spot where he thinks Lily must have hit the water. 'Where the fuck is she?'

'Turn the boat round,' Nicole says. 'Can she swim?'

'How the fuck do I know?' he says. 'Mum, turn the boat round, you're nearest.'

'I'm not sure I know how,' Anne says, standing bolt upright in the middle of the boat, swaying a little, with one hand on the edge of the canopy, and the other on her forehead. 'Oh my God,' she says, making no effort to grab the controls. 'Oh my God. I knew something awful was going to happen.'

'Just turn the fucking wheel, like a car,' he says.

'It's not far to the bank,' Nicole says. 'If she can swim she could easily make it. Here, Mark, hold Gemma, I'm going in.'

'Don't be silly,' he says. 'You might get stuck in weeds or something. Maybe that's what's happened to Lily. Then that'll be the end of both of you. You always hear about people drowning like that – going in to help other people.'

'There she is,' Nicole says, letting go of Gemma, pushing the child towards Mark and climbing on to the back of the boat, ready to jump. 'Look. There. That's her, isn't it?'

OCTOBER

I

'You don't really expect me to come as well, do you, Mark?' Nicole says, standing in the kitchen, with her back to the sink and the naked, black window. Looking beyond Nicole, almost through her, at the window, at the smears of silver drizzle, makes Mark feel cold and shivery, despite the light and the warmth in the kitchen. The kitchen is always warm as it contains the boiler and a large radiator – much too large for the room, but Mark was offered it cheap and he wasn't going to miss out on a bargain. Besides, he and Nicole were determined to make the house as cosy as possible – their nest, as they used to call it, their snug little nest where no harm would come to them, where they would be safe from the world, where he'd always be able to protect her. He wonders whether he's getting flu. Gemma was off school last week. 'All the way to Newbury?' she says.

'Yeah,' he says. 'Why not? You came last time.'

'That was different,' she says. 'I felt you needed my support. I was there to hold your hand, not that you wanted to be seen holding mine. Remember? Things seem to have changed quite a bit since then, don't they? And what about Gemma? I definitely don't want to drag her all that way, especially since she's been unwell.' She pauses, looks behind her at the dark, wet weather, shaking her head slightly, almost mockingly, as though, Mark thinks, she has it in her power to turn night into day, rain into sunshine, that she can really do these things.

'Who knows what'll happen when we get there,' she says.

'Gem will be fine,' he says. 'She'll play with anyone. She'll fit in.'

'I wasn't thinking about her,' she says. 'I was thinking about Kim. How she's going to be with you, and me for that matter. And Lily, what she'll do to get a bit of attention this time. I could have died jumping into that bloody river.'

Mark laughs, thinking that perhaps Nicole isn't quite so all-powerful, so mighty – picturing his wife finally pulling herself on to the bank, her white top smeared with great streaks of mud and being soaked through, of course, and clinging to her so he could clearly see her bra through the material from where he was out on the water, from a mile away, like she was in a wet T-shirt competition, with her jeans having come undone somehow and slipping off her too, revealing half her bum and the tiny waist band of her thong, with Lily already on the bank trying to help Nicole, trying to grab her by the hand, in her bare feet, having lost her stilettos, and her dripping, muddy Babe T-shirt and tight skirt. And with all these people watching from a number of other boats which had formed a semicircle around the area – with groups of bare-chested lads laughing and jeering, realising that everyone was all right, thinking that the whole thing was some sort of drunken stunt put on especially for their entertainment.

'I've done enough for that girl,' Nicole says.

'She didn't do it on purpose, for God's sake,' Mark says. 'How many times do we have to go over it. You said you might have done the same thing yourself, didn't you? Had you been her age and had blood trickling down your legs because your period had just started, one of your first ever periods – catching you completely by surprise. Had you been on a boat you couldn't get off with a load of people you barely knew – all these grown-ups. And you were too embarrassed to let them see what had happened, with all this blood on your legs and skirt, and on the seat.'

'She's always been pretty forward with us, Mark,' Nicole says. 'She just plays at being shy when it suits her. I don't think anything could embarrass her. And anyway don't make it sound like she was haemorrhaging or something, there was never blood all over the place. That doesn't happen.'

'You sympathised with her about it earlier, saying how awkward girls can be about their periods, especially at that age,' he says. 'You even laughed about it, remembering all those people watching you as you tried to get out with your jeans falling off. Didn't you?'

'So maybe I don't any more. Now I've had time to mull it over. Lily made a fool of me, Mark, apart from putting my life in danger.'

'You're the one who jumped in after her.'

'Well, you weren't going to, were you? You'd have just let her drown. And you're her father. A pretty useless one at that.'

'Fuck you,' Mark says, walking out of the kitchen, hearing the ping of the microwave, realising their supper is ready – a Sainsbury's ready-made sausage and tomato pasta bake he'd been really looking forward to, being starving after spending the day in the garage sorting out his tools – feeling the heat of the room on the back of his neck. Feeling the growing weight of Nicole's annoyance with Lily, with Lily's existence, on his shoulders, pulling him down, crippling him. 'It is her fucking birthday, Nicole. It would mean a lot to her if you and Gemma were there also. You're her family too, don't forget.'

2

The hotel and the pool and the stretch of beach near the hotel were everything Mark hoped they'd be – big and noisy and boiling, with lots of activities on hand such as trampolining, crazy golf, all-day karaoke. There was also a baby-listening service and an on-site nightclub, and jet-skiing and parasailing, not that he was interested in the deep-water stuff. The brochure hadn't misled them and he soon forgot about the heatwave back home – it was still better here, miles better. To begin with.

Nicole and Gemma were thrilled with it all, too, at first, from the moment they stepped off the coach. From the moment they left the city. Driving to the airport Nicole said, 'We're going to have the holiday of a lifetime. Aren't we, Gem? Mark? Our first family holiday abroad. Can you believe it?' Even the bad tummy Gemma picked up on the second day did little to dampen their spirits, to curb their expenditure on the extra-curricular activities, especially the trampolining and the crazy golf, and the jet-skiing, which Nicole found she loved.

Normally, it's Mark who has the dodgy stomach, but he didn't have a problem with his guts, with his bowels, this time abroad. His problem began inside his head, and got steadily worse as the fortnight progressed. What set it off were all these near-naked women. They were everywhere, by the pool, on the beach, walking along the flat, dusty promenade into Alcudia, often wearing nothing but bikini bottoms. He'd forgotten how much naked flesh you saw in the Med – flesh belonging to women, to girls, girls he took to be Lily's age. He found it both arousing and shocking.

These girls didn't remind him specifically of Lily, he didn't suddenly realise he fancied Lily, his own daughter, or anything appalling and incomprehensible like that, but they reminded him of how vulnerable she was, of how attractive to older men she could be, men his age. She had periods, after all. She was capable of getting pregnant. He could be a grandfather before he knew it.

As it was, he didn't want to let Lily take the train home after her stay with them, especially as he'd overheard her tell Nicole about this man buying her drinks and holding her hand on the way there – even though she hadn't mentioned it again and he wasn't convinced she'd been telling the truth. That she could have just said it to shock them, like, he suspected, and hoped, was the motive behind much of what she did say. However, he suddenly didn't have time to drive her to Newbury before they went on holiday. There was no option but to put her on the train.

He actually thought about asking her to come to Mallorca with them, to the Hotel Bon Alcudia – he would have been prepared to pay for her ticket, or at least borrow the money from Nicole or his mum to pay for it, had there been one available last minute – but he knew how much Nicole would have hated Lily coming. And anyway Lily did tell him she didn't have a passport – 'I've never needed one, have I,' she had said – and he wasn't prepared to start organising a passport for her – getting all the forms and photos and liaising with Kim over who had to sign what. He wasn't prepared to liaise with Kim over anything complicated. He knew how brilliant she was with forms, with bureaucracy, how she would make him sign away things he shouldn't. Like rights of access. He knew she would screw him over it if she could.

3

And being in Mallorca reminded him, of course, of when he was last there with Nicole. When they were still getting to know each other and he was still trying to forget about his failed marriage and his lost daughter. When in reality he was doing a pretty good job at it, letting the balmy weather and the smell of Nicole naked – a sweet, sweaty, after sun-lotion smell – intoxicate him. They had plenty of sex – in the shower, on the balcony, once on the beach at night behind a pedalo. Nicole was never as energetic or as abandoned as Kim. She was never as uninhibited and didn't let him put so much as a finger up her arsehole, let alone the tip of his cock – but he preferred her body. He appreciated it so much more and in those early days loved to caress her thin thighs, her flat stomach, the soft, tight skin behind her ears – her neat strip of pubic hair. 'Nice fuzz,' he used to say. And he loved the way she pushed her fanny towards him while he was playing with her fuzz, wanting him to apply pressure to her fanny lips, to her clitoris, to rub it gently with a couple of fingers, exactly as she taught him how. He loved, too, the way she quietly moaned when she came.

Kim used to scream. Kim used to pant and scream and shout things like, 'Harder, Mark. Fuck me harder. I can't feel you. I want it to hurt. Hurt me, Mark.' Or when they really went at it, 'Fuck me. Fuck me to death. Go on. Put your hands round my throat and throttle me. I don't want to breathe. Breathing's too easy.' Kim scared him even in bed.

It was a mistake, Mark thinks. They should have gone to Greece, because being in Mallorca this time reminded him of not only the period in his life he was trying to forget, but the fact that his whole relationship with Nicole was founded on Lily's absence. What they had, they had built for themselves, in isolation of his past. As if they were castaways on a desert island, a paradise island, where no one could suddenly intrude, and where, Mark thinks, he must have been under the impression that they had washed up without any baggage.

Being in Mallorca this time, without Lily, but with Lily so much on his mind, with Lily being talked about again and again (usually something about her need to shock people all the time, or her eating habits, or her clothes) by him, and by Nicole and Gemma, made him begin to realise, and obviously well after Nicole had seen it, the serious threat she posed to the stability of his second family, to the family that meant everything to him, to the great second chance in his life. To his bit of paradise.

During tea one evening, in the large, packed, low-ceilinged dining room which overlooked the pool, after Gemma had mentioned that Lily was brilliant at doing jigsaw puzzles, because she was struggling with one herself when she should have been eating her spaghetti and chips and no one would help her with it, Nicole said, 'Do we have to talk about that girl any more? Can we just get on with the rest of our holiday without mentioning her again, please.'

'Yeah,' Mark said, sick of the very idea of Lily too. 'Let's give it a rest.'

'But she's my big sister,' Gemma said, deliberately pushing some of the puzzle on to the floor. 'She's my best friend.'

Gemma was sharing their room, but Mark believed that that wasn't why Nicole was so reluctant to have sex with him on holiday, for Christ's sake. Lily was the person getting in the way. He knew that. Despite being abroad without Lily, despite all the attractions and activities surrounding them, Nicole couldn't forgive him for letting Lily crash into their lives and then slowly ruin their first ever family holiday abroad. Plus Nicole said she had forgotten her contraceptive pills and he didn't know where you bought condoms from in Mallorca. He wasn't just going to walk into some foreign chemist's where he wouldn't be able to understand a word.

Nicole was paranoid about getting pregnant again. This had troubled Mark for ages – the way she had gone from being so desperate to have a kid, to not wanting to have any more children almost as soon as Gemma was born. She made out that she didn't want to interrupt her career once more, as she was clearly going to have to be the major breadwinner. Especially as she was in line to head her own division, the peachy consumer division too, and she didn't see why one day she wouldn't be in charge of the whole company. Anyway she kept saying she was quite happy with one child, she liked that dynamic, there being just the three of them. As she saw it the smaller the unit the more efficient it could be, the more secure, the happier. It was what they believed in at her office and the business she worked for was hugely successful, out-performing everyone in their sector. He believed in that too, didn't he? Their cosy little family unit. He was always saying as much, wasn't he?

Of course he went along with her, as he went along with most of her wishes. Not wanting to be seen to be a pushover, he did protest a bit, though he always felt his past record didn't exactly give him much authority and he knew how lucky he was to have her. Though in Mallorca that second time, when in reality they didn't have sex once, when Nicole didn't even quickly wank him off as she might have done if he were dying for sex and she had her period or was too tired – seeing as they were on holiday – he began to look at it differently. He wondered whether in fact the reason Nicole had not wanted any more children with him was because she was no longer convinced about him or their marriage, and that she was possibly looking to run off before it became even more complicated – despite always maintaining that she was a 'sticker', that she would never just walk out on someone. However bad it got.

She wasn't another Kim, she used to say. She believed in working things through, especially if kids were involved. Her parents had managed to stay together for all those years, hadn't they? She took after them. She was definitely their daughter –

dependable, loving, solid. A sticker, as she kept telling him. Tougher than Sellotape. Tougher than Super Glue. Besides, she fancied the pants off him.

Lying awake at night, listening to Gemma snoring on her kid's bed in the corner of the room, and Nicole sighing and turning fitfully in the close heat on her lumpy single bed which was pushed next to his, with Nicole totally naked under her sheet, just inches away, so he kept thinking about her nakedness, her proud nipples and still trim fuzz, and all the nearly naked bodies he'd seen that day, becoming increasingly aroused, finding he had his stiff cock in his hand, while listening also to the intermittent high-pitched buzz of a mosquito near his head and the sound of someone having a shower in another room, the sound of distant laughter too and perhaps the knocking and moaning of a couple shagging – which only made him even more aroused and lonely – and with absolutely no sound of the sea, because their room faced inland, without the comfort of hearing waves gently breaking, but high-revving scooters instead, he had this strong feeling that his world was suddenly coming apart, that he was in the middle of a full-blown crisis. That he was drowning in a buzzing, airless room.

He didn't know who to trust. He didn't trust himself, his own feelings to start with. And lying there with his erection he felt haunted, too. He felt that he'd never escaped his past – how could he have? – that history hadn't nearly finished with him yet. That he'd got away with nothing. Part of him had always suspected that what you do to others, they'll do back to you, given time.

Beginning to stroke his super-hard cock, aggressively, angrily – as if that would somehow relieve him of all this anguish – he sensed himself drifting further and further away from reality, from the last vestiges of truth. There had been too many lies in his life, too much insincerity, too much deviousness. Too much crap. People were always ultimately letting him down. Breaking his fucking heart. Weren't they?

Trying to picture Kim his mind somehow settled for a brief moment on the image of Lily in her soaking Babe T-shirt and tight black skirt, on her growing breasts and shapely, womanly hips, as she helped Nicole on to the river bank, then, almost at the last moment, he managed to recall Kim, Kim with her back to him,

Kim kneeling on their old bed, in their scruffy housing association house which backed on to a field, Kim wanting him to do it doggy style, wanting, expecting, indeed urging him to pull apart her big buttocks and to let the tip of his cock tickle her arsehole, to make her arsehole sticky with her own juices, before entering her vagina, before leaning forward and grabbing her around the shoulders, the neck, and ramming into her as hard as he could, with her beginning to moan and scream and fight for breath, and while carefully holding the sheet away from his body with his left hand, he ejaculated upon his stomach, a warm, wet dollop of semen which slowly sank into his belly button, as the tears slid down his burning, crumpled, unshaven face.

4

He now only plays the Rod Stewart when he's in the car on his own as Nicole hates it. She says he's sick. She says her dad wouldn't even listen to it, nor her mum. But Mark loves Rod Stewart, he especially loves the greatest hits compilation, which has all his favourites on it – 'Hot Legs', 'Maggie May', 'Da Ya Think I'm Sexy', 'Sailing' – one after the other. When he was fourteen, when 'Sailing' was released and immediately went to the top of the charts where it stayed for something like twenty-eight weeks on end, he wanted to be Rod Stewart. He peroxided his hair and had it cut short and spiky on top while leaving it long and shaggy on the sides and back. He had his left ear pierced and wore a big gold hoop, and in his high waisters and wide-collared, long-sleeved pink or maroon satin shirts – mostly from Top Man, the high-street store where all his best clothes came from then – people were always remarking on his resemblance to the singer.

And how he, too, could look moody yet sort of innocent at the same time – standing in a corner of a pub, or a disco, scowling a bit and not dancing, not making any effort with the girls but letting them eye him up and eventually come over to talk to him, in giggly groups of twos and threes, which they invariably did. Because he looked the part. Because he was fucking gorgeous. And, invariably, he'd end up snogging someone, still in the corner, or outside, where he'd touch their breasts and maybe try to slip a hand inside their knickers. He can remember a few of the girls' names – Kate, Hazel, Emma, Becky, Gail. Especially Gail, as she was the first person who dared put her hand inside his Y-fronts in return, having spent ages struggling to undo the waist band of his trousers. Especially Gail, with her straight, mousy-blonde hair, squashy, pig-like nose and large tits, abnormally large for a girl her age, he and his mates used to think. Yeah, especially Gail, as she was the girl who he lost his virginity to in Chapel Field Gardens, in shadowy moonlight, behind a rhododendron bush, on damp muddy grass.

It is not raining at the moment but the motorway is thick with spray from an earlier downpour – from a month of autumnal downpours – and the sky is a dim, patchy grey and 'Sailing' has just come on the Astra's well-cranked-up eight-speaker Blaupunkt hi-fi system, which Mark thinks is spot-on given the weather, given the sheer amount of water on the road and the water that is airborne too. For a moment he imagines he's on a warship, ploughing through the waves, the open sea, sailing, sailing into the stormy distance, like Rod in that video. But a car pulls out of the middle lane and into the fast lane right in front of him without indicating and he has to brake hard to avoid going into the back of it. He continues to brake to get out of the plume of spray being kicked up by the car – so he has some idea of where the hell he's going. Once in the clear, rather than accelerate again, perhaps on an inside lane, rather than go after the guy for cutting him up, he decides to keep his distance, not wanting a scrap today, soothed by the music, and finding, as always, that without Nicole in the car, without Nicole around, he doesn't get so wound up – that he has no need to prove anything to anyone. Besides, he's not in a rush, he doesn't want to get to Kim and Lily's too early. He's still savouring all this stuff he has to talk to his ex-wife about. These things he's been saving up since the summer, since Easter, while waiting for the chance to speak to her in person – when he knows he'll at least be able to string more than a word or two together in one go. When, hopefully, he'll be able to get across everything that he wants to, these very important questions and some other stuff, in one go, more or less, as he's always been crap on the phone with her, with anyone. He's actually pleased, if he thinks about it, that Nicole is not with him to keep him calm and reasonable. He's pleased he'll be able to really let rip.

Strictly, of course, in an attempt to get to the bottom of exactly what has been going on with, for starters, Lily's schooling. He wants to know why she's been asked to leave yet another school, a special needs school at that (for kids with learning difficulties, with physical disabilities, with all sorts of disorders). He wants to get to the bottom of her eating problem too, her bulimia, Nicole's convinced him she has, and her clearly excessive drinking and smoking, and probably chronic drug abuse. Her glue-sniffing, her E-dropping, her dope-smoking – which he can just imagine. He wants to know what is going on with her clothes too, this new tarty look of hers, plus her ever-increasing number of tattoos and body piercings – on flesh so young it makes him want to weep. Why, in fact, she has to look so grown-up anyway, and whether Kim's warned her about strange men, about how easy it is to get yourself into trouble at that age, and while they're on to this he thinks he ought to be told once and for all what really happened to her when they were travelling, in the hippy, New Age peace convoy, or whatever it was – whether she was sexually abused by a series of her mother's boyfriends. Whether, as she has claimed, a host of these hopeless hippies, these disgusting vagrants, really did make her suck their scabby cocks. With that out of the way, calming down, possibly, but still looking Kim in the eye, he'll want to know precisely what she's been doing with all this money he's been sending her on Lily's behalf – for Lily's school clothes, and her summer clothes, for her books, and phonecards (seeing as she never rings him on it) and her special food. His hard-earned cash, cash he could have spent on Gemma, and should have spent on his own bills and debts at the very least. Cash which is in increasingly short supply owing to the serious downturn in his business – so much so he's been thinking about giving up cabinet-making and doing something completely different. Or rather Nicole's been urging him to explore other avenues. At the moment she wants him to retrain as an engineer, a cooker engineer for a John Lewis-affiliated call-out firm, which is currently recruiting in the city and providing free training. 'It's the sort of skill that'll always be required,' Nicole said. 'You'll never have a problem getting work. Think how useful you'll be at home.' He said he'd rather rob a bank. He said, never having been so blatant about his criminal past in front of Nicole before, not caring in the slightest whether she might believe him, that he'd rather hook up with some old mates and get a few scams going. He said he'd rather go back to thieving and burglary. He wouldn't need any retraining here, he said, it's all still in his head. 'Like riding a bicycle, Nics,' he said.

But he knows all this can wait a short while longer. These questions, still so many questions. This showdown with Kim, the first for a decade, which he sadly realises will have to come on the occasion of Lily's fourteenth birthday. Well, there is nothing he can do about that, he thinks, because these issues he's been saving up since April clearly have to be dealt with in person, thoroughly, firmly – if he's ever to assume some sort of father role, if he's ever to exert a bit of paternal authority.

He's certainly not in so much of a rush to tackle Kim over what has happened to his daughter, over what she has let happen to her, by being a neglectful mother, by being deceitful and manipulative too, and violent, oh yes and most definitely that, that he's going to risk his life getting there. He's quite happy to dawdle along the sodden M25 at ninety, at ninety-five, with Rod Stewart booming from the speakers, reminiscing about Gail, about giving Gail one in Chapel Field Gardens. His own fourteen-year-old face nestling between those massive boobs. With mud on his knees, his elbows. Fumbling with the Durex. Not sure which way it should roll down, and finally her steady, helping hand – her soft intake of breath as he slowly entered her. She'd done it before, of course. She'd done it loads of times.

5

Lily said on the phone a week ago, her voice breaking, 'Mum won't let me have a birthday party. She says she doesn't want tons of people round here she doesn't know making a mess. Not when she's just redecorated the lounge, and has the baby to look after. There weren't going to be tons of people anyway. Just a couple of friends, Zara and Kylie and maybe Dan. Mum used to say I could always bring my friends back. That we lived in an open house. You know, peace, man, and all that hippy dippy shit. Now all she thinks about is money and the new carpet and her screaming brat. I'm barely allowed to breathe in here any more. Ever since Dave went she's become this real pain.'

'I'm sorry, sweetheart,' Mark heard himself saying. 'I'm sorry your mum's being so unreasonable. But you know what? If you want to have some friends round on your birthday, ask them anyway. You'll be fourteen, for Christ's sake. You're not a kid any more. She's not going to throw your mates out. Not on your birthday.'

'Oh no?' said Lily. 'She's become like this fascist. I get told off all the time.'

'How about if I'm there?' he said.

'Yeah, sure, Mark,' she said.

'No, I mean it,' he said.

'Mum'll love that,' she said. 'That'd be really cool.'

'There won't be much she can do about it,' he said. 'It's your birthday, your special day. Besides, I've got to talk to her about some things anyway, in person. I've been meaning to for ages.'

'What do you want to come to my birthday for?' she said.

'You're my daughter,' he said.

'You ignored the last ten, though, didn't you?' she said.

'That was different,' he said. 'I would have come had I known where you were, wouldn't I? You can talk to your mum about that. It was her fault I wasn't around. Ask her. See what she has to say about it. See if she can get out of that one. In fact put her on the phone now, Lil, will you? Is she there?'

6

'Hello, Mark,' Kim said.

'Hello, Kim,' he said, not just surprised that Kim had come to the phone but that she was on it almost immediately, as if she had been standing in the room beside Lily all along, listening to her daughter slag her off to her ex-husband. Or, it occurred to him, perhaps even encouraging her to slag her off to him so he'd feel more sorry for his daughter, more protective and fatherly, and hand over even more cash or something.

For a couple of seconds, with Kim on the other end of the phone, hearing her breathing, hearing the softly humming distance that separated them, he wondered again whether Lily was as manipulative, as deceitful as her mother, and whether the two of them were simply out to screw him for everything they could get. Or whether he was just being paranoid – something Nicole is always accusing him of being. 'Stop being so paranoid, Mark,' she says. 'Not everyone's out to get you.'

'How's things?' Kim said.

'OK,' he said. 'Not bad.' What else could he have said?

'Good,' she said. 'I'm happy for you.'

'Yeah, I bet,' he said.

'I am,' she said. 'I'm glad things have worked out for one of us.'

'So what's up with you, then?' he said.

'Nothing much. I'm just on my own again, that's all. It's just me and the kids again. But you don't want to hear about all that.'

'No,' he said. 'No, I don't. I want to talk about Lil. She's the only person I'm interested in.'

'Yeah, sure, Mark, like when she was little,' she said. 'I remember all the interest you took in her then. Bothering to feed her and change her. Making sure we had enough money to feed her properly. Yeah, I remember all that.'

'You're the one who took her away from me, right?' he said.

'I had no choice,' she said. 'I acted out of self-defence. With the full knowledge and encouragement of the social services.'

'Put Lily back on,' he said. 'I don't want to talk to you any more.'

'Can't handle the truth?' she said.

'I can't handle you,' he said. 'Not on the phone. I'm coming up for Lily's birthday, by the way. I'm bringing her a present. We'll sort this out then. And the rest of it.'

'Yeah, of course we will,' she said.

'OK then,' he said, not mentioning anything about how upset Lily seemed on the phone moments earlier – supposedly because Kim wouldn't allow her to have a small birthday party. Confused, not sure whether he was being tricked, again, he was suddenly desperate to end the call.

'I look forward to it, Mark. Like mad,' Kim said, slowly, quietly, slurring a little, but not angrily – perhaps teasingly even – just before he removed the cordless from his ear and pressed the red disconnection button, swearing to himself, saying fuck you, even more uncertain of Kim, and for that matter Lily's motives.

7

Stopping at a set of lights on the outskirts of Newbury, Mark takes the time to look over his shoulder at Lily's huge present strapped to the back seat because he didn't want it sliding around or tipping off if he had to brake sharply and maybe getting damaged, or worse, damaging the interior of his car. He wasn't able to put the present in the boot because as usual the boot was full of his tools – in fact there are more of them in there than ever because he recently lost the use of the garage and has nowhere else to store them. Apart from knowing Nicole wouldn't have them in the house he didn't want her getting suspicious of what he was up to had he unloaded them into the lounge, where they've always been banned from anyway.

So far she doesn't have a clue about the present, which he had to wrap in a lay-by, using four rolls of wrapping paper he bought from a newsagent's on the way out of the city. He spent ages trying to make it look neat but he's pleased with the result, especially the bright pink wrapping paper, patterned with hundreds of Happy Birthdays in glittering silver – the same tone of pink, and sparkly silver, he reckons, as Lily's Babe T-shirt, before it got ruined by the mud.

Nicole inadvertently gave him the idea to buy Lily the computer.

When he asked her what he should get Lily for her birthday – after she'd made it more than clear that she and Gemma weren't going to Newbury with him – she said, 'What about a new life?' He told Nicole to stop being stupid, so she then said, 'I don't know, she's your daughter. How about a T-shirt with "silly cow" or something on it? Or what about a new pair of stilettos? She could share them with Kim. Though I didn't think you had any spare money, Mark. To be quite honest, the only present you should be thinking about at the moment is Gemma's computer we've promised her for Christmas.'

Well out of Nicole's earshot, he spoke to Darren – his most trusted electrical goods supplier – who said he was certain he could fix him up with something. Darren wouldn't be drawn on the make or even whether it would be the most up-to-date model, but he was willing to guarantee that it would be totally unused and still in its original packaging – for 200 quid tops. Mark collected the computer, a Compaq he noticed, this morning from Darren's lock-up out near the airport, having got the cash from his business bank account (which though badly overdrawn hadn't quite reached its limit). He didn't have time to check the Compaq over, he doubts whether he would have known what to look for, not being at all computer-literate unlike Nicole, but Darren has never let him down before. Everything he's supplied has always worked without a glitch, except, Mark thinks, they keep losing that blasted hands-free.

Soon stopping at another set of lights, a set of pedestrian lights, with the red stop light piercing the falling rain and seemingly pooling on the empty pavement – a glimmer of red in the oily, dark water – Mark looks at the Maurice Lacroix on his wrist then the digital clock on the dash, seeing that, as ever, the two are perfectly synchronised. It's 3.24. He said he'd be there at teatime, at least he told Lily when he spoke to her on the phone last night that he'd be there in plenty of time to wish her a happy birthday and have a word with her mum before her friends pitched up, and he had to leave to drive home before it got too late. She told him not to bother coming, but he ignored her, saying he looked forward to seeing his birthday girl tomorrow.

Pulling away from the lights, he feels proud of himself for

making so much effort for Lily's birthday, for driving all this way on his own, and then back – a round trip of over 300 miles. He feels particularly proud of the large pink parcel on the back seat, which is partly obscuring his view in the rear-view mirror. He doesn't think his father ever bought him a birthday present. When his dad was married to his mum, he knows his mum always got the presents. He wonders whether his dad ever bought Robbie a birthday or a Christmas present once they were in Canada. Or whether he just relied upon Sue to do that, and then the women he's been with after her. Mark hopes his father never made that sort of effort for Robbie, that he never did such a thing entirely off his own back. He hopes that once they got to Canada his father pretty well ignored Robbie, as he had certainly ignored him when they were all living together in the UK.

Though something makes him think his dad didn't ignore Robbie in Canada. Indeed, he thinks, partly out of jealousy but mostly because it is how he would have behaved, that his dad showered Robbie with presents and attention, with love indeed, to make up for the fact that he'd destroyed the family, that he'd dragged his youngest son away from his mother and his brother, and deposited him in another country, on another continent. He'd have done it out of guilt, Mark presumes. He thinks his dad – this man who had the same slightly hooked nose as him but who was in fact quite short and stocky and dark, much more like Robbie – would have tried his hardest to please Robbie, to be there for him, because he would have felt so guilty.

Mark thinks this because that's how he would have behaved had he been his dad. And because he knows just how parents and stepparents are when it comes to the families they've fucked up – always trying to secure the love of various kids, always trying to atone for their actions. Pretending they are better people than they really are. He knows how it is with parents. With the guilty. Lawrence bought him a birthday present once, the year they all started living together. It was a watch, an Omega, with a big gold face and a shiny brown leather strap, complete with a matching gold buckle featuring the Omega Ω trademark. He immediately hated it, despite knowing it must have cost a lot of money. He also knew his mother had nothing to do with it, that it was all Lawrence's idea. Something the man wanted to surprise everybody with, especially his mum. Indeed, Mark became convinced Lawrence only bought him the watch to impress his mum, so she'd think her new husband was amazingly generous and big-hearted, which of course he wasn't.

Mark wore the watch around the house for a couple of weeks, then he took it into the city centre, together with its plush red box and fancy-looking guarantee, and sold it to an antique and second-hand jewellers. He didn't get much for it, nothing like what it was worth, but it made him feel good and he spent the money, he can clearly remember, on a shirt and a new gold earring and a couple of albums – by Thin Lizzy and Earth Wind and Fire. Neither Lawrence, nor his mum, ever asked him why he no longer wore the watch though he's sure they knew what he'd done with it. He played those albums to death.

8

It says number 12, but the house doesn't look a bit like how he remembers it. The front door is smartly painted, a mauve gloss, and the small window panels, which were damp, graffitied cardboard, are now new-looking, florally patterned glass. The path has been neatly paved too, and the front yard covered with bright shingle. There's no litter, no sign of any cat or dog shit.

He's so disorientated, before venturing further up the path he decides to go back to the car to check the address. From where he's parked he can read the street sign at the beginning of the road and, checking the address which he'd written on the back of an envelope and left by his road map on the front passenger seat, sees he has got the correct place all right. Climbing out of the car again his first thought is that he wishes Nicole were with him – this drastic change to Kim's house having only added to his unease – though reaching into the back of the car and carefully lifting out the computer, then struggling with it, this massive pink parcel, across the short, even path to the shiny front door, he also feels once more this growing thrill that she isn't with him – the fact that he can behave however he wants, totally unchecked.

Waiting for somebody to answer the door, having put the package on the doorstep and knocked, he recalls the last thing Kim said to him on the phone when he unexpectedly spoke to her a week or so ago – the tone of her voice, the half-pissed teasing that has trapped him before – and standing in the wet cold he starts wondering what it would be like to have sex with Kim now, after all these years. He imagines her leading him into her bedroom where she slowly, teasingly removes her dirty orange hippy gear to reveal she isn't wearing any underwear and that her armpit hair, plus her pubic hair, has grown bushy and wild, as all hippies and travellers and vagrants have their body hair, he thinks. She smells, not of some fancy, overpriced perfume from Boots, but of stale sweat, of unwashed skin. It is almost an animal smell, which he finds surprisingly exciting. He imagines her reclining on her bed, spreading her legs, offering up this great tangle of dark pubes, beckoning for him to join her, which he does, burying himself in her smell, her hair, her body. Her wildness. After all these years.

The door opens, making him jump, and it takes him a moment or two to realise he's facing Kim, but Kim doesn't look much like a hippy any more. Her hair is no longer scarlet, it's still short but neat and blonde, at least brightly highlighted, and there's no trace of her straggly ponytail. She's wearing numerous earrings and a nose stud, but she's replaced the loose, home-made-looking orange clothes with a tight-fitting, bright red rollneck top and a pair of seemingly sprayed-on stone-washed jeans.

'So you've come,' she says.

'Yeah,' he says, remembering how Kim was always changing her look to fit in with whoever she wanted to fit in with, and how obviously Lily has inherited this trait.

'Well, Lily's not here.'

'Where is she?'

'At a friend's, I think. I don't know. I think she got fed up with waiting for you.'

'What do you mean? I said I'd be here at teatime.'

'Did you? She thought you were coming to take her out for lunch, like last time. That's what she told me.' Kim tightly folds her arms in front of her, under her breasts, which has the effect of pushing them up, of making them look huge – Mark can't help noticing. Nor can he help noticing her large nipples pressing against the fabric.

'But I never said that,' he says. 'I said I was coming at teatime. I only spoke to her last night.'

'You can't expect her to take in everything you say,' Kim says. 'She's hardly used to you yet. Anyway, she's not very good with time. She never knows when lunch or tea is meant to be – it doesn't mean anything to her. She operates in her own little world. We could try to ring her.'

'Isn't she having some friends over?' he says. 'I thought she was having some sort of party. But maybe that's later.'

'Not in this house,' Kim says. 'Look, do you want to come in?'

'No, I thought I'd just wait out in the rain, getting soaked,' he says, knowing that he would never have been able to help Lily defy her mother over whether she could have a party, however small.

'What's that?' Kim says, as Mark picks up the giant pink parcel.

'A present for Lily.'

'That's a first,' she says, leading him into the lounge. 'Mind the wallpaper, Mark. It's new. You idiot, I said mind the wallpaper. And watch out for the carpet too.' Letting the box bump against the wall again, he follows Kim into the lounge, wondering how on earth he could have fantasised about having sex with her while waiting on the doorstep just moments ago. OK, she might not be so much of a scummy-looking New Age traveller as when he last saw her, indeed she might have retained something of her former sexiness – her top-tease attributes – but she still revolts him. Her voice, her attitude. Everything she's done to him. How can he divorce that from what she looks like, from her physical self? He can't, of course, not when she's in the same room as him, just inches away, breathing hard.

And what a room, he thinks, settling the computer on to the carpet. It has totally changed since he was last here. He might have only seen it over Kim's shoulder then but he distinctly remembers how grim it was, being largely without furniture, except for a hammock thing and a grubby old bean bag, and with bare floor-boards and stained and peeling walls. Now it has plush beige carpet and smart red and gold flock wallpaper, shiny brass light-fittings and a large, dark brown three-piece suite. There's a big wide-screen telly on a stand in one corner and a small hi-fi system in another. It's just the sort of room, he thinks, his mum would go for.

It's the sort of room – if Kim hadn't had anything to do with it – he'd fancy for himself.

'What's happened in here?' he says, wondering whether in fact his mum has been involved with the redecoration. He's had very little contact with her since that day on the river in the summer and was under the impression that, having witnessed Lily at her most wild and destructive, she had decided after all to keep well out of her eldest granddaughter's life. He knows how his mum can turn away from situations that bother her, from people who get in her way. People who are too difficult to handle. People who cause her too much grief.

He has long suspected that it wasn't simply the case that his father found someone else and left, with his youngest son, for another continent, but that his mum played a part in pushing his dad out, in pushing them both out – at least she can't have fought very hard to keep them. She found his dad was eventually not worth the effort, being tough and single-minded, and not at home much – because he was always at his industrial park, or drinking with his mates – and that looking after both Robbie and himself – these wicked, uncontrollable boys – in a small house, near the city centre, was way too difficult – didn't she? Didn't she decide she could cope with one boy, but not two, and that she would keep Mark because he was most like her? Didn't she?

However, taking in the full splendour of Kim's new-look lounge he wonders whether it's possible that his mum hasn't given up on Lily already and has been down here helping Kim with the decorating, with choosing the carpet and the wallpaper and the three-piece suite, the light-fittings and the frilly-edged Venetian blinds hanging in front of the nets. That she's done this all behind his back. He certainly wouldn't be surprised to hear that she's helped to pay for it. Along with him, of course, he suddenly realises. That this is where the money he's been giving to Kim supposedly for Lily – for her summer clothes and school books, and her phone-cards and food, or as Kim's been calling it, Lily's 'day-to-day living costs' – has been going.

'Who's done this place up?' he says, because Kim either didn't understand or decided not to answer his first question.

'Oh, I have. With a bit of help,' she says. 'It's taken months.'

'From who?' he says. 'Who's helped you?'

'You know, Dave, before he fucked off. He had his uses, though he wasn't really into it. A couple of neighbours have been pretty handy. The people round here are very friendly.'

'So what, have you done the rest of the house? Does it all look like this?' he says.

'I've done the bedrooms. I'm really pleased with them. I'd show you upstairs but Zak's having his afternoon nap. Maybe later.'

'How much did it all cost?' he says, poking the arm rest of the settee, feeling how amazingly soft and springy it is, feeling the sheer quality. 'Where did you get the money?'

'Grants mostly, though I've been working a bit. And as I said, a number of people from round here have helped me out.'

'They must have,' he says, looking over the room once more, surprised that she seems to have even bothered to decorate it, and, in his mind, so tastefully, when she never made any effort with their place in Norfolk, and especially when he thought she was supposed to have become a New Age traveller, when she was meant to be used to living rough, in the backs of old buses, in tree houses and wigwams or what have you, and not meant to be in the least bit concerned with material things. Isn't that what hippies and travellers are all about?

'Working, doing what?' he says. He still can't imagine her fruit-picking – scrabbling around in a dusty field with a punnet of mouldy strawberries.

'Working in a club,' she says.

'We're back doing that, are we?' he says. 'Aren't you too old?'

'It's a very exclusive club,' she says. 'For gentlemen, not yobs. Besides, it doesn't stay open that late.'

'Who looks after your baby?' he says.

'Lily. She usually baby-sits. I pay her well for it, too. I earn good money, you know, the evenings I work.'

Lily told him on the phone her mother had changed since she's had her baby and especially since this Dave character pissed off, and how she has become this fascist, obsessed with money and the carpet and the baby, and looking at Kim in her tight rollneck sweater and neat stone-washed jeans, leaning on the windowsill, peering proudly through the net curtains at her once scruffy front yard, he can see how Lily might think that. And he reckons he knows just how disorientated, how displaced, his daughter must be feeling about it all, too – if she's anything like him. He always likes to know where he is with someone, to have people sized up. He hates it when people suddenly change, turning themselves into this or that, and then maybe back again when it happens to suit them. However, he's not so sure how much Kim has changed, inside. OK, she never used to care for the decor of a place, or, in his mind, Lily when she was small – she didn't care too much about that particular baby, being only too willing to make a joke of her – but when he was married to Kim she was certainly obsessed with money, constantly going on to him about how little they had and why he couldn't do something to earn a bit more because she would love to make herself half-presentable, she would love to simply be able to feed them all properly. Kim, he senses, is just as slippery, as devious as ever, operating to her own agenda. He never did know where he was with her (with her one minute wanting to live in the middle of the country, in isolation, ha-ha, and the next wanting to be chatting up men in some club in the centre of the city – for starters), now he's sure her own daughter doesn't either – their daughter, whose fourteenth birthday it is today, and who has decided to slope off somewhere, when, he thinks, she should have been at home waiting for him. He has only just driven 150 miles on treacherous roads for the occasion, and on top of that, he's brought her a whacking great present, which cost him a small fortune.

'So if you're making so much money, Kim,' he says, moving into the middle of the room, moving closer to her, moving into a position where he'll be able to block her way out of the room, should she decide to make a run for it, 'why do you keep asking me for more?'

'I've got a lot of mouths to feed, haven't I?' she says, with her back to the window now, hooking her thumbs inside her jeans pockets. 'Your daughter's great gob to begin with, Mark.'

'It doesn't seem like you're doing a very good job at that,' he says.

'There are clothes and uniforms and books as well, and kids these days are always wanting new CDs and DVDs, and make-up and money to spend going out in the evenings with their friends,' she says. 'And phonecards too. About a million of those a day.'

'Wait a minute,' he says. 'Tell me why Lily won't eat properly, Kim. That's what I want to know. We reckon she's, you know, bulimic. That's what Nicole says.'

'It's just kids today, isn't it?' Kim says. 'All her friends are the same. None of them eat anything.'

'Well, what about the clothes I keep giving you money for?' he says. 'She looks like a fucking tart, Kim. That stupid Babe T-shirt. She's going to get herself into a lot of trouble wearing skimpy things like that, at her age. She nearly did when she came to see us on the train in the summer. Did she tell you about that? How some fucking paedophile tried to pick her up? Do you warn her about what happens out there? What men are really like?'

'Mark, she's fourteen. She knows what she's doing. She can take care of herself. Besides, some of those clothes were mine – don't you remember? You never used to complain about them.' Kim winks at him. But so briefly and in a way that Mark has no idea what she means by it, whether it's a come-on, whether she's actually being flirty, or whether she's teasing him, being ironic or something.

'That's a great fucking attitude, that is,' he says, stepping closer to Kim, who has remained by the window with her arms crossed, and feeling his neck flush, feeling that this is the moment he's been waiting for, with Kim backed against the wall. 'Encourage her to dress up like a tart and then not tell her how to protect herself, right? Just let someone else deal with it. Let her teachers talk to her. Is that what you do? But she doesn't have any teachers at the moment, does she? She hasn't got on very well at school so far, has she? Why's that, I wonder? Might it have something to do with the fact that she never even went to school until she was thirteen? And how before that she was carted up and down the country in the back of some clapped-out old bus, being abused by hippies left, right and centre? I know what went on. She's told me what those men used to do to her – all your fucking so-called boyfriends.'

'Mark,' Kim says, picking at a bit of fluff on the front of her sweater and laughing, 'I don't know what you're getting at, but she is just fourteen. She's got a big imagination. She's always making up stuff. That's what kids her age do. They're not straightforward. They're always saying things for effect, to shock or whatever. I should know, I have been through it before, twice.'

'You can't get out of it that easily,' he says. 'I hold you one hundred per cent responsible for what's happened to her. I'm not going to let you get away with it. Not this time.'

'No?' she says.

'You've just got to start looking after her properly, Kim,' he says, unsure of the way forward, unsure of where he wants this to go and what commitments regarding Lily's future he's willing to give right now. 'She's not a joke. She's a human being. She needs a lot of love and attention. More than she's obviously been getting. You've abused her enough, Kim – you and your fucking hippy traveller convoy friends. I won't let you abuse her any more.'

'Mark,' Kim says, 'do you want to fuck me?'

9

Over a period of about a year and a half he supposes he must have hit her again and again. Mostly across her face with the back of his hand. Though he jabbed her in the ribs once, and once pulled her across the room by her hair. He probably kicked and kneed her a few times too – if he thinks about it hard. It wasn't just her bragging about her sexual conquests that set him off – about sleeping with Chris, the nightclub owner, about slipping out of the fire exit at Henry's and into the alleyway with any number of punters, especially the pilots from RAF Coltishall ('You should see their muscles, Mark,' she'd say, 'their chests are as finely tuned as their cocks'), about having a frig with Robin, her best mate Claire's hubby, one afternoon in the kitchen, up on the counter, with her legs wrapped round his back, so she said, while Lily was having a nap and the boys were at school, in fact having a couple of threesomes with Claire and Robin – but the way she would use her sexuality, the fact that she knew he fancied her because she was so uninhibited, because she was so eager and vigorous, to make him feel weak and constantly mocked.

During arguments, when they had started screaming at each other, and perhaps jostling a little as well, she would suddenly shout something like, 'I bet you've got a stiffy, Mark. Come on, big boy, let me feel how hard you are. Let me have a suck.' Or, 'This is really turning me on, Mark. You're such a man. I just love it when you're so aggressive, when you threaten me. You're making me wet through. My knickers are completely soaked.'

She even said in front of this woman from social services, this small, skinny, timid-looking woman, with long, black, greasy hair and large glasses, who had turned up one evening completely out of the blue, as far as he was concerned, though Kim, he later found out, knew she was coming because her GP had been in contact with both social services and the domestic crime unit of the local police, she even said in front of her, when the three of them were sitting in the kitchen and he was getting increasingly heated because though Kim was telling this woman, this social worker, how violent he could be and detailing the sort of beatings he would give her, totally exaggerating everything, of course, and not mentioning her own escapades out of the house, her affairs and sexual promiscuity, which obviously wound him up so much in the first place, with Kim not letting him say a word in his defence, certainly not letting him get his side across, so he could only shout and thump the table in frustration, absolutely done in by the lies, by the complete injustice of it all, she said, in front of this really very timid-looking woman, suddenly quite calmly, 'Mark, why don't you go upstairs and have a wank? Go on, do us all a favour. I don't want you getting your cock out down here in front of this nice young woman. I can see how desperate you are. How frustrated. You men are all the same.'

And here she is, he thinks, in Newbury but it might as well be Norfolk ten years ago, up to the same old tricks. Side-tracking him. Pushing him way off course. Mocking him. Making him want to explode. Saying, 'Do you want to fuck me?'

10

Does he want to fuck her? Is that what he really wants to do? He's contemplating this as the doorbell goes. As a deep, melodious ding-dong – exactly the same sound his mother's bell makes, an old-fashioned sound, he thinks, a sound from his childhood – reverberates through the small house.

Standing back, he lets Kim walk past him to the front door, then he moves over to the far corner of the room where hopefully he's well out of view from whoever it might be. Knowing that they've been shouting and that maybe they were about to become physical – just like years before – he doesn't want to be seen here by anyone. He certainly doesn't want to be revealed as Lily's dad – not in front of some friend of Kim's, not in front of one of her handy neighbours. He doesn't want to be caught by Lily even, not off his guard like this. Not when he's always denied to her that he was ever violent towards her mum.

He's suddenly ashamed of himself, despite knowing he was being seriously provoked and couldn't possibly be blamed for any defensive action he might have been preparing to take. Or any other action. Like rape, it occurs to him, except he knows it wouldn't have been rape because Kim asked him whether he wanted to fuck her. She wanted to do it. It was her idea. Wasn't it?

With huge relief, he hears a child's voice, at least a young, female teenager's voice – a voice not at all dissimilar to Lily's – but definitely not Lily's voice. He hears this voice say to Kim, 'Is Lily in, Kim?'

'No, sorry, love, she's out somewhere,' Kim says. 'I thought she might be with you, love. Have you tried Zara's?'

'Yeah,' Mark hears the girl say. 'She's not with her.'

'Dan's?' Kim says.

'Yeah, tried his too,' the girl says.

'What about her mobile?' Kim says.

'I've been trying that,' the girl says. 'And I've sent loads of messages but she's not replying.'

'She's probably run down the battery,' Kim says. 'You know how much she uses that thing. Perhaps she's gone into town shopping. Her gran sent her some money, so maybe she's buying herself something to wear.'

'Yeah,' the girl says, 'probably. I'll call round later.'

'OK,' says Kim, 'but not too late, love.'

'See-ya, then,' the girl says.

Mark watches Kim shut the door and move back into the room, stopping for a moment to take a look at his present for Lily, which is still sitting on the floor near the front door.

'What's in that box, then?' she says.

'A computer,' he says. 'Brand-new.'

'No expense spared for Lil, all of a sudden,' she says.

'Yeah, that's right,' he says.

'Well, it's a pity she's not here to open it, isn't it?' she says. 'Who knows when she'll be back. She usually skips tea. I don't know what you're going to do, but I've got to get Zak up. I'm not sure I want you snooping around my house while I'm upstairs. I know what you're like.'

'A minute ago it sounded like you wanted me to come upstairs with you,' he says.

'You have never understood me, Mark, have you?' she says. 'You've never got it.'

'I don't care about trying to understand you,' he says. 'I don't care about you one tiny little bit – surprise, surprise. All I care about right now is my birthday girl.'

'Sure you do,' she says.

'Which is more than I can say for you,' he says, not sure whether that sounds right, but he thinks Kim knows what he means – that he's the only one who truly cares for Lily, who really cares about her well-being, her whereabouts, her sanity, on her birthday. On every fucking day.

DECEMBER

I

'She looks different,' Gemma says, waving from the back seat. 'She's got black hair and her face is skinny.'

'She hasn't been well, that's all,' Nicole says.

'Does being ill make your hair black?' Gemma says.

'No, sweetheart,' Nicole says, laughing. 'She's just dyed it, to make herself look different. People are always dyeing their hair.'

'Like Mum,' Mark says. 'And Gran.'

'And Daddy when he was younger, too,' Nicole says. 'When he wanted to look like Rod Stewart.'

'Who's Rod Stewart?' Gemma says.

'Daddy's favourite pop singer,' says Nicole. 'You know that terrible music he was always playing in the car until I banned it? Daddy loves that. He loves that so much sometimes he used to start crying when he listened to it.'

'Shut up, Nicole,' Mark says, stopping the car as soon as he can on a band of wavy yellow lines a short way past Lily, who they spotted waiting by the entrance to the train station, out on the pavement, next to the huge Christmas tree. He knew they were going to be late the moment they hit the heavy, last-Saturday-before-Christmas-shopping traffic on the inner ring road, but they are only four minutes late, due to the fact he jumped two sets of lights, and he didn't imagine for a moment that the train would actually be on time. He gets out of the car, presuming Lily didn't notice them drive in with Gemma waving from the back seat. Lily's still waiting by the Christmas tree, her black hair and white skin standing out against the dark green foliage.

Like Nicole, he had no difficulty recognising her, having been warned by Kim that she had dyed her hair black and had lost a bit of weight because of a virus. Though he thinks he would have recognised her anyway, from the way she was standing, or sloping indifferently, with her hands stuffed in her pockets and her head bowed. From the shape of her frame, which of course is his frame, being so angular. However, he is surprised by just how thin and pale she does look, how fragile, even from a distance. He's never liked black hair on women, or girls, he supposes, finding it too extreme, too untrustworthy, too frigging punkish. He's always been into blondes, whether artificial or not. With tanned, healthy complexions.

'You're late,' Lily says, looking up at him as he approaches. 'It's bloody freezing.'

'You could have waited inside the building,' he says.

'You could have been on time,' she says, beginning to jig on the spot.

'Yeah, well, at least I'm here,' he says. 'When I drove all the way to see you on your birthday you couldn't even be bothered to be there at all, could you?'

This is the first time Mark has seen Lily since he put her on the train to go back to Newbury last summer – nearly half a year ago, it occurs to him, and in a way he feels like he's seeing her for the first time in a decade again. His long-lost daughter. His wild child who, after he was excluded from her life, was brought up on the road with a bunch of New Age travellers, and who when he last saw her in August had metamorphosed into some slapper and who now appears to be only half tart, but half hippy traveller again, too. She's wearing a tiny black skirt, thick black tights dotted with large holes and tears, clumpy, DM-style boots, and a baggy red, loosely-knitted jumper over a well-worn white T-shirt – he can see her scrawny, bare arms, this pale, goose-pimpled flesh, through the wool.

He doesn't get her new look at all, nor does he know whether he should hug her, or be cross with her, about her appearance, about her confusing him. About her, also, not bothering to show up for her own birthday after he'd travelled all that way in a torrential downpour to see her, bringing with him a pretty serious present, which she has still never thanked him for.

As a kid, his mother always made him thank people, his gran or his aunt, for any birthday or Christmas presents they gave him. But he thinks he would have done it anyway because he knew what was right, he knew how to treat people even then – when he was just a kid, a teenager. When, he supposes, he should have been rebelling. When he should have been rude and difficult, and drugged out of his head half the time.

It was because he was so angry with Lily for not showing up when he went to see her – leaving him to spend hours on end with Kim, in her fancy lounge – and then not even ringing him to thank him for the computer, in the weeks and months since, that he decided there was no way he was going to drive all the way to Newbury to fetch her for Christmas. He was quite happy for Kim to put her on the train, which Kim didn't even ask him to pay for, and let Lily cope with whatever weirdo approached her. He wasn't going to worry about her being taken advantage of, about her being persuaded off the train at Ipswich and dragged back to a squalid bedsit and then raped.

'Where's the car?' says Lily, continuing to jig on the spot. 'Where's my sister? Where's Nicole? I don't want to stand here talking to you all day, freezing my tits off.'

'Over there,' Mark says, pointing to the Astra stopped illegally on the yellow wavy bands, in the dim early afternoon light but with the station's Christmas decorations quietly playing on the dark blue metallic surface – he thinks it's odd that they should bother to smother the exterior of the station with fairy lights, but leave the tree bare.

'Where's your coat?' he says, sure she has grown, though he realises he could just be thinking this because she's so much thinner, and because her sweater, like her T-shirt, is far too short and doesn't cover her bare stomach, her still pierced belly button.

'Don't have one, do I,' she says, bending to pick up her large bag, which Mark recognises from before.

'I'll take that,' he says, pushing Lily away from her bag, not being able to let this thin, pale, shivering daughter of his, this pathetic-looking figure with black hair and deathly white skin, and too-small clothes, drag her own stuff over to his car, not this time. The bag, he finds, is ridiculously heavy, almost as heavy as his tool box. He can't imagine what she has in it.

'Get off,' she says, trying to grab the handle back from him, fighting him for the bag on the pavement. Shoving her thin body against his. She's so light he feels it is as if Gemma is pushing into him. 'It's mine,' she says. 'I don't want you touching it with your grubby hands.'

'I'm only taking it to the bloody car,' he says, humping it along the ground, barely able to lift it clear himself but determined to hang on to it. Quite ashamed of how weak his daughter seems, as if he's somehow to blame. 'I'm not running off with it. Don't worry about that. What have you got in it, anyway?'

'Stuff,' she says.

2

In the car, crawling once more through thick traffic on the inner ring road, but with the road now sunk below a blanket of orange light dashed with reds and shattering silvers, with all this artificial light lingering on the damp, still, mid-December air, Nicole says, 'You must have been freezing out there. But at least you can't have been waiting for long.'

'An hour or two, maybe,' Lily says.

'An hour or two?' Mark says. 'You've got a mobile, haven't you? Why didn't you ring? Anyway, I thought your train was getting in at three-forty.'

'It was probably early or something,' Lily says. 'And my phone-card's run out, hasn't it?'

'You got the two o'clock from Liverpool Street, right?' says Nicole.

'How do I know what time it was?' Lily says. 'I just got on the first train that they said was coming here. The heating didn't work and no one bought me a drink, or anything to eat. Nothing. The passengers were all horrible. I couldn't even bum a fag.'

'But your mum took you as far as Liverpool Street, didn't she? She made sure you got on the right train?' Nicole says.

'Sort of,' Lily says.

'What does that mean?' Mark says. 'Sort of?' he adds, trying to mimic her voice, her moody, shrill West Country accent.

'It means sort of,' Lily says.

'So did she put you on the train in London, or not?' he says. 'As she told me she was going to do on the phone at the beginning of the week.'

'What difference does it make?' Lily says.

'All the difference,' Mark says.

'What if I didn't want her to take me to London to put me on a train, like I was some little kid? What if I did it on my own? What if I spent last night round my friend's, anyway? I'm not five. I've been to London loads of times before on my own. I can handle it. I'm wise, man.'

'So she didn't put you on the train?' Mark says. 'I should have fucking known it.'

He's not just angry with Kim, he's angry with himself, for not having sensed something like this would have happened, for not having thought that Lily could have been wandering around London, of all places, on her own, getting into who knows what trouble – for him having been too proud to have driven to Newbury to collect her after she stood him up before. Especially as Kim had mentioned Lily hadn't been well and had lost a bit of weight and had recently even been talking about running away. But how is he meant to believe a word Kim ever says?

'Mark, don't you dare swear in front of Gemma,' Nicole says. 'How many times do I have to tell you not to do it? I just won't have it.'

'Yeah, Mark,' Lily says, 'watch your tongue.'

'Yeah, Mark,' Gemma says, laughing, 'watch your tongue, or it'll drop off.'

3

They were in the lounge watching telly, watching the adverts, which all seemed to be for special Christmas compilation CDs, or cheap jewellery, or the prices of three-piece suites slashed in the forthcoming furniture warehouse sales starting on Boxing Day, when Mark, standing up and making as if to go into the kitchen, but stopping short, said, 'What do you think about Lily coming for Christmas?' They had eaten their tea ages ago and Gemma was fast asleep, having gone to bed early, believing Christmas would come sooner that way – having been told that by both Mark and Nicole for the last few nights.

'Not much,' said Nicole, keeping her eyes fixed on the telly, not even flinching, Mark noticed, as he looked over his shoulder to catch her reaction.

'Yeah, well, no one else is coming, are they?' he said, moving back into the room and standing next to the settee, where Nicole was curled up with her feet tucked under her in her usual position. 'Your mum and your dad are going to your sister's. My mum will be with Lawrence and his stupid family, so we won't be seeing much of her this year.'

'That's not the point,' she said. 'I thought we could have a nice, quiet, family Christmas on our own. Just the three of us. That's what I'd been looking forward to.'

'So then there'd be just the four of us,' he said. 'She is my daughter, Nicole. If she wants to come for Christmas I can't really say no.'

'Yes, you can,' she said. 'You can easily say no. Besides, does Lily really want to come here at the last minute, or does Kim just want to get rid of her? What's that woman up to now?'

'Kim told me on the phone that Lily's been saying she wants to be with us for Christmas. She's sick of spending it with her mum – Kim even said that.'

'Yeah, well, maybe we don't want to spend Christmas with her.'

'Who's we? You have your opinions, I have mine.'

'I don't understand you, Mark,' Nicole said, untucking her feet and looking away from the telly, but not quite at him. 'Half the time you've got nothing but bad words for Lily and the other half she's like the most important thing in your life. The last time you saw her, when you went to Newbury for her birthday, you came back slagging her off, didn't you? You went on about her not having any manners and ignoring you, and wanting to be with her friends instead.'

'That doesn't mean she's not my daughter,' he said.

'No, that's certainly true.'

He hadn't told Nicole he hadn't actually seen Lily when he went to Newbury for her birthday. He couldn't admit to his wife that Lily had failed to be around to see her dad, just as he hadn't mentioned anything about buying Lily the computer – which obviously made the fact that she hadn't been there so much worse. And he hadn't mentioned anything about his confrontation with Kim either, the fact that he nearly fucked her.

'That doesn't mean I don't have certain responsibilities,' he said. 'Blood's blood, isn't it? There's no escaping that.'

'Responsibilities – you don't know what the word means,' Nicole said. 'How about your responsibility to your wife, your current wife, and Gemma, the daughter you share with her, the daughter you live with full-time?'

'Look, Nicole, Kim said she was worried Lily might run away or do something stupid, if she doesn't get her way over Christmas.

Apparently, she's feeling really sensitive about it, especially as her brothers, her half-brothers, you know, Jake and Sean, are no longer living at home. Kim says Lily keeps telling her she doesn't have a proper family.'

'Whose fault's that?' Nicole said, flicking the TV off with the remote, which had been on her lap, and standing. She then brushed the creases out of her work skirt, before reaching down to straighten her tights – something Mark is always catching her doing – inadvertently pulling up her skirt a little. 'I don't know why I've stuck with you, Mark,' she said. 'I mean, I must be mentally retarded or something. It can't just be for Gemma's sake – you hardly know the girl. What good are you as a father to her? Or this stupid thing I have about sticking to my guns, sticking with things, however bad they get. God, Mark, I don't know what I ever saw in you in the first place, come to think of it, except perhaps some idea that you were, you know, warm and caring under that thick skin of yours. The trouble people get into because they fancy someone once, for a millisecond, because they think that that person's someone they're not – it's mad. But maybe I just felt sorry for you. You know, with all that stuff having just gone on – with all that stuff that you bloody well caused. Right?'

Finally looking straight at Mark, unblinking, Nicole continued, 'You're nothing but trouble, Mark, and stupid me has just let you get away with it – spoiling everything for Gemma, our daughter. Putting everything at risk. How did I let that happen – I've got a good job, people respect me? I'm not surprised you've run out of work, or that firm of engineers didn't employ you, when they seemed to be hiring everyone else in the city. Who'd trust you? You're a liability, Mark, just like Lily. And you're as pathetically childish. Blood's blood as you say, all right. It's as thick as anything between you two, that's for sure. Like some horrible glue.'

Walking into the kitchen, Nicole had to budge Mark aside with her shoulder. He wasn't going to step out of her way, but he couldn't answer her back. He couldn't say anything in his defence. He'd never felt quite like this with Nicole before – not so blocked, so crushed. Though it was a feeling he experienced when he was with Kim often enough. Having followed Nicole into the kitchen and facing his livid second wife close up in the confined space, this

Kim mark two, so he thought, in her short, tight, navy work skirt and white near see-through blouse which revealed almost every detail of her lacy black Wonderbra – who was she trying to impress at work, who was she knocking off from the office? Some rich executive with a swanky company car? With a top-of-the-range, five-series BMW, as her immediate boss had? – all he could say, with his mind flashing between Nicole and Kim, between anger and hurt, but experiencing also a dizzying rush of adrenalin – a sudden need to be physical, a need to use his body not his head, a need to use his limbs, his cock – all he could say was, 'Do you want to fuck me?'

4

Like the first car, the first house was easy. They knew the owners were away because they'd been observing the street for a number of nights as they walked into the city centre and back – egging each other on at the same time, daring each other, building a common will, a momentum, which soon clearly couldn't be diffused without some sort of action, without going through with a break-in. All four of them were novices when it came to burglary.

Mark didn't lead the group down the side alley, but he followed readily enough, with his heart thumping and his fists balled and clammy. The back gate was bolted but it needed only a small push to prise the bolt off the soft wood – they didn't even have to climb over the fence. Once inside the small yard, a couple of them started giggling, with the ease with which they'd already got so far, with sheer nervousness. They were closely surrounded by the brightly lit houses of the terraces to the rear and the sides, and they knew they had to be quiet, but still they giggled and jostled, pushing each other, trying to get one of them to make the next move.

That person was eventually Mark. Having come this far, he suddenly felt emboldened, and more than anything else he wanted to impress his mates. It was his turn to prove how tough he was, how wised-up, how crooked. Similarly, when he broke into his first car, a Ford Granada Ghia (the same model his dad had once had), he initially stood back, letting Steve open the doors, letting Lee start the engine, but once out of the city, in the dark and empty early hours of the morning, he made sure he had a spell behind the wheel, and having had a bit of driving practice on an old World War II aerodrome with his dad a year or so before – which was one of the few things he and his old man ever did together, just the two of them – he proved how competent he was, certainly how wild, how incorrigible, by driving on the wrong side of the road and slipping on to the verge, by U-turning on a dual carriageway and bumping over the central reservation, by shooting across almost the middle of a roundabout when coming back into the city. If they were spotted by the police they had decided they'd attempt to outrun them. They'd aim for near enough where they lived and hopefully lose them in the series of one-way and blocked-off streets there, and once clear they'd dump the car and scatter.

Indeed, over the next few weeks and months he began to show off a skill for getting into cars as well. Often he simply used keys he found in car doors or ignitions, or more commonly those he noticed lying around various friends' and relatives' houses. He took car keys belonging to his mum, to Lawrence (before he'd officially become his stepdad), to his gran, to his mum's sister – finding that some keys happened to fit most of the particular models they came from. Italian and French cars were the easiest and most consistent, then the British, though he eventually learned how to hot-wire ignitions and knock out alarm systems of the more sophisticated German and Swedish makes, the Audis and Mercs and Volvos. He wrapped his swelling key collection in an old T-shirt which he kept behind a false back on the top shelf of his built-in bedroom cupboard, along with the other tools and bits of refashioned coat hanger he came to use. However, for his very first break-in, in front of Steve and Lee again, and Lee's younger brother Paul, Mark nervously, perhaps shyly, stepped up to the badly rotten sash window, placed his hands on the glass and shoved upwards. Much to his relief it shifted, sliding and rattling open, with almost as little effort as the gate had given way. Lee pushed past him and climbed straight in. Mark went next, then Steve. Paul was meant to wait outside to keep watch but he climbed in, too. The house stank of damp and was very dark, and they soon realised none of them had thought to bring a torch. Lee had some matches but the first one he struck seemed suddenly far too bright so he quickly blew it out, though not before they could see that the room, with a small kitchen leading off it, was completely empty. There was no furniture, there was nothing. The owners weren't just away, they had moved out, probably ages ago. But determined to come away with something, to prove to themselves that they'd done it, that they'd actually committed their first burglary, they scoured the house, downstairs and upstairs, with their eyes having grown much more accustomed to the darkness, and making ghost noises while they were at it – pretending the house was haunted, pinching each other, shutting Paul in a small room upstairs and jamming the door.

Apart from piles of old newspapers and a couple of cardboard boxes full of empty wine and whisky bottles, all they could find were an old metal anglepoise lamp, without most of its springs or a plug, and a dirty, cream ring-dial telephone. They left the lamp because it was too heavy and bulky though they took the telephone, Lee stuffing it inside his jacket. They didn't attempt to sell it later but kept it as a memento, a trophy, a good-luck charm – seeing as they weren't caught – passing it from one to the other. Mark had the phone for a couple of months, and didn't even bother to hide it from his mum, leaving it on public display in his room, by the portable TV at the foot of his bed. The TV didn't work either, though he always thought it looked really impressive sitting there. Like it was the height of luxury. Like he was a pop star or something. Like he was Rod Stewart.

5

Lily says, pointing at Top Shop across the packed pedestrian street, 'Mark, I want to go in there.'

Mark looks towards the building, at its windows filled with large posters of models in frilly underwear, high heels and floppy, red and white Father Christmas hats, and again at the street, this great, seething obstacle between them and the shop. He spots numerous snakes of people wearing various Father Christmas hats too, with each group wearing exactly the same style of hat, like a uniform, he thinks, a membership badge. Some groups are clearly drunker and more unable to walk than others, with people using lengths of tinsel to hang on to each other, and with the odd stray bloke inadvertently latching on to total strangers, lunging at them, making a complete idiot of himself. Office workers after their Christmas lunch piss Mark right off. He's been trying not to think about Nicole at a work Christmas lunch today – about the fourth she's had this year – but he can't help himself now, wondering who she's sitting next to – this guy she's been knocking off with the gleaming five-series? – wondering what sort of state she'll be in when she gets home. He hates seeing people drunk on the streets. He hates it when people don't control themselves in public.

'Yeah, Dad,' Gemma says, holding Lily's hand. 'I want to go in there too. It looks wicked.' She giggles quietly, self-consciously.

'Forget it,' Mark says. 'We haven't come shopping for the benefit of you two. We've got a load of stuff to get, including a present for your mum, Gemma – haven't we? – but it doesn't include anything from Top Shop, I can tell you that. Though just look at the place, you won't get anywhere near it.'

'It is meant to be Christmas,' Lily says. 'Isn't that when people have to be nice to one another? When people let you do what you want – and get off your back?'

'Not where I come from,' Mark says. 'Where I come from they always do what I say. I thought you didn't have any money, anyway. What are you going to buy with no money?'

'Who said I wanted to buy anything?' she says.

'What do you want to go in there for, then?' he says.

'Have a look,' she says.

'Right,' he says, 'well, we're going to Boots instead and then we're going to Habitat, and then the market, and we've got to get Nicole's present somewhere along the way too.' He reaches for Gemma's hand, the hand Lily's not holding, fearful that Lily might try to drag Gemma off to Top Shop, and that he could then lose both of them in the crowd. He pulls Gemma in the opposite direction, towards Boots, feeling Lily pulling her the other way, at least Lily not budging from where she's standing.

'Dad,' Gemma says, 'you're hurting me.'

'Tell Lily to let go, then,' he says.

'Mark,' Gemma says, attempting to sound like Lily – she keeps doing this, and using words like 'wicked' and 'wise', and 'grebo', knowing how much it annoys him – 'you're really hurting me.'

'Gem, please,' he says. 'And Lily, don't make this any more of a pain in the arse than it is. Stop mucking about. Look, after Boots I'll buy you both a cake and a drink. We can go to that Starbucks in the Castle Mall.' Nicole gave him extra money for such emergencies, and if he's careful in Boots and the market he reckons she gave him enough money for the Christmas present he'll have to get for her too.

'Funny man,' says Lily. 'Why can't you buy me something proper? You know I don't eat cakes. Cakes give you diabetes.'

'The last time I bought you a present, you weren't even there to open it – remember?' he says. 'In fact you've never even thanked me for it, either. You ungrateful cow. You're not my daughter. Who are you?'

'Thanks, Mark. Thanks for everything,' she says. 'See, I've thanked you now. But that wasn't a proper present anyway. That was a boring computer, which Mum uses all the time. She won't let me near it because she thinks I'll break it. Why can't you buy me a new top, or some jewellery, or make-up? What are you getting Nicole? I bet you're getting her something pretty. Well, I want to look pretty too, Marky Mark.'

'You're fourteen,' he says. 'And anyway I've been giving your mum loads of money for your clothes, and make-up, probably.'

'That was wise,' says Lily. 'What do you think she spends that on, simpleton? Only herself, or her precious house, and her fucking Dave man, now he's come back with his dick between his legs.'

Since the serious downturn in his work, and having been refused a job with the call-out firm, Mark has mostly been picking up Gemma from school and giving her her tea before Nicole gets home, as Nicole has been staying at the office late, overseeing a new marketing campaign, often not getting back until 6.30 or so, which completely infuriates him. The fact that he's at home giving Gemma her tea while his wife's still out at work – supposedly. However, he does feel he's recently become much better at handling Gemma. He knows how to keep her calm and out of trouble, usually by letting her watch her favourite video, which is currently *Lady and the Tramp III*, or if that fails giving her these mini Swiss rolls she loves. (What else is he meant to feed her on when she refuses to eat the ready-made meals Nicole's left out for her? Spaghetti bolognese? Chicken Kiev? Fish pie? He's no cook.) And he now feels competent taking Gemma into town on his own, to the Castle Mall, or Anglia Square, and not just to the supermarket. But he doesn't have a clue how to control Lily, how to keep her quiet, how to keep her shut up, and standing on the packed pedestrian street, being bumped into and jostled, he's suddenly concerned, just as Nicole was ages ago, he remembers – what with Lily's swearing and her continual rudeness, with her dark moods and her weird, all-over-the-place dress sense, not to mention her eating habits – that she'll be a terrible influence on Gemma. On his precious little Gem, who he might not have paid much attention to in the past though feels he's been doing more than his fair share of looking after recently – as a firm though always affectionate dad. A role model.

'Gem,' he says, tightening his grip on her hand, 'let go of Lily this instant, we're going this way. And you, Lily, you're coming too. I'm not having you sneaking off looking like that, without a coat and with those stupid clothes on, getting yourself picked up by some pervert. You're sticking with me too, missy, whether you like it or not.'

6

Walking into Boots on London Street, the city's flagship store, with his two daughters, with this vast list of stuff Nicole's asked him to get from here, with such things on the list as shampoo, and toothpaste and tampons, a packet of Non-Applicator Tampax Super-Plus Tampons at that, with Gemma and Lily suddenly, amazingly – and he has no idea quite why, though he hopes they're not just plotting something, he really hopes that they're not just gearing themselves up for another bout of stubbornness – actually behaving themselves, with the two of them walking quietly and obediently behind him, and with masses of women, masses of mothers and fathers and other children too in the shop to observe this, plus with the shop smelling so fragrant, so feminine – of this great mishmash of perfumes and toiletries – he feels like he's stepping into another world. He feels as if he's become one of these new men. A dad taking his kids to Boots. While his wife tucks into an office Christmas lunch. While at this very moment his wife is no doubt putting on her floppy Father Christmas hat and draping tinsel all over herself – letting the top two buttons of her blouse come undone, and probably letting her skirt ride up her thighs a little as well to purposefully reveal the tops of her stay-up stockings, which he noticed she put on this morning as opposed to her normal tights. And soon she'll be tossing her head back as she sweeps her hair from her eyes, and laughing loudly, flirtatiously, and patting men's shoulders and knees, the way she does after she's had a few. The tart, he thinks. The bitch. How on earth did he end up in this position?

'Hey, Mark,' says Lily, picking up a hairdryer, a light pink and purple hairdryer very obviously designed, he thinks, for trendy young women, 'why don't you buy yourself one of these for Christmas? I've seen you use Nicole's in front of the mirror enough. And what is that thing you are always doing to you hair?' Mark watches as Lily uses the fingers on both her hands to flick her black hair forward, but keeping it puffed up and bouncy too – exactly, he realises, how he tries to get his hair into place, especially when he uses a bit of gel. 'This thing,' she says. 'Is this right, Gemma?'

'Shut it, Lily,' he says, looking away from her and at the shopping list Nicole prepared for him.

'This is boring,' Lily says, putting the hairdryer back on the wrong shelf. 'This shop's boring.'

'I'll give you something to do then,' Mark says, handing her the basket, 'you can bloody well hold this.'

'Thanks, Mark,' she says, 'I've always wanted to be your slave.'

'And you can keep an eye on Gemma, too. Gemma, come back here,' he says, as Gemma walks to the end of the aisle and disappears from view. 'Don't you bloody go wandering off on your own.'

Despite having been in this particular Boots countless times over the years, he's still unsure of the layout, realising he's never had to pay attention in here before, always having let Nicole, or Kim before her, he supposes, guide him around while he carried the basket, while he tried to keep an eye on the kids. That was his role. Now he's in charge, being the stroppy woman, trying to find the aisle with the Tampax, while running after his younger daughter because the person he just delegated that responsibility to can't be arsed, not that he could probably trust her anyway.

He jogs to the end of the aisle to find Gemma has walked halfway back along the other side, the side which seems to contain all the make-up, most of which has been brightly packaged with

Boots' special silver and red Christmas packaging. Gemma giggles and moves further down the aisle as he approaches, but she doesn't run away fast enough and he snatches her by the arm, pinching her hard, so he thinks she'll get the message and not try to run away again today. She whimpers though she doesn't cry.

'Bully,' Lily says, having caught up with them. She has still got the basket, and turning away from Mark and Gemma and moving back down the make-up aisle, she starts to fill it with Christmas packs of lipstick and bottles of nail varnish, with mascaras and eyebrow pencils and compacts – grabbing the cosmetics by the handful.

'What the hell do you think you're doing?' Mark says. 'Who's going to pay for that lot?'

'You are,' she says. 'Oh, please, Marky Mark. Just a few little things. Please. No one ever buys me anything. I am your daughter. Don't you want me to look pretty for Christmas? Like Nicole?'

'No,' he says. 'No bloody way. How many times do I have to say no to you? Now put it all back.'

'No,' she says, picking up various items from the basket with her skeletal right hand and putting them in her jeans pockets.

'I said put it back,' Mark says.

'No,' Lily screams. 'No, no, no. It's mine. It's all mine.'

Mark checks the rest of the aisle to see who's watching. Remarkably, no one else is anywhere near, and no one appears to have yet been drawn closer by Lily's screaming fit. 'Right, we're going,' he says, grabbing Gemma by the arm again, not quite so viciously, but firm enough to make sure she won't escape, and making for the door with her, thinking he's had quite enough of Lily, thinking Lily can stay where she is until she's detained by the security people for shoplifting and then carted off to the central police station. He's not going to help her any more. He won't bail her out this time. He's done all he can for her. 'I've had enough of you,' he says over his shoulder. 'I'm sick of you.' But she follows him to the exit, dropping the now almost empty basket on the floor, though not emptying her pockets, making no effort to do that, he observes, sneaking looks back. She follows him and Gemma out into the street, setting off the security system buzzer – at least Mark's certain he can hear its shrill, intermittent beeping above a group of carol singers who are performing by the entrance, and the singing and shouting and screaming of the people pushing to get in and out of the store, and the, 'ho, ho, ho,' laughing coming from Boots' own Father Christmas, who is also out on the pavement, competing with the carol singers while trying to entice the last shoppers in before the store shuts early today at 4 pm.

'Wait,' Mark hears Lily shout some way behind him, as he in turn elbows a passage through the desperate crowd, pulling Gemma with him, further and further into the packed street, under the dim flicker of the high street's digital Christmas lights. 'Don't leave me,' she shouts. 'Don't leave me, Dad.'

7

Abba were performing 'Fernando' on *Top of the Pops*, the song being number one then, when his father wandered in with the news. Mark had never admitted to anyone he actually liked Abba, that he really fancied the blonde girl, and especially loved the song 'Fernando' – he put it right up there with 'Sailing'. Not to his dad, and certainly not to his mates.

Lee or Steve didn't have a clue about him and Abba, he's sure of that. However, he thinks he was less successful in his attempts to hide from them the fact that he couldn't handle a lot of alcohol and that dope made him sick almost instantly, and that the one time he tried speed, which Lee bought off a neighbour, he thought he was going to die of a heart attack, or a brain haemorrhage, or both – all he could see were these blinding flashes. He was fine with the joyriding, with the thieving, he positively shone there, but he just couldn't hack the drinking and the drugs. Which is why, he's since thought, he eventually fell out with Lee and Steve, and Paul, and the few others they used to hang around with. As hard as he tried he couldn't keep up. He couldn't compete physically. His body wouldn't take it, his head wouldn't. He was a complete wuss when it came to drink and drugs, when it came to any mind-altering substances.

Mark knows he's spent half his life trying to hide bits of himself from others, his weaknesses mostly, like his pathetic constitution, like his fondness for soppy songs. Yet who should catch him listening to 'Fernando', glued to the blonde one's bum gently swaying in a pair of super-tight white satin trousers? When Mark was already feeling a little emotional because of the music? His dad. His fucking dad, who said he had something important to say to him.

Being so embarrassed at being caught watching Abba on TV, not just caught watching the Swedish group performing their number-one hit 'Fernando' – which Mark thought actually deserved to be number one for longer than 'Sailing' – but also having been emotionally affected by it, maybe he was even weeping a little, Mark said, immediately getting up to turn off the TV, that whatever it was he didn't want to hear it.

Though his dad stood there, not looking at his eldest son, or the suddenly blank TV screen either, with his pale, grey-blue eyes (Mark's eyes), Mark noticed not seeming to focus on anything, so Mark returned to the settee, resumed his slumped telly-watching pose despite the telly being off, and stared ahead himself – silently, moodily, shamed. Then after a minute or two his father said he was going away, with Robbie, and that they had decided it would be best if he stayed here with his mum. That he and his mum had decided this, though obviously having his best interests in mind. Because Robbie was younger, his dad said, it would be easier for him to change schools and make new friends abroad. It didn't mean, however, his dad said, but still not looking at Mark, that he didn't love him as much as Robbie. Of course he loved his two boys the same. They were a couple of tykes, though he loved them both, nevertheless. He was gutted he had to leave, and leave for abroad too, as was Robbie, he could assure Mark, even if his brother hadn't yet told him so in person, though he was certain it would ultimately be for the best, having this proper break. Marriages don't always work out, he said. Families don't always stay together.

Words began to drift hopelessly around Mark's head so he didn't know what his dad said and what he interpreted him as saying. He couldn't look at his father by this point either, as his own eyes had become far too watery to focus properly, so he doesn't know whether his father had started to look at him by then, to actually clock him, as an individual, as a human being. As his son. Or not.

Sometimes it was better for families to split up, his father went on, Mark thinks. And for both parties to start afresh. And a long way away from each other, out of all contact. That didn't mean he wouldn't always have a special place for him in his heart – a soft spot, he even said. A soft spot? Mark thought at the time. A fucking soft spot – is that all? Of course he would, his dad said, leaning down to kiss Mark, who was still slumped on the settee. Trying to embrace him at the same time. But Mark pushed his dad away – this short, stocky man, this solid lump of muscle and rage beginning to melt in front of him for the first time. Mark couldn't bear it and flung up his left elbow and started jabbing at his father with it, while using his right arm to cover his face, wrapping his right arm tightly around his head so there was no way his father could get anywhere near him.

His dad didn't force himself on Mark for long. Instead, he ruffled Mark's hair, something which always used to infuriate Mark, anyone doing such a thing, and then he backed slowly out of the room. Mark watched him go having lifted his arm a little, though still keeping it wrapped tightly around his forehead – sensing just how out of place his hair suddenly was. He didn't say anything. He didn't tell his dad he loved him. He didn't tell his dad not to leave. He definitely didn't say, 'Don't leave me, Dad.'

8

'I was going to give this to you tomorrow,' Mark says, walking into Gemma's bright pink bedroom, where he knows he'll find Lily on her own, as Gemma is watching a video downstairs. Lily is lying on the bed, the bed he made for Gemma, surrounded by Gemma's soft toys – the giant rabbit and badger and numerous teddies and dolls – with her headphones on and her heavily made-up eyes wide open. She doesn't look at him as he walks over to the bed, she doesn't flinch, continuing to stare straight at the ceiling, her skinny body dwarfed by the enveloping duvet. 'But I thought you might like it now,' he says, holding out the small box, which the jewellery shop gift-wrapped for him specially, using gold paper and a purple ribbon. They also wanted to attach a small card but he said no, not knowing what he'd write on it. 'And I didn't want Nicole seeing it,' he says. 'Let's keep it a secret between you and me, hey?'

Lily sits up slowly. She takes the package without looking him in the eye, while leaving her headphones firmly in place and the volume obviously on high – not that he has any idea what she's listening to, as ever. He stands back, feeling himself flush because he's not at all sure he's doing the right thing – up until this afternoon he still hadn't definitely decided to give it to her – or what her reaction will be, as she rips off the packaging, opens the box and pulls out the pencil-thin, gold-plated electronic lighter, which he acquired when he was on his own in the city centre last week and knew Lily was definitely coming for Christmas. She immediately uses the tiny switch to turn the small, yellow flame on and off, making the lighter click rapidly.

'Cool,' she says. 'Cool flame. Thanks, dude.'

'That doesn't mean you can smoke in bed,' he says, smiling. 'Not in Gemma's room, young lady, not in my house, but I won't mind any more if you want to smoke out the back – as long as you shut the kitchen door after you.'

Hoping she'll say something else, he stays where he is, looking at his elder daughter's jet-black hair held back by her headphones, at her eyes encased in too much dark eyeliner, at her lips smothered in bright red lipstick, at her wildly contrasting deathly pale skin, and her awkward, now desperately fragile-looking frame hunched up and surrounded by his younger daughter's fat, cuddly toys. Any response will do, so he can then attempt to get some sort of conversation going, during which, he thinks, he'll be able to explain that he would never have really just left her in Boots, in the centre of the city, for the authorities to deal with. He wouldn't actually have done what he might have implied he was going to do at the time. No, of course he wouldn't. But Lily says nothing further, while continuing to play with the lighter, and still feeling flushed, Mark turns and walks out of the room, hearing the rapid clicking. The flame igniting and then being extinguished, again and again.

9

'Here on the settee?' says Nicole. 'Come on, then. Quick. Let's do it *sans* protection, as they say. *Au naturel.*'

'What?' says Mark. 'What the hell are you talking about? You're drunk. You're still arseholed.'

'No one will hear,' she says. 'Gemma's asleep.'

'Yeah, well, I bet Lily isn't,' he says. 'She could come down at any moment.'

'She won't, though, will she? She never does. She's up there all the time, moping around, listening to her music, isn't she? Come on, Mark, a Christmas shag with your missus on the settee. It was originally your idea, anyway, wasn't it?' Nicole pats one of her mum's cushions then puts her hand on his crotch. 'I'll even let you video it.'

'Don't be disgusting,' he says, pushing her hand away from his flies and crossing his legs. 'You stink of alcohol. How much did you have to drink at this lunch? Were you the only one to make a total idiot of themselves?'

'No way,' she says. 'We were all on the floor by the end.'

'So who else have you been trying to shag today? Your boss? Your immediate boss? What's his name? John? John Read, isn't it? With that brand-new five-series? I've seen you talk to him in the car park.' Mark doesn't understand why he's recently been convincing himself that Nicole's having an affair. He never used to be jealous of her. It was always what made his second marriage so much more bearable than his first. Why he always felt things would be different. Why, this time, he thought it would work out. That it was meant to be. A perfectly balanced union. Nicole didn't wind him up. She didn't tease him. She didn't encourage him to imagine the worst. She didn't fuck half of the city behind his back.

'Mark,' Nicole says, unbuttoning her blouse, 'you know I've only got eyes for you. You know I can't resist you – for some daft reason.' With her blouse undone she pulls her skirt up around her waist, revealing her bare thighs above her stay-up stockings, and her largely transparent black knickers (knickers Mark's sure he hasn't seen her wear before today), and swings her right leg over him until she's sitting firmly on his lap, letting him support all her weight.

'Stop it,' he says, grabbing her by the legs, but not pushing her off, while feeling a tinge of excitement in his crotch, at least the fact that his cock is being squashed and has no room to expand. 'You're nuts.'

'Maybe I fancy you because you're always so angry,' she says. 'So cross.'

Mark turns his face away from her in an attempt to avoid her boozy breath, and finds himself looking instead at their perfectly triangular silver Christmas tree in the corner of the room. It has been hung with red tinsel and gold balls and flashing, multi-coloured fairy lights which only Gemma can turn on or off. What a joke, he thinks. What a sham.

'And I feel I'm the only person in the whole wide world who can calm that anger, who can mother you,' she says. 'In fact, I'm doing everyone a favour. Keeping you in order. I should get paid for this.'

'You probably do,' he says, suddenly pushing her legs apart on his lap and staring at her knickers, checking for any sign that she might have fucked someone this afternoon, for a silvery stain on the crotch, for a trace of dried-up spunk and fanny juice on the thin black material – he knows exactly what to look for, having been used to checking Kim's knickers, and to feel for. Oh yes. That sudden ease of entry, he thinks. That extra slipperiness when you start fucking. 'How else do you make so much money?'

'You could be a little nicer to me, Mark, a little more charitable, it is Christmas,' she says.

'I am charitable,' he says. 'More than you'd ever know.'

'Then fuck me,' she says. 'Fuck me like you used to fuck Kim.'

10

Kim says on the phone, after she's wished Mark a happy Christmas, after she's told him she and Dave and Zak are having a right old time in Newbury, – 'thank you, very much' – after she's asked him whether Lily's been behaving herself and he's said, in not so many words, of course, she has, in my house she wouldn't dare not to, Kim says, 'I'm pleased to hear it because I found her pills under her bed. She's been prescribed these thing to calm her down, I should have told you, but I didn't want to worry you any more than I had to, seeing as she just had that virus and has lost so much weight. It's not strong stuff, it's only Ritalin – quite harmless, really. In fact, her head teacher at her new school recommended it. Loads of kids take it, apparently, for this thing they call Attention Deficit Hyperactivity Disorder, one of these big poncy medical terms, but which, if you ask me, just means they're a bit skitzy and don't concentrate in class. Lily's always saying she feels skitzy, doesn't she? You must have heard her. Anyway, the head teacher said if she didn't take it she'd have to leave, and this is the second school she's gone to since we've been here, and it is already meant to be a special school for troubled kids, so what more could we do? Though it's possible she might get a place at this live-in adolescent unit in February. Has she told you anything?

It would be great if that happens. The social services here are being really helpful. Best I've come across.'

Drugs, Mark thinks, Ritalin? He has a problem with paracetamol. He certainly doesn't see why his daughter should have to take drugs. To calm her down? For some mental problem? She's not a loony. He doesn't think she's been particularly mad since she's been with them. Apart from the scene in Boots, she's just spent ages in Gemma's room, lying on the bed, listening to her music. And the possibility that Lily might be sent to a live-in adolescent unit? Whatever that is. Lily certainly hasn't mentioned anything to him about it. As for the social services being really helpful – he knows just how Kim must be manipulating them this time.

All he can suddenly think, with Kim on the other end of the phone, in her newly renovated house in Newbury – which he believes he's more or less paid for – but with all her old wiliness intact, is that he should not only have fucked her when he saw her in October, he should have properly clobbered her for once as well. He never hit her hard enough all those years ago. They were just playful slaps. A few jokey jabs. Nothing serious.

'It's Christmas Day,' he eventually says, with his mind beginning to clear. 'What am I meant to do about this now? Why did you even have to tell me about it today, of all days? Why can't you return to your Zak and your Dave – what made him change his mind and come back anyway? – and your right old time?'

'Keep your lid on, Mark,' Kim says. 'I was just worried that Lily hasn't had her medicine, and whether she's feeling OK, and thought that maybe you could get another prescription for her if necessary. And I also wanted to wish her a happy Christmas. I have to speak to my daughter on Christmas Day. I have to speak to all my children on Christmas Day. I miss them, Mark. I want to be with them. Is Lil there? Can I speak to her? Put my darling on.'

11

'She's drunk,' says Lily, switching off the cordless handset and dropping it on the well-padded arm of the settee.

Mark looks at Lily, still enraged with Kim, more enraged than ever, remembering that he should have asked Kim why she hadn't even managed to take Lily to Liverpool Street the other day and ensured that she got on the right train – whether she had any idea of what Lily might have got up to in London, seeing as the girl still isn't telling him anything. And how come Lily could claim that she was used to being in London on her own anyway? – he loathes London, believing it to be full of drug addicts and foreigners. He should also have asked Kim what made her think she was capable of being a fit mother to his daughter. What gave her the right to control Lily's upbringing, to control his daughter's future. To abuse it endlessly.

However, he has this heavy, nauseous feeling that this is how it will always be. He'll always be enraged with Kim, and he'll always be worrying about Lily and whether she's being looked after properly. Yet he'll be unable to do very much about that because he doesn't have the back-up, because he knows Nicole doesn't want Lily becoming too dependent on them. She certainly doesn't want Lily moving in, which she believes Lily had been planning to do, given the amount of stuff she had packed into her case. Though he knows it's not just Nicole's fault. Standing in the lounge on Christmas Day with Lily turning shyly away from him – as if, for once, she's said something she shouldn't have – and with Nicole and Gemma on their knees by the Christmas tree, going through the presents, making their separate piles, competing with each other playfully, he realises that when it comes down to it he just doesn't have it in him. He's way too much of a wuss to even take control of his daughter's future.

Less than a year ago, he was perfectly happy. In fact right up until Easter, when he got that call from Kim, everything seemed to be going his way. Life was probably much better than he had any right to expect – halfway up the hill, in their cosy slice of paradise – and now he feels miserable, and trapped, and full of crushing self-doubt once more. On Christmas Day, of all days.

As fed up, as gutted, as he's sure he felt the first Christmas he spent with his mum and Lawrence, in Lawrence's precious house, where you couldn't touch anything in case you left a dirty mark, in case you broke it. With just the three of them, Lawrence, his mum and himself, and obviously no Robbie (who he realises he'll not be hearing from for another Christmas, presuming he hasn't lost his battle with AIDS, or his dad, though he's never seriously thought that was at all likely) pretending it was a normal Christmas, pretending the three of them had done it together numerous times before. That it was the most natural thing in the world.

There weren't even Lawrence's snotty sons around for him to take the piss out of, or the girl for him to terrorise and then of course eventually screw – in her bedroom, in her very own single bed, as he did one Saturday afternoon when everyone else had gone into the city shopping. He'd been working on her for a while, at least during the few instances when he did see her, capitalising on the fact that she believed him to be tough and streetwise and something of a stud, as well as being dead fucking gorgeous, of course. 'You're a man, Mark,' she once said to him. 'That's what I like about you. The fact that you're always dead straight with people and don't put up with any nonsense.'

Though he felt he'd achieved something by screwing his step-sister, by dirtying, if not damaging Lawrence's most precious daughter – and thus exacting some revenge for having a revolting stepsister pushed on him – it was nothing compared to what he felt when he set fire to his mum and Lawrence's bedroom. That was the biggest thrill of his childhood. Better than breaking into any car or house. Better than losing his virginity to big-bosomed Gail in Chapel Field Gardens. A hundred times better. Plus he very nearly got away with it.

'She's always worse when Dave's around,' Lily says, now standing by the stairs, holding the banister, ready, Mark thinks, to run to her room. 'The two of them sit around drinking all day,' she says, her shrill voice beginning to crack, 'only getting up to feed bloody Zak, or have a smelly shag. I don't know why Dave had to come back. He's disgusting. When he's not trying to shag Mum he's after me, isn't he? And she lets him do it. She never tells him to leave me alone. She doesn't love me. How can she and let Dave do those things to me, with his grubby hands, with his stinky cock, right in front of her? Jake and Sean were lucky, they got away, didn't they, but I'm stuck there, with nowhere else to go. No one wants me. No one loves me.'

Lily's out of sight, nearing the top of the stairs, having crashed her way up much more noisily than Mark thinks could be possible for someone so light, before he manages to shout, 'I love you. I love you, Lily. Your dad loves you.' It comes out involuntarily, it bursts out of him, with the force of projectile vomit (he was always vomiting as a kid, the moment he had one sip of lager too many, the moment he had a puff of a joint, the moment his dad shut the lounge door behind him for the last time – he puked all over the carpet then, on his shoes and best Burton trousers too) – but he doesn't follow her up the stairs and when he looks behind him, at Nicole and Gemma still on the floor, with their piles of unwrapped presents (with Gemma's pile clearly not including a computer, because he managed to persuade Nicole that it would be unfair to give Gemma such an expensive present in front of Lily, when all they had decided to give Lily was a CD and a hat, and that they could give Gemma the computer for her next birthday, besides, he couldn't get hold of Darren), the two of them flushed with the heat from the gushing gas fire, Nicole more flushed than Gemma because of her chronic hangover, and both of them clearly saying nothing on purpose, not coming to his rescue, not willing to intervene, and so just compounding the embarrassment he feels at being the object of Lily's latest public tirade, at having been singled out, and then the fact that he shouted, all right, he screamed, that he loved her. In front of his wife and daughter, his calm, restrained, mostly rational wife (not that he reckons she's been behaving totally normally recently, suddenly being so frisky and wanting him to fuck her like he used to fuck Kim, wanting him to do it without a Durex Avanti as well, despite never having gone back on the pill after Mallorca – out of guilt for having an affair, he wonders?) and his full-time daughter, his gorgeous, his precious, his one and only little Gem.

Unable to say anything further, in explanation – in his defence? – he has an almost overwhelming, uncontrollable, urge to disappear himself, and to run out of the house and head for the city centre once more. Or the river, which he thinks he might as well plonk himself in, head first.

However, he looks again at Nicole and Gemma crouched by the Christmas tree – this perfect triangle of throbbing reds and greens and blues and whites – knowing Gemma's been up since four in the morning, desperate to open her presents (not that she'll be getting what she was expecting), knowing how worried Nicole was at the prospect of having Lily for Christmas, believing that she would just cause a scene and ruin it for everyone else, especially Gemma, and knowing he assured Nicole numerous times that he would not let Lily disrupt the day, and thinking back also to those disastrous Christmases he had when growing up himself, with his dad, who was always drunk and would start smashing plates, or taking swipes at his mum in the kitchen (he can suddenly recall that, all right), and then those spent with his mum and Lawrence, and no Robbie, which were worse in a way because no one said anything, because they were so false, he feels he owes it to Gemma, especially – to his one grip on reality, to her as yet untainted, not abused childhood, to her innocence – and Nicole – who's stuck by him for all these years, who's put up with his baggage and his moods, hasn't she? – not to help ruin another Christmas, by running simply off, by spoiling everything for everyone. There's no way, he thinks, he can let history keep repeating itself. For him to carry on making the same mistakes his dad made – as his dad and mum, as his parents and stepparents clearly made with their kids. As grown-ups make all the fucking time. It's up to him to set an example at long last. After all, he is charitable, more than anyone would know. There is a decent side to him, a warm, happy, good-natured, loving side, he's certain of that. He's certain too that he's strong enough – inside, mentally – to hold everything together, to build a future for his family, his extended family. Sure he is. He's not the only person who thinks he's a man.

'Nics,' he says, 'why don't you pop upstairs and tell Lily we're going to open the presents now? You'll be able to bring her back down, I know you will. She listens to you. Tell her everything's all right. We forgive her. We forgive her everything. Tell her we want her here with us.'

12

Early the next morning, Mark knows what's coming before Nicole opens her mouth. From the way she's trying to stop her mouth from quivering by holding it tightly shut, by using her teeth to make the well-cleansed skin on her cheeks and upper lip taut. From the way her eyes are bulging and unblinking, and all filmy and rapidly becoming bloodshot too. From the way she's standing, with her legs slightly apart and slightly bent, with her left hand pressed flat against the wall, with her head bowed and the muscles on her neck clearly tensed, as if she's unsure of the ground beneath her feet, of the firmness of the soft pile, light brown carpet, and the Cloud 9 underlay underneath that, of the very floorboards and joists and supporting walls and the late Victorian foundations keeping the house in place, keeping it together. As if she's bracing herself. He knows exactly what's coming, so before she does open her mouth, before she says a word, he looks away from her – just as he's always looking away from people the moment anyone tries to connect with him, the moment anyone pushes him emotionally – and at a patch of blank wall, a patch of wall he once stripped and filled and repapered, and which Nicole then carefully rollered a light pink, a Dulux Magnolia, if he remembers the specific paint correctly – of course he remembers it was Dulux Magnolia, the

whole house apart from Gemma's bedroom and the kitchen is
Dulux Magnolia – and says, 'Don't tell me. Please don't tell me, I
don't want to hear it.'

FEBRUARY / MARCH

I

'We've been through all this before,' Mark says.

'Hardly,' says Anne. 'I want to hear the full story, while Nicole and Gemma aren't here.' His mother is sitting at his kitchen table, slurping her coffee, having already sucked the sugar spoon clean, and put it back into the sugar bowl. For someone who thinks they are so refined, so cultured, so middle class, he's always been surprised by his mum's completely gross table manners – often he can't believe he was brought up by her. 'Come on, Mark, tell me what happened from the beginning, please,' she says. She demands. He knows that sharp, no-nonsense, tone of voice – the threatening way she said 'please'. The same voice that spoke to him endlessly when he was a kid, though he mostly ignored her then. He's not sure why he doesn't still ignore her – another sign, perhaps, of his increasing confusion about who to listen to, who to trust.

'All right,' he says, 'if it makes you happy. Apart from everything else that had happened that day Lily overheard Nicole saying all this stuff to me about her.' How he wishes he could make Nicole's words unravel and slowly disappear. How he wishes he could make everything start again at the click of his fingers, so somehow no one would get hurt. He wants yet another second chance. 'But I've already told you this.'

'Not in any detail,' she says. 'For once in your life, Mark, try to be a bit more forthcoming. It might help.'

'OK,' he says, 'OK.' Pleased in a way that he's finally been given the chance to explain to his mother who is ultimately to blame for what happened over Christmas. 'Lily obviously overheard Nicole saying that she was sick of her, you know of all her hysterics and loopiness, and how she'd become a really bad influence on Gemma,' he says. 'And she said she didn't want Lily hanging around the house for another minute. It wasn't my fault, Mum, honestly. I'd have let Lily stay for however long she wanted, I'd have let her move in. She knew that. In fact I think that's what she wanted to do. You should have seen the amount of clothes and things she brought with her. All Christmas I just tried to keep the peace, honestly. I should have got an award for it, one of those humanitarian things. The Nobel Peace Prize.' He laughs. 'But Nicole had had enough. She'd finally lost it with Lil. She was like ranting at me in our bedroom and of course who should be listening out on the landing but Lily, who'd only spent most of the day in her room in a huff about something anyway.'

He can remember all too clearly Nicole almost shouting, despite Gemma being asleep on the fold-out in there with them, 'I don't believe a word of all that nonsense Lily talks about being sexually abused by her mum's boyfriends. It's just designed to get attention, as usual with her.' He can remember Nicole then going on to say that actually she'd made a lot of effort with Lily over Christmas, she hadn't even kicked up a fuss when the girl had refused to eat any turkey roll or watch TV with them. But, she'd said, there was a limit. She'd said there was no way she was going to allow Lily to move in, however much the silly girl went on about nobody loving her. 'Besides, what if we have another child, Mark?' Nicole had finally said – he hasn't forgotten those words.

Or what Nicole had said to him early the next morning, Boxing Day morning, after she'd stood in the doorway for a moment or two, with her hand pressed against the wall and her eyes bulging, her face contorted with anger and frustration – with her doing that thing she does with her teeth and her upper lip. She'd said, simply, 'Lily's gone, Mark. She's taken her bag and everything, I've checked.'

Mark tells his mum about the note Lily left on the kitchen table, on that Boxing Day morning, of all special days, and which Gemma found when she went down for her cereal, and which for a short while Nicole and he were convinced Gemma had written because the handwriting was so like hers, at least too childish, Nicole thought, for a fourteen-year-old to have produced. What did he know?

He doesn't just tell his mum about it now, weeks later, he decides to show it to her – fetching the roughly folded piece of light blue drawing paper from the over-stuffed drawer by the sink, where they keep all the kitchen-appliance manuals and take-away menus and Blockbuster Videos flyers. He's not sure why he has kept it, perhaps because it's the only bit of writing he has of Lily's, and thinks he might ever have.

'There's no need to snatch, Mum,' he says, handing her the note. The words of which are lodged in his brain for ever, he reckons – I never want to see you again, I hate you all. He recites them to himself as he watches his mum read, as he watches her lips move, but not he thinks exactly to the shape of the words. Slowly he realises she's attempting to redistribute what's left of her lipstick after leaving her coffee cup ringed with crimson.

'I thought she couldn't read or write,' Anne says. 'She's only made one spelling mistake. She's spelled see, S E A when it should be S E E, of course. She must have learned something at that special school then. I'm impressed. Though her mother's not stupid.'

'Mum, give us a break,' he says. 'It's not an English test.'

'But it shows promise, Mark,' she says. 'Promise, at least.'

2

He didn't plan to set fire to his mum and Lawrence's bedroom, not like the tyres – he'd been thinking about slashing those for a while, having got the idea from Lee, who was always puncturing people's tyres because he said he enjoyed the noise they made deflating. This loud pop followed by a gushing sound. And if he was quick, the hole not too devastating, and the tyres weren't low profiles, he liked to watch the car sink as well. They all did, from their various concealed vantage points. What they especially liked was the way a car would maybe tilt towards one corner first, then another and then even up with a low, muffled clunk as the rims hit the asphalt. Lee's favourite tool for this was a specially sharpened screwdriver, which he used to stab at the rubber, normally needing only one go. On Mark's mum's car, her clapped-out Austin Maxi, Mark found the second, thinner blade on his Swiss Army penknife – which his mum had given him for his fourteenth birthday – was sharp and strong enough. It punctured the worn rubber as easily as if he had been attacking a bike tyre. Almost as easily as if he'd been slicing up the stretched, furry, brown fabric of the settee at home – something which used to occupy him for hours.

Apart from hating the Maxi – it was maroon with beige leatherette seats, which always stank of plastic and stuck to his skin when it was hot – he was feeling particularly cross with his mum at the time. She'd tried to ban him from going out of the house on week nights, yet she was always going out herself – with her sister, with her friends from Tops the estate agents, where she worked part-time then, with Lawrence, he discovered, one evening when he saw her being dropped off, when in fact he caught his mum virtually snogging this small, silver-haired man on the pavement outside their house. In the middle of the city. In front of the whole street.

Shortly after that they kept getting these strange phone calls. Mark would pick up the phone to hear the line go dead. But this never happened to his mum, it never seemed to go dead when she answered it, though if he was nearby she would usually whisper into the receiver, shielding her mouth behind her hand, or she'd take the handset into another room entirely, shutting the door behind her, squeezing the cord square into the door frame. After he witnessed another snogging and groping session on the street – it honestly made him retch – he realised what was going on and if his mum wasn't in the house he'd shout 'fuck off' the instant he grabbed the phone. 'Fuck off, granddad,' he'd say.

Because he was getting worse and worse reports, and was threatened with suspension, his mum eventually tried to ban him from playing with his mates after school as well as in the evening after tea. She said he had to come straight home to get on with his homework. That was when he decided to retaliate, when he felt it wasn't enough to just think about doing something wicked. Plus he knew she possibly wouldn't suspect him as numerous cars in their street were currently being vandalised – not by anyone he knew, of course. Not by Lee or Steve, or Paul, or himself. They weren't vandals. They were good boys. They were mummies' boys. Weren't they?

However, he didn't plan to set fire to his mum's bedroom. That came from one small thing rapidly leading on to another. It was chance, really. And something he doesn't feel he should be held totally accountable for. He thinks he was acting as if possessed. Later it frightened him, what he was capable of doing under such circumstances. When, he supposes, he was a little out of his mind – with, suddenly, rage, and loneliness, and the feeling that no one cared about him. He doesn't remember there being some obvious build-up, either. He hadn't been getting on with his mum, or Lawrence, any worse than usual. They hadn't suddenly banned him from doing anything they hadn't already banned him from. Maybe, he thinks, people, kids even, especially kids, really do just crack, when one more thing, however tiny, tips them over the edge. Or maybe it was to do with his hormones – Kim was always going on about her hormones, how instantly moody they could make her, how dangerous – and to do with him being an adolescent, when all these hormones were supposedly shooting around his body. He and Nicole saw a thing about it on telly recently and Nicole kept saying, 'That's Lily. That's Lily all over.' Perhaps it was a bit of both, he thinks. Perhaps it's always a bit of both.

What he does remember is arriving home from school early one afternoon – it is possible he hadn't been to school at all that day – to find the house empty. He went straight to his mum and Lawrence's bedroom and started going through their cupboards and drawers, having no idea what he was looking for, but being constantly surprised, by the style of his mum's underwear, these lacy black and red knickers and bras and suspender belts, he swears, and by her short nighties and this drawer full of weird toiletries, including an almost empty tube of K-Y Lubricating Jelly, which didn't smell of anything though he got dried flakes of it on his nose when he sniffed the lid.

Somehow, he couldn't get the contents to fit neatly back into their drawers, or on their hangers, or in their plush little boxes. For he came across some of his mum's jewellery, and Lawrence's jewellery also – these gold and silver and gem-encrusted cuff-links and tie-pins and a couple of dress watches, plus a number of rings and chunky bracelets. He briefly admired Lawrence when he saw all this stuff – indeed, he thought of him in a totally new light, as this flash git. Mark put one of the watches in his pocket, knowing where he could sell it, even if he knew he'd be ripped off.

At the back of what he took to be Lawrence's jewellery drawer he also found a hallmarked silver matchbox container, with a nearly full box of matches slotted inside. He had no idea how long the matches had been in there – neither his mum nor Lawrence smoked – though they still worked, perfectly.

He began by singeing bits of coloured tissue paper which some of the jewellery had been carefully wrapped in, then the corners of the jewellery boxes, before moving on to various items of clothing, much of which he'd let fall on to the floor and the bed, discovering that his mum's négligées and fancy underwear took the easiest and quickly melted.

With the air in the bedroom becoming fumey, and with blobs of molten fabric having dropped on to the bedspread, creating mini craters in the wadding, Mark soon realised he wouldn't be able to cover up the damage, that he'd already gone too far. But anyway he didn't want to stop, he was enjoying himself. With each item he burned, whether it belonged to his mum or Lawrence – though his mum's stuff did burn that much better – he felt a thrilling surge of power shoot through his body. It was a sexual, almost orgasmic feeling, and being so turned on he was tempted to lie on the bed, a part not covered by burns anyway, loosen his trousers and get out his cock. He contemplated using a pair of his mum's knickers to hold around it, knowing he'd then be able to use them to ejaculate into, as he had done once before with a pair he'd pulled from the dirty laundry basket, a pair already thick with whitish stains, and which he later buried in the garden. But he found he couldn't stop setting fire to more and more items of clothing, making a big pile of this smouldering material at the foot of the bed, thinking it was more fun than wanking into his mum's pants any day.

When the smoke became too thick and noxious, with all this artificial material catching as easily as wood shavings, as old car tyres, as hair, he left the room, taking only the watch with him.

3

'Sorry, Mark,' says his mother, shaking her head. 'That was insensitive of me. I can see how desperate you are about this. I suppose it's like it was, all over again.'

'No, it's not, it's worse,' Mark says, sneering at his mum, annoyed with her also for still doing that thing with her lips – he wishes she'd just apply some more lipstick and get on with the business of trying to hide her badly aged lips, which she's always been embarrassed about. 'I know where she is this time,' he says, 'but she just doesn't want to see me. She won't even talk to me on the phone. Kim's not helping, either. She says I've ruined my chance. She says I've blown it.'

'So when Lily left here on Boxing Day,' Anne says, 'she went straight home? On the train?'

'More or less,' he says, knowing that Lily got herself to London, where, according to Kim, she spent two days with a friend – though he reckons she spent that time on her own, wandering the streets, sleeping rough, being stuffed full of E and crack and methylated spirits by drug dealers and dossers, who then forced her into give them blow jobs and doing who knows what else – before she turned up in Newbury, on Kim's doorstep, and convinced her stupid mum that he and Nicole had kicked her out and that as far as she was concerned she never wanted to see her dad or his stinking family ever again. Though he doesn't want to divulge his worst fears to his mother, so she can think he's even more negligent and uncaring. So she can think he's just another hopeless, absent father. Because that is what women always think, isn't it? They're always only blaming the dads, the men – from what he's heard and experienced.

'You didn't call the police or anything?' she says.

'No. We managed to reach Lily a couple of times on her mobile, until she either switched it off or ran the batteries out,' he says, 'so we sort of knew she was all right, at least to begin with. But I wasn't going to get the police involved anyway. Apart from the fact that they wouldn't have been able to do anything – they don't care about teenagers who run off these days – they'd hardly have listened to me, would they? They'd have only banned me from seeing her again or something. Or maybe they'd have taken her away all together and put her in a home.'

'I thought she was in a home now?' Anne says.

'It's not a home, Mum,' Mark says, trying to sound hopeful. 'It's a live-in adolescent unit, in Berkshire. A place for kids with problems. Behavioural problems mostly. You know, kids who are complete nightmares and then those who don't eat properly or keep harming themselves.' He tries to laugh but what comes out is more of a snort. 'Kim says it's a bit like a boarding school, except the state pays. Apparently, Lily's really lucky to have got a place. It's not a nuthouse, she's not kept locked up or anything.'

However, Mark suspects that that is exactly what it is, and is what has happened to Lily. He has this idea that Kim has not only managed to get rid of Lily because she can't be bothered to care for her any more – as she is way too much trouble (and he knows exactly what mothers think about children who are too much trouble) – but that she's had her put away in place where even he can't get to her. He's sure Kim has stitched him up once more and can't believe he didn't see it coming this time.

'I've been stupid,' Anne says, finally standing and moving over to the sink, where she starts to wash the few things in the bowl, squirting far too much washing-up liquid into the water. 'I should have been here at Christmas to take control of the situation. But I was keeping out of your way on purpose, hoping it would be easier for Lily that way. I thought it would be better for there not to be too many interfering relations around. I trusted you, Mark. I thought you'd grown up a lot – I said as much to Kim. I thought you'd be able to deal with Lily. She is your daughter after all, your eldest daughter. But I was wrong, wasn't I? And now you've lost her again. For both of us, as Kim's not even being cooperative with me at the moment. I suppose I've let her down.'

'That's rubbish, Mum, and you know it,' he says. 'It wasn't my fault Lily left. She didn't overhear me slagging her off. Besides, the real reason you weren't rushing round here to see her at Christmas, or any other time for that matter, is because she freaks you out. Doesn't she? After that boat trip in the summer you've almost completely ignored her. You're the one who can't deal with her, just as you couldn't deal with me and Robbie together.' He pauses to wipe a drop of washing-up water off his cheek. 'What did you do then?' he continues. 'You got rid of one of us. That's how you dealt with that particular problem. And stop washing up, for Christ's sake, will you? We have got a dishwasher. A Bosch, which is much more effective than you could ever be.'

'Don't be ridiculous,' his mother says, turning round to face him with soapy wet hands, and large patches of damp on her pale, tight-fitting jumper. 'That's just not true. It had nothing to do with you and Robbie. It was what your dad wanted, and I stupidly listened to him. The man had ground me down so much I didn't have the strength to fight him. Or this bent solicitor who came up with this scheme that if your father got Robbie I'd get to keep the house and a considerable lump sum, which would obviously go towards your upkeep. So I'm afraid, Mark, I eventually gave in. All I could think about at the time was that at least I'd be able to care for one of you properly. But don't think I don't regret it. Don't think I don't regret it every single day.'

Mark has rarely seen his mother cry. She cried when he told her Kim had disappeared with Lily, but the time before that, he thinks, was probably when she confronted him about setting fire to her bedroom, all those years ago. However, she's wiping tears from her eyes now with her wet hands – her bent, arthritic hands she's so ashamed of – making her cheeks glisten with popped washing-up bubbles. For a second or two he thinks about walking over to her and putting his arms around her, giving her a squeeze, then he remembers Lawrence, how his mum had suddenly dropped everything for Lawrence, how this wimpy, white-haired man very quickly became the most important thing in her life, and he doesn't move.

'You should never let go of your children,' she says, snuffling, using the sleeves of her sweater to wipe her face. 'Never let them out of your sight for long. They're too precious.'

'Yeah, right,' he says.

'You know what I think?' she says. 'I think you should go and see Lily, if you know where she is. Make it up to her. Kids can be very proud. Too proud.'

'I don't have to make anything up to her,' he says. 'I haven't done anything wrong. And anyway from what I can gather it's a nightmare getting into that place. According to Kim there are all these official procedures you have to go through just to visit.'

'I thought you said she wasn't kept locked up,' she says.

'Yeah, but that doesn't mean it's going to be easy,' he says.

'Kim's probably trying to put you off, knowing what you're like in those situations,' she says. 'Be a man, Mark. Look, don't lose this chance. You can't afford to lose her again. Believe me.'

4

Had he left the house a minute or two earlier he's sure he would have got away with it, certain that his mum and Lawrence, that the police too, would have blamed it on a burglary which had somehow gone wrong, or had just been plain malicious. A few kids more intent on causing havoc in someone's house, in someone's bedroom – turning over the owners' most personal items, doing despicable things to pieces of fancy female underwear – than stealing anything of value. Bored, middle-class kids Mark might have come across in the area. On the way home from school, perhaps. But definitely not kids he would have hung out with. None of his close mates.

As it was, however, he calmly left the house, at about two-thirty in the afternoon, having smashed a kitchen window with a saucepan (to make it look as if someone had broken in) while leaving the front door ajar behind him – with smoke beginning to drift downstairs and into the hall. He started walking through the close towards the bus stop on the main road. Although he didn't want to draw attention to himself, he wasn't trying to be particularly covert either, he certainly wasn't nipping behind hedges or slipping across people's back gardens. He simply stuck to the pavement, head down, but being careful to dodge the manhole covers, thinking that if he accidentally stood on one he'd be caught and done for arson.

His mum spotted him crossing the main road at the bottom of the close just as she was turning in, on her way back from Safeway. She slowed, though he didn't look up or wave, and convinced himself she hadn't seen or recognised him, as he should have been at school then anyway, and he continued across the road and to the bus stop, from where he caught a yellow Hoppa into the city, with the sudden intention of never coming back.

Because she alerted the fire brigade when she did, and the fact that they were on the scene so quickly, as he later heard, the damage was really only limited to the bedroom and a bit of the landing. Still, he thought his mum and Lawrence acted as if the whole house had burned down.

When he did turn up later that evening – realising, while he'd been shuffling about the city with little money (the jewellers wouldn't buy this particular watch because Mark didn't have the box it came in or the guarantee, so he threw it in the river, not wanting to be caught with it on him either) and no spare clothes, that if he didn't return it would only appear as if he were definitely guilty – he found them loading the car, preparing to move out, with his mother quivering uncontrollably and barely able to speak.

He said that he'd been at a friend's since school finished, and tried to look shocked when they showed him the damage, which was so much less than he had been imagining he'd encounter. In fact, he thought it was totally pathetic and rather wished he'd started fires in other rooms also.

Of course they suspected it was him, not just because his mum had clearly seen him walking away from the house shortly before she arrived to find the fire, but because the police said that whoever had smashed the kitchen window had not been trying to break in because it had been smashed from the inside.

Mark initially denied that he was involved when his mother first accused him in the hall, well out of earshot of the neighbours, who'd been hanging around in the drive, but after finding her voice for a moment, that stern, no-nonsense tone of hers, and swiftly proceeded to talk about how all her trust in him was now destroyed, and how she had only ever had his best interests at heart, how she had always striven to be a good, loving mother, sacrificing her own wants and needs for him, he said something like, 'Yeah, well, it's not how it felt, is it? I wish the whole lot had gone up. I wish you had gone up with it too. I hate you. And this fucking life.' That was when she really started crying. When these glistening drops of hurt began streaming down her face.

5

Why does this woman still want to help me, Mark thinks, watching his mum attempt a U-turn in the street, not paying any attention to the camber of the road and allowing her car to roll heavily backwards into the kerb, crushing the bumper almost in half, after all the grief I've given her?

But as she finally manages to get the car facing the way she wants, downhill, and accelerates away with a brief, stiff-lipped nod and a wave – her royal wave, he thinks, the wave she adopted when she married Lawrence and moved into his swanky executive home – clearly not in the slightest bit concerned about her bumper, about whether she's permanently damaged her car, Mark has an idea that he knows why she still wants to help him, why she hasn't written him off yet. He thinks it's because a parent can forgive a child anything. Because it is only natural to constantly make allowances and exceptions for your kids. To give them the benefit of the doubt – so they'll love you back.

However, he's not sure whether it works quite so smoothly, quite so naturally the other way round, which makes him immediately start worrying about Lily again. About whether she'll forgive him (even though it should really be Nicole she has to forgive), and come and stay with them again. About whether she'll ever forget the fact that he was missing for most of her life. About whether she'll stop this Mark crap and always call him Dad.

He doesn't know exactly what is happening inside his brain, quite what is whizzing through his creaky emotional circuit board, but he feels increasingly hung up on Lily. As if he's developed an addiction. Which amazes him. An addiction. And he was the person who never went anywhere near drugs, for fear of losing control and making an idiot of himself, for fear of collapsing on the deck, dead as a dodo, after only a couple of drags, for fear of becoming hooked, and he now finds he seems to be addicted to Lily. A harmless, skinny fourteen-year-old girl who he's only seen a handful of times in the last ten years. He can't get her out of his mind. He can't stop feeling guilty one minute, for not having been able to take closer care of her, and revengeful the next, towards those who should have been looking after her when he couldn't – those people, those scum who so badly abused the authority they had.

It's time for action, he thinks. Time he took control of the situation. With force if necessary, considerable force. Words have never got him anywhere. Words have always failed him. As far as he's concerned, words are for wimps. Besides, he's said far too much for him as it is. He feels he's been gassing on like a madman – to his mum, to Nicole, to Kim – exhausting his mind with the sheer effort of explaining himself, of justifying himself, of simply trying to exist. He's the one who should be locked away.

6

Nicole says, before he has a chance to tell her of his plans, to inform her of what he finally intends to do regarding Lily, and with the rest of his life too, he reckons, she says, still breathless from walking up the hill in the wet and the wind, and the freezing early evening, late February dark, at least breathless with excitement if not the exertion, 'Guess what?'

'What? says Mark.

'You've got to guess,' she says, standing with her back to the sink, her hands on her hips, with her chest thrust forward, making her anything but massive breasts actually appear a half-decent size for once, Mark thinks, at least fuller than he ever remembers them being, while grinning wildly, and nodding her head too, attempting to flick an especially highlighted curl off her cheek with the move-ment, this fleck of almost pure white – she's let her hair grow longer than normal, which he likes, though is slightly uneasy as to why she's decided to do this, as he's always suspicious when she changes her look, her style, of any change of course. In the morn-ings, before she's washed and styled it, when it's all tousled, she looks dead dirty to him and he can't help but imagine her appearing like this to other men, to her immediate boss at work, this John Read character, after he's just shagged her. After they've driven out of the city at lunchtime and done it on the grey leather seats of his top-of-the-range five-series, in a lay-by, or just pulled over in a quiet lane somewhere near Salhouse say, as that's what people are always doing in their cars around there from what he saw when he lived nearby. With this fat, balding man having run his sweaty, chubby hands all over her body, through her hair, inside her fancy new knickers.

'How the hell do I know?' he says. 'I don't want to think about what you get up to when you're out of the house.'

'Don't be mean, Mark,' she says, raising her eyebrows – these wafer-thin strips of down that she spends so much trouble over, plucking and tinting, reshaping and colouring. 'Go on, guess?' she says, thickly, softly, while pouting a little. This obvious attempt of hers to be alluring, to be seductive, to be sexy, revolts Mark as he considers what she's been up to recently, and with whom.

'Whatever it is, I don't care,' he says, moving towards the doorway to the lounge, thinking he can't even be in the same room as her at the moment, that her presence is destroying him.

'Thanks a lot,' she says, suddenly sounding both angry and accusatory. 'The minute Gemma's out of earshot you can't help but be unpleasant and aggressive. Well, sod you, I'm not going to tell you what it is now, anyway. You've ruined it, as usual. My big surprise. I was so proud too. You pig.'

'Sorry, Nicole,' he says. Sick of saying sorry, feeling that that is all he ever does say to Nicole nowadays. But even though he feels Nicole's presence is destroying him more than ever, tonight he doesn't want to lose her. He doesn't want to say or do anything fatal. He could never bring himself to swipe her, to actually make contact.

For some stupid reason, he thinks, he still feels drawn to her, he still feels aroused by her, and that life without her in their cosy terrace halfway up the hill – their slice of paradise, he laughs to himself – would be much worse than life with her. The prospect of her just not being around terrifies him. Plus he does feel that there's some hope left in the marriage, that they'll pull through once he's done what he has to do regarding Lily – once he's executed his plan of action, once he's asserted his authority, once he knows she loves and respects him really. He'll feel a lot better about himself then. Sure he will.

'I'm sorry,' he says. 'You know I've been under so much stress over the last few months, what with my work situation, and the police sniffing around Darren, and all the Lily stuff going on, of course. Do tell me, Nics, please. Come on, love. I can't guess. I haven't got a clue. I'm sorry, sweetheart.'

Then he gets it. Then he realises what Nicole was about to tell him, standing there with her swollen tits and long, shaggy hair, being saucy, and excited and proud, being every bit the woman he first met in the queue outside KFC on Prince of Wales Road – she was with a couple of friends and though he was on his own he made himself noticed and eventually started talking to her, wanting to know whether she'd like to share a Bargain Bucket with him, just the two of them. He can't believe he's so thick, that he's so fucking insensitive. That he never sees what's right in front of his eyes. 'You're pregnant,' he says, smiling. 'You're fucking pregnant. How about that?'

'No, Mark,' she says, laughing. 'Don't be silly. You don't honestly think I'd consider having another child with you at the moment, being the way you are?'

'You mentioned something about it a while ago, over Christmas,' he says. He hasn't forgotten Nicole saying, 'What if we have another child?' of course. And her wanting to do it *au naturel* – he eventually realised what that meant. 'You were up for it then.'

'No?' she says. 'It must have been because I was pissed, or more like pissed off with Lily for taking up so much space. I mean, I'd rather have a baby than have her hanging around here for ever. Perhaps I thought if we had a baby you'd come to your senses and stop running after some teenager who just wants to take advantage of everyone, who's totally manipulative and destructive, who you can't trust an inch. OK, I recognise she's got problems, serious problems, and needs help but there must be ways of doing that which don't have to sacrifice everything else around her. Maybe, Mark, I thought it was about time you realised where your priorities should lie and get on with looking after Gemma and me, and the house. Our little set-up, which used to work so well, didn't it?'

'What do you know about priorities?' he says. 'Who's the person who mostly picks up Gemma from school and gives her her tea? Who sees that she does her homework? And who's always tidying up the house, hoovering and putting the washing on, wiping the sinks with Cif? It's me nowadays, isn't it?'

'Yeah well, who's out at work, earning the money to pay for it all?' she says. 'The stupid floozie, as you keep calling me. The old tart. And you know what, you know what I was going to tell you? That you couldn't guess because you're too busy worrying about yourself to ever think about anyone else? I've been promoted, haven't I? I've been made a director and given a whacking great pay rise, and I'll be getting a company car as well. A BMW, hey? One of those five-series things you love so much.'

He looks at her, unable to smile, unable to change his expression, unable to move a muscle in his face, hoping his mood will suddenly change. Hoping the right words will come, and quickly.

'Well, say something,' she says. 'Don't just stand there like a gormless chicken.'

'So who did you fuck to get that?' he says. He can't help himself. He doesn't want to be like this. He wants to be pleased for Nicole. He'd like to feel proud of her. He's tried. He's constantly trying. But he just feels duped. How else could she have got such a big promotion if she hadn't fucked the boss, at least if she hadn't done some major flirting – he knows how the office world works, certainly how it works in this city. But he realises it's not only Nicole who's drastically let him down, by making him feel so useless, so insecure, it's his mum as well, and in their very separate ways Gemma and Lily too. It's all these women, these females. This alien species.

He sees her approaching from the corner of his eye but not in time to stand back or duck – maybe not believing for a second that she has it in her either – and not having braced himself, the sudden force of her swipe, the sheer weight of her clenched fist landing square on his cheekbone with a loud thwack – a sound that explodes inside his head – sends him sideways into the fridge. Despite the ringing in his ear, the rapidly intensifying pain, and the shocking realisation that Nicole has attacked him, with real force, he's conscious of hearing the contents of the fridge, and the fridge shelves and compartment dividers no doubt too, smashing and rolling all over the place. And holding the side of his face, he can't help imagining the mess in there. The shards of glass in Gemma's tea leftovers – a sausage and a couple of potato dinosaurs. The ketchup splattered on the interior light casing. The vinegar from Nicole's pickled gherkins seeping into his streaky bacon, and pooling in the empty vegetable compartment. He only defrosted and cleaned the fridge last week, spending ages over it.

Shouting in his ear, his other ear, the one that he's not clasping and which still seems to be working, Nicole says, standing in front of him, having pinned him against the side of the fridge, having totally stunned him, having knocked him into submission, Nicole shouts, 'Why have you become so bloody suspicious of me all the time? Do you honestly think I'm having an affair? That that is how I really got a promotion? You sexist arsehole. Or are you just jealous of the fact that I'm the one who goes out to work, while you spend your days moping around here feeling sorry for yourself? Is that it? You're not the person I married, Mark. You've changed. Beyond all recognition. You're pathetic. I don't know what I'm still doing with you. I should have kicked you out months ago.'

7

Waiting for Kim to answer the phone, with the phone pressed against his ear, his sore ear, he quickly realises, changing the phone over to his other ear, he starts thinking – lightly rubbing his bad ear and the lump on his cheekbone with his free hand, while listening to the ringing tone in his good ear, and suddenly not wanting anyone to answer, even though he's sitting on the toilet with the handsfree, well out of earshot of Nicole – that he never hit Kim as hard as Nicole hit him in the kitchen the other night.

If he is to be completely honest with himself, if for once he doesn't let pride get in the way, the fact he's not as tough as he'd like to think, he can only draw the conclusion that he never hit Kim anything like as hard as she hit him either. When he did nudge and poke her, and maybe kick out at her shins, at her arse if he could reach – after, of course, she had driven him to despair, and words had failed him – she certainly clobbered him back. And how. With her fists, with her feet. She bit him too, on the arms mostly, though occasionally on his legs and neck, and pulled his hair, often managing to wrench out handfuls of the stuff, totally spoiling his latest cut – he was always having to return to Miranda's, and getting Wendy, the pretty junior stylist who did men's hair there, to rework what he had left, his beautiful, shaggy hair.

Kim maintained she'd learned to fight back as a kid, when her dad and her uncles, followed by a whole series of her mum's boyfriends, had a go at her. She said she'd always retaliate if they tried to touch her up, or whack her for misbehaving, or most commonly just whack her for getting in their way. She warned him before he married her, when, he will never forget, they were in bed together and he hadn't managed to get much of an erection because he'd drunk one lager top too many, that if he ever tried any funny business behind her back, if he ever snuck off with some slag, she'd have him, she'd totally floor him, because she could be a right dirty little fighter.

Believing, when they did resort to scrapping, that he always got the better of Kim, that he at least gave her what she deserved – because he was the man, because he was obviously the stronger of the two, the dominant sex (so he liked to think) – made him feel better about himself. This lie, this self-deception helped him through those many months when he had lost all status he'd ever had within the relationship. When he could have easily let it get to him and spent the time worrying about whether anyone would ever take him seriously again – as a normal bloke, warranting a bit of respect. How could he have ever inflicted much damage on Kim, anyway? He was never vicious enough. He was no match for her.

'The game's over, Kim,' he says, as soon as the phone is picked up, but before anyone on the other end of the line says anything, before he even knows who's answered.

Though it is Kim on the other end and she says, 'Hello, Mark, what's got into you today?'

'Don't say anything you're going to regret,' he says. 'Or I'll use it as evidence against you. I'm warning you.'

'You haven't given me a chance to say a word yet,' she says.

'I'm not going to be pushed around by you,' he says. 'You've done enough harm over the years, having everything your way. Fucking off with my daughter when you felt like it. Well, I'm in charge now. I'm taking control of Lily. I don't want you to have anything more to do with her. Just count yourself excluded from her life from now on.'

'You think you could do any better with her?' Kim says. 'You wouldn't know where to start, you useless twit. Anyway, have you spoken to her recently? She doesn't even want to know you, not after you, and your pretty blonde wifey and cute little Barbie kid, made her feel so welcome at Christmas.'

'Of course she wants to know her dad,' he says. 'I'm going there tomorrow if you have to know. Maybe I'll even take Lily home with me. See if you can stop me. See if anyone can stop me.'

'Oh, Lily's really going to listen to you,' she says. 'And the consultants, they'll be all ears. I bet you haven't even cleared it with them. They won't let you in the gates. That place is not a joke. It's run by the local council. They keep tabs on everything. I made sure of that – I wouldn't have had Lily sent to just anywhere. I wouldn't.'

'I have, actually,' he says. 'It's all above board. You'll find out. When you no longer have any access yourself. When it dawns on you that you'll never see Lily again, at least not for a decade.'

'You're not living in the real world, Mark,' Kim says. 'You're unhinged. That's probably where Lily gets it from.'

'I've already warned you,' he says. 'I can make this a lot harder for you than you ever made it for me. You think you're a dirty fighter, you just wait. You've got a big surprise heading your way, Kim.'

'All right,' she says, 'I give in. You can have her. She's all yours. If that's what you want. If that'll make you feel better about yourself, for being such a lousy father. For being such a lousy human being more like. She's yours, Mark. You're in charge. You're responsible. Good luck to you.'

'See,' he says, 'I knew you never really cared for her. I knew you were always trying to get rid of her, palming her off on those dirty hippy travellers, and all sorts. You selfish cunt. How can you live with yourself?' He switches off the phone, realising Kim's already hung up, and having no idea whether she meant what she said about him having Lily. However, rubbing his cheekbone again with the tips of his fingers, softly massaging this disfiguring lump of still acute pain while sitting on the toilet with the lid down and locked in the bathroom, with the door closed and locked to keep Nicole not just out of earshot but at bay too, he at least knows he's serious about taking control of Lily, of her life. It is just the beginning of his plan of action – the reversal of his fortunes. Maybe he will remove her from the so-called live-in adolescent unit, from this Berkshire House, if he doesn't think it's suitable. If it doesn't meet the high standards of care he believes his daughter deserves. She's not a loon. She's not disturbed. How could she be? She's just a kid. His kid.

8

It feels totally illegal. Like a getaway in a stolen vehicle. A real tear-up. As if he's fourteen again. Despite being at the wheel of the Astra, and leaving the city on the A11 in broad daylight. However, he hasn't told Nicole where he's going, he doesn't think she has a clue – he left the house while she was upstairs dressing Gemma. Normally when he's stomped off, without saying a word or otherwise, he's headed into the city on foot, now he's really flying, doing a ton on the Wymondham bypass – with plenty of oomph left under the bonnet, more than he reckons Nicole's new BMW will have anyway – watching the white lane markings merge in front of him and the countryside squeeze into tight, camouflage-coloured bands on the periphery of his vision.

There are few other vehicles about, and with his head feeling suddenly so much lighter than it has done for ages, he begins to enjoy the sensation of pulling out to overtake the cars and trucks which he does come across and then slowly moving back into the near-side lane. Out and then in. He does this manoeuvre when there are no cars in sight also, imagining he's leaving a perfect snaking trail behind him. One of those wavy lines Gemma is always having to draw for homework to practise her eye–hand co-ordination, her motor skills. Well, he's practising his motor skills, he thinks, while having embarked upon his mission, his nearly secret mission.

Just as he hasn't informed Nicole of his intentions today, well, he hasn't told Lily, or any of her supervisors, what he's up to. He didn't want to be rejected before he'd even got there, and knew that his best chance of getting access, his best form of attack, as ever, would be to take everyone by surprise. Which, obviously, was how Kim managed to whip Lily away from him all those years ago.

Hitting a snarl-up at Snetterton, with lights and lane restrictions, and heavy road resurfacing equipment travelling in his direction, he realises he shouldn't have told Kim what he intended to do on the phone last night, but he couldn't resist the urge to taunt her, to tease her, to get a little of his own back. He wanted to hear the concern, the fear, the anger in her voice when she realised she might lose Lily for good. Not that he then heard that. She simply handed Lily over, didn't she? Which could at least mean, he decides, with the traffic now completely halted, with this massive asphalting machine attempting to turn off the single carriageway but having taken too acute an angle and got stuck, that Kim hasn't warned Lily, or any of the officials at Berkshire House, that he might be coming. That because she's so unconcerned about him taking charge of Lily – ultimately wanting to wash her hands of her – she hasn't sought to protect her interest. But whatever the opposition he's determined to see Lily. Perhaps he will take her out of Berkshire House and disappear with her. Why not? As he sees it there is nothing much to keep him at home, as Nicole is barely speaking to him, except to outline her plans for kicking him out, except to say she can't stand the sight of him any more and will whack him even harder if he dares come anywhere near her, while Gemma, copying her mother as usual, has also violently taken against him and won't even be in the same room as him. He doesn't have any work. The possibility of him doing some transporting for Darren collapsed the minute the police started sniffing about Darren's business interests – in fact, he wouldn't be surprised if they turned up at his soon, with the amount of stuff he's bought off Darren over the years. He could easily get done for handling stolen goods. The more he thinks about it the more he realises it might be the only option left to him – to disappear for a while, to

make himself scarce, to begin yet again. He and Lily could hit the
road big time. They could trade in the Astra for an old camper van
and become New Age travellers, hooking up with some tribe in a
lay-by in Dorset, or North Wales, or the Outer Hebrides. Lily
would show him the ropes. She'd sort him out with the right gear
– a pair of baggy orange trousers, a holey mohair sweater, and a
pair of German-made sandals. She'd show him where he could get
his nose and eyebrow pierced and where he could get a tattoo of a
cannabis leaf on his shoulder. She could teach him to inhale the
bloody stuff too, without throwing up. And to drink gallons of
scrumpy and eat veggie burgers, and shit in the woods using leaves
for toilet paper.

His Lil, he thinks, as the traffic starts to flow and he flicks the
Astra into first, gently squeezing the hyper-sensitive accelerator,
his precious Lil, his only hope – all that he's got left in the world.
He wonders whether she needs him anything like as much as he
needs her right now. How he wants her to adore him, to love him.
To forgive him.

Reaching inside the glove pocket, while taking his eye off the
road every few seconds to check the tapes he's tossing on to
the passenger seat, he eventually manages to find the one he's
looking for, in its distinctive bright green casing, and slots it into
the Blaupunkt. It is already rewound to exactly the right spot, he
finds, as the pipes and drums at the beginning of 'Fernando' slowly
fade in. It's a kids' tape, *Kidz Abba*, which he bought for Gemma
knowing he'd be able to listen to it as well without Nicole mocking
him, without her accusing him of having awful taste, worse than
her dad's, and though the songs are not sung by the original
members of Abba, the production is plenty good enough for his
dulled eardrums, for his long-battered senses.

As he starts to sing along, and accelerate harder, he begins to
realise quite how much he's going to miss his car with its old
though highly responsive 16-valve, 1.6-litre engine, its eight-
speaker hi-fi system and numerous other top-of-the range accessories. But he's prepared to sacrifice it all for Lily. So she can have a
happy and fulfilling future. A life free from neglect and abuse.
With a loving, caring dad always on hand. Like a shield. Like a
great sword and a shield in one he'll be, for ever marching a few

steps ahead of her. Banging on his drum. Protecting her from any danger.

9

Nobody stops him. Nobody checks who he is – there are no gates or checkpoints, no barbed wire or electric fences. He's not sure what he was expecting but it certainly wasn't a big country house with a long, tree-lined drive and sweeping lawns. Though as he parks in the nearly empty car park and walks towards the building, hugging himself tightly in a hopeless attempt to block the freezing wind, he sees that the place is in a bad way. A number of the windows are broken and the dark red paint on the woodwork appears to be either cracked or flaked off completely, while wispy trails of graffiti cover large areas of wall. Rounding a clump of unkempt bushes to the side of the house, he comes across three or four dilapidated Portakabins, one signposted Reception, another Out-Patients. So far he has neither seen nor heard anyone and for a moment he begins to wonder whether the place is in fact deserted and that Kim actually gave him the address of a defunct loony bin on purpose, when Lily started in January – which, he thinks, might explain why last night on the phone she seemed so happy to say he could have Lily if that's what he wanted, knowing he'd never find her.

When he tries the door to the Reception Portakabin and finds it is locked he's sure he's been duped by Kim once again – and that it will be the second time he's driven all the way to Berkshire and not seen Lily. Shaking his head in disgust – with himself, mostly, for being so stupid, and trusting of other people – he slowly walks over to what appears to be the main entrance of the big house, dragging his feet through the slimy shingle as he goes, leaving long skid marks. Because of the gusting wind and the apparent lack of any human activity and the fact that he's in an unfamiliar environment, an almost derelict setting, he's becoming increasingly spooked and starts to wonder about what terrible acts must have occurred here in the past. Abuse on a scale he can barely imagine, abuse way beyond what a few hippy travellers are capable of – with people being tortured and raped and then throttled to death. With girls Lily's age, with girls as young and vulnerable as Lily having being done in on a massive scale.

Approaching the double door, two girls wander out and try to pass him on the worn steps. One of them stumbles into him so heavily he has to check she hasn't damaged his sweater. She hasn't, nevertheless she doesn't say sorry, which he thinks she should do, or acknowledge him at all. He turns and watches them as they make their way across the shingle, noticing how Lily-like they are, being tall and scrawny, and wearing skimpy, ill-fitting clothes. They both have bare midriffs and no coats, which amazes him given the ferocious weather, and he's sure he can hear the jangling of their hooped earrings and studs and chains and whatever else it is they pierce themselves with today, above the gusting wind and the sound of their unsteady footsteps on tiny stones.

It is not until he's inside a second set of double doors that he comes across anyone official-looking, discovering a large woman in a blue nurse's uniform sitting behind a boxed-in counter. On the drive here Mark had thought he'd ask some kid to locate Lily for him, hoping he'd be able to bypass the proper route – as, of course, he's never got very far with people in authority, with the police, or with the social services – but this woman catches his eye and he nods back, knowing he'll have to go through her.

However, he quickly discovers that she's not at all difficult or officious, introducing herself in a friendly enough manner as the nurse-in-charge. When he says he's Lily's dad and he's come to see his daughter, she says that's nice, because Lily never gets visitors.

Signing himself in, he asks her how Lily is, and the nurse says, looking at the ceiling and huffing, 'How are any of them? I try to keep out of their way. You should have made an appointment with the consultant, or her keyworker if you wanted an assessment. I'm just here to hand out the medicine and to stop the place from burning down.' She points him in the direction of the TV lounge where she thinks he'll find Lily, if not he's to come back and she'll send someone to fetch her from her room, as visitors, even parents – he's sure she winks at him when she says this – aren't allowed in the patients' rooms.

Feeling he's achieved much already, that he's passed some sort of test, with, amazingly, a person in a position of authority, with a proper uniformed official, and that things will maybe edge his way after all – delighted with himself, in fact, for having finally embarked upon this mission – he follows the nurse's directions past a wide staircase and along a freezing, grubby corridor, until he comes to the second door on his left. From the corridor he can clearly hear a TV. He thinks he can hear people talking and laughing excitedly too. Plus a crackling sound he can't pin down. A spitting, crackling, sandpapering sort of sound.

IO

There was no way he suddenly walked out on Kim and Lily and the boys, he thinks. He didn't make some dramatic departure. He just started spending the odd night at Darren's and then his mum's and Lawrence's, unable to bear Kim's tantrums and violence, her lies and deceptions any longer.

The relationship had reached the stage where he couldn't even confront her about the men she was seeing on the sly – notably Chris and then this taxi driver called Ian. Despite Mark having plenty of proof, like overhearing her tell Chris on the phone that she thought he was 'one sexy beast', and calling him 'darling' on several occasions, and saying she couldn't wait to see him next, and that she loved him too, and then seeing her kissing this Ian character in his taxi as he dropped her off late at night after she'd supposedly been working, seeing them actually groping each other in the front of the car, with their hands absolutely nowhere in sight because they were obviously buried under various layers of clothing, because his hands were up her skirt tearing at her under-wear and hers were well dug into his flies. Despite Mark having endless proof, including of course prime examples of Kim's stained knickers, which he'd hidden away in a compartment of his tool box, she still wasn't prepared to accept any of it, only fiercely lashing out at him if he dared discuss the subject. She became especially useful with her titchy, size-four feet, somehow being able to boot him in the kidneys from quite a distance. That always made him bend over double, gasping for breath, which was when she'd move in for a bit of hair-pulling – with her arms and legs flaying, with her screeching wildly too. She sounded like a fox, like the foxes that went for the rubbish in the cul-de-sac in the middle of the night. This terrible screeching rang in his ears for days.

No one warned him Kim was seeking an exclusion order. He had no idea what an exclusion order was until a court-appointed solicitor rang him at his mum's to explain the charges and the details, and to inform him also that a temporary exclusion order had immediately been put in place. That was when Mark realised just how much Kim had been distorting the truth behind his back. How she'd been telling anyone who would listen – the police (who admittedly had had to come to the house a couple of times to break them up, but thank God, Mark's always thought, as he might have been completely finished off otherwise), her doctor, and especially the social services – that her husband beat her up, that he physically and mentally abused her and was constantly threatening the kids too. The social services were her biggest ally, of course. They believed every word she said. They thought she was the victim.

What has always struck Mark as being particularly unfair about Kim getting the exclusion order placed on him, an order that effectively banned him from seeing Lily too, was that he never once harmed his daughter. She might have witnessed the odd scene, but he never deliberately hit her. Not even when she was being a right pain in the arse. If anyone did smack her on purpose, or shake her, or grab her by her thin, tufty red hair, it was Kim. Kim was much tougher with Lily than he ever was. She was forever losing her temper with her kids. She was always on the verge of walloping them.

And what also gets Mark about the exclusion order is that no one ever wanted to hear his side of things. Not the social services, not the police, not the magistrates. Even his solicitor didn't want anything to do with his evidence, his proof, saying she couldn't possibly produce a pair of Kim's soiled knickers in court – that that would only have an adverse effect. Mark didn't see why. He didn't get it at all.

However, as things materialised he discovered that the exclusion order wasn't the worst possible thing to have happened, it wasn't the crisis his mum made it out to be. That came a few weeks later when his family disappeared, and no one would tell him where they'd gone. The police, the social services, Kim's solicitor weren't saying anything about their whereabouts, only bothering to inform him that he was still obliged to fulfil his maintenance obligations, by direct debit, he seems to remember, which he certainly wasn't going to do. Quite what sort of a mug did they take him for? Though as it was in the days before the Child Support Agency (which managed to snare Darren a few years ago) no one eventually seemed too keen to pursue the matter. Maybe, it has occurred to him, they slowly realised he had been punished enough.

'How else are we meant to keep warm in there?' says Lily.

'Can't they turn up the heating?' says Mark, aware how quickly boiling his car gets, sensing the feeling coming back into his fingertips as he drives away from freezing Berkshire House, with his daughter safely in the passenger seat beside him.

'Nah, they're too mean,' she says.

'So they just leave you to start fires all over the place?' he says.

'Yeah,' she says.

'They don't mind about the furniture?' he says, alarmed to have found Lily, and a few other girls in the TV lounge, sprawled on the floor in front of a huge open fireplace, with flames roaring and spitting from the grate, where clearly a couple of broken chairs had just been heaped. As far as he could tell there was no fire guard in the room, no sense that the fire was being monitored by anyone in charge, even that it should have been started. It looked completely dangerous to him. Like it could topple over and set the carpet alight.

'I suppose they get a bit narked when we use the chairs and stuff, and try to ban us from the TV room or from going out for a bit,' she says. 'But it's not me who usually starts them. A couple of girls here are really crazy.' She laughs, a forced-sounding, high-pitched cackle Mark hasn't heard from her before. 'They burn everything. You should see their arms.' She laughs again. 'And Gaynor's bum. It's covered in scars.'

'No thanks,' he says, glancing at Lily, worried about what else she might have picked up from her short time at Berkshire House apart from the terrible laugh, though he's surprised by how well she looks. She has put on a considerable amount of weight – her face is no longer so caved in, indeed it's almost puffy, and her arms, encased in a tight-fitting, long-sleeved white top, appear thicker and stronger, and he notices her bare midriff actually bulges slightly, that flesh is beginning to spill over the low waistband of her flared jeans. Her skin is smooth and shiny too, waxy almost, while her hair is now a much lighter reddy brown. He's not sure whether it's still dyed, or is at last its natural colour and that she somehow managed to wash out the black. It's the colour he always imagined her hair would be at this age.

He was also surprised by how she reacted when he appeared in the TV lounge. She didn't say, 'Hi, Dad,' and leap to her feet and run over to kiss him, but she did immediately acknowledge him. She smiled and waved, at least she flicked open the palm of her hand at him and then held up three fingers. When she did finally get to her platformed feet and walk over she continued to smile, despite her mates jeering and wolf-whistling, and one girl shouting, 'Where did you pick him up, Lily?' And another, an extremely overweight black girl with braided hair Mark couldn't help noticing, saying, 'Save some for me, honey.'

Mark is sure Lily's smiling and waving was genuine enough, that she was truly pleased to see him. Perhaps, he thinks, gripping the steering wheel tightly, making a special effort to concentrate on the road, to be fully prepared to cope with any dangers that might spring out at them, it was recognition of her love for him, of her love for her father. At least she hasn't yet mentioned anything about disappearing after Christmas and leaving the hate-you note. She definitely hasn't mentioned anything about not wanting to see him ever again. In fact, she was more than willing to get in the car with him, having encouraged him to simply tell the nurse-in-charge that he was taking her out for the afternoon, which apparently he was allowed to do seeing as he was a parent and it was a

Saturday, and the nurse-in-charge never bothered to check who had prior permission from one of the consultants anyway, or who was currently banned from leaving the premises.

As far as he can see everything is back to normal with him and Lil. Better than normal – there's no way he's going to jeopardise the situation by bollocking her for having run off on Boxing Day, or interrogating her about what she really got up to in London for those couple of days. Right now he feels they'll make a great little team, motoring around the country, in a clapped-out van, living from day to day, doing away with material comforts, behaving like proper hippy travellers. Without any ties. Always one step ahead of the authorities. Not catchable. Quite unstoppable.

Except he hasn't driven more than a couple of miles when Lily says, 'Where are we going, Mark?'

And he can't bring himself to say Scotland, or Wales, or Dorset, all places he's never been before. He can't bring himself to say, I thought we'd run away together. I thought we'd sell the Astra and maybe buy a van – which, of course, he should always have had for his work – and tour the country, stopping off here and there to do some fruit-picking perhaps, some craft-making, some jewellery-making. Only looking out for each other, as a father and daughter should every so often, he reckons – with all things being fair.

It's not in him. He might be a hopeless fantasist, but he'll never be a hopeless hippy. He can't seriously see himself in a pair of baggy tie-dye trousers, behind the wheel of a Dormobile, listening to a warped recording of *Astral Weeks* on a cheap cassette player. He's still not sure he can see himself taking sole care of Lily, actually accepting that responsibility despite making all this noise about it. So he says, in the same way that he'll always defer a difficult decision, that he'll always let someone else make the next move, the defining move, and before he's obviously had time to think about an alternative plan of action for giving Lily a new start in life, for extracting her from Berkshire House, and thus from Kim's influence for good (just because he realises he might not be quite ready to manage Lily on his own full-time, to make that commitment, doesn't mean he's not still certain about wanting Kim to have nothing to do with her), he says, while loosening his grip on the steering wheel and letting his shoulders drop, maybe sensing a small bit of him collapsing internally, as if he's finally started to break up from the inside out – crushed by the sheer weight of his paternal and emotional inadequacy, by his failure to be a strong, decisive dad, by his failure to be a decent human being for once – he says calmly, distractedly, knowing he should be screaming, 'Where do you want to go? I've never been to this part before. I don't know what there is. You tell me.'

12

She directs him to the pub. She tells him, in between loud bursts of her sickening new laugh, that the supervisors at Berkshire House are always searching their rooms and nicking their alcohol. She says she's lost loads this week. A whole stash of Hooch. And that she's dying for a drink.

The pub is large and bright, standing just by a roundabout with no other buildings in sight. Though because it is set against the backdrop of bare fields sunk in gusty twilight, it looks warm and comforting to Mark, with the spotlit Harvester sign running along the top of the building acting like a beacon. He's pleased Lily suggested the pub and that the pub was close because he knows it will give him time to collect his thoughts. There must be plenty of options left open to them, at the very least there still has to be time for them to scarper (if he could just be a little more of a man about the situation), especially if they're now going in the Astra. They'd make Scotland in a flash.

Lily has clearly been to the pub before and he follows her through the wide, fully carpeted entranceway and across an empty bar to a side room which stinks of crisps and stale smoke. There are a number of flashing video-game machines, a big, blank TV screen in a far corner and three or four chest-height round tables with matching high stools.

'We always go in this bit,' she says, walking up to a video machine – a TT Racer motorbike game, Mark sees – and running the backs of her fingers over the controls. 'They don't mind us in here and it's the only place you can smoke. Have you got any change?'

'Yeah,' he says, handing her the few loose coins he can find in his pocket. 'I'll get you a drink. What do you want? One of those Bacardi Breezer things?'

'No way José,' she says, sorting through his money, obviously unimpressed by the lack of it. 'That's really naff. I want a Dooleys.'

'What the hell is that?' he says.

'Never mind, Grandad,' she says, 'just order it. And get me a straw too, will you?'

Mark leaves Lily inserting coins into the machine, crouching in her platforms, with the soft flesh on her sides bunching over the frayed waistband of her jeans. He walks out of the room and back towards the main bar, thinking that Berkshire House might have managed to fatten Lily up a bit but no one there seems to have taught her any manners. However, he's determined not to make an issue of it, desperate not to upset Lily in any way and have her storm off, bang in the middle of nowhere.

The two barmen chatting to each other at one end of the main bar either remain unaware of Mark as he walks up to the counter, or ignore him on purpose. 'Oi,' Mark says, not knowing whether the pub is empty because it is the middle of a Saturday afternoon or because it really is isolated. Or most likely, he thinks, because the staff are complete jerks. 'How about some service?' he says, though he immediately regrets saying it quite so aggressively, knowing that he should try to avoid having a confrontation with anyone this afternoon, and he adds a 'please'.

A tall, thin, spotty kid with heavily gelled dark brown hair eventually sidles over, though he serves Mark pleasantly enough, even finding a couple of straws. Dooleys, Mark discovers, popping the straws into the bottle, is a creamy, toffee-flavoured vodka, and walking back to the video-games room, with the Dooleys and a pint of lager top for himself, it occurs to Mark that maybe Lily has been putting on weight because she's been downing massive quantities of this stuff, of Dooleys, and Hooch and probably the odd Bacardi Breezer for old times' sake as well. That these drinks with their sickly mixers must be incredibly fattening. OK, he's never been keen on straight alcohol and needs a dash of blackcurrant in his lager, and some lime in his vodka, but he thinks toffee-flavoured vodka sounds disgusting, a real girl's drink. A tart's drink.

'What do they feed you on?' he says, placing the drinks on one of the high tables near the TT Racer machine which Lily is still playing. 'You know, at the place.' He doesn't know what to call Berkshire House. School? Nuthouse?

'Drugs mostly,' Lily says, not looking away from the machine, with her right hand grasping a small joystick and with the forefinger of her left hand maniacally tapping a panel of buttons. 'They give us this stuff which is meant to stop us getting edgy and being like disruptive and depressed all the time. To keep us cool, man.'

'Ritalin?' he says.

'They used to give me that,' she says, still not looking up, 'but they give me different pills now. It's weird, sometimes they can really knock me out, and other times I feel as skitzy as ever. You're not supposed to drink alcohol or smoke spliff with them but everyone does. You think I'm fat, don't you?'

'No,' he says, reaching for his drink and taking a small sip. 'No way.'

'Well, why did you ask me what they feed me on, then?' she says, inserting more money into the machine. 'Because I am fat, aren't I?'

'You're not fat,' he says. 'You're not as skinny as you were when I last saw you, that's all. But you look better for it, Lil. You don't want to be too thin, it's not nice. No one wants to see your bones sticking out all over the place, like some famine victim. That's horrible. That's disgusting.'

'So I used to look disgusting and now I look fat?' she says, letting go of the joystick and thumping the row of buttons. 'Give us some more change, will you?' Mark hands her what coins he has and she slots 50p into the machine and pockets the rest, then takes a long sip of her Dooleys before placing the bottle back on the nearest table and pressing the start button, being careful to avoid looking directly at Mark. 'I've scored eighteen thousand three hundred and thirty four on here before, the top score ever,' she says, beginning to move the joystick and maniacally flick the buttons once again.

'Is this what they teach you up the road?' he says. 'How to be champion video-game players?'

'They don't teach us anything,' she says, releasing a rapid burst of her high-pitched cackle, either because of what she's just said or because she's caused a massive pile-up on the screen – he's not sure. 'We just sit around having these sessions, and consultations with our keyworkers, and these community meeting things where no one ever says anything. It's a joke, man.'

'Something must be said. What do your teachers, or whatever they are, say?'

Mark feels awkward addressing the back of Lily's head, standing behind her while she attacks the machine. He wonders whether he should just sit down and wait until she finishes. Though he thinks it's possible she'll never finish, and in a way he's finding talking to her without actually looking at her, while indeed she's almost totally occupied doing something else, easier than if he were sitting face to face with her, and with her giving him her full attention – if she's capable of doing that.

'They just try to get us to talk about ourselves and stuff,' she says.

'What stuff?' he says.

'I don't know, Grandad, just stuff.'

Mark would like to think that being called Grandad was a step closer to being called Dad, than just being called Mark, but he knows it isn't, that if anything it's worse. 'What, like your past, your upbringing, things like that?' he says.

'Yeah, yeah, yeah,' she says. 'All that shit. What, are you going to interrogate me all day, too?'

'Are you going to be on that machine all day?' he says.

'Until you get me another drink,' she says.

So he gets her another drink. He goes back to the bored barmen and orders another Dooleys and another lager top for himself, wondering what she has told the people at Berkshire House about her past, whether she's told them she was abused by her mum's boyfriends, or about the fact that she didn't see her dad for ten years because her mum decided he was too violent – and too much of a threat to the other kids as well as her, that's what Kim told the court – and he returns to the side room to find that Lily has moved over to another machine.

'What did you tell them?' he says, placing her new drink on the gently sloping top of the machine this time. She ignores him, concentrating hard on the screen, where an animated snowboarder is racing down a mountain, zig-zagging around boulders and other snowboarders, and suddenly doing somersaults and split-second leaps and twists, and he asks her again, 'What did you tell the teachers about when you were younger, and were a traveller, and lived with all those dirty hippies? And why your mum ran away with you in the first place?'

'I don't know,' she says, 'what I felt like.'

'Did you tell them about, you know, being abused? Did you tell them what you've told me? How those men made you touch their what's-its?'

'Maybe,' she says, stopping for a second to have a drink.

'Did they believe you?' Despite wanting to remain calm and not wanting to wind up Lily, despite thinking he's done exceptionally well so far today, Mark finds he's becoming increasingly agitated – at the very thought of his daughter being abused, at the thought of her not being abused but making out she was. What does he know? What does he know about anything any more? No one has ever told him the truth.

'Why don't you ask them? They take enough notes,' she says. 'I'm sure they'll tell you what's wrong with me. Every single thing.'

'What is wrong with you?' he says, sensing how sticky and clammy his hands are, with spilt Dooleys and sweat, but not wanting to rub them on his trousers, and not for a moment expecting Lily to give him a straight answer.

But she says, turning towards him as well, and letting go of the controls, leaving the snowboarder to career down the mountain unaided, free to do his flips and twists at will, to make yippee sounds and to splatter into other snowboarders and jagged grey rocks with an electronic groan and an 'oh no', she says, facing him at last with her bluish-grey eyes, her puffy cheeks flushed from the screen and probably too much Dooleys, 'They say I suffer from low self-esteem. That's what's wrong with all of us at the unit, apparently. Low self-esteem. Like we don't respect ourselves. Like we want to harm our bodies by not eating, or cutting our arms, or burning bits of us. Like we want to do ourselves in all the time.'

Stepping back, reeling from the warm blast of Lily's sweet, sickly, alcoholic breath, reeling from her forwardness, her frankness, Mark says, 'How do you get that then?'

'From having shit parents,' she says, pulling a squashed cigarette packet out of a front pocket. 'From not having a dad around. From not having a dad to tell me I looked pretty when I was seven. That's what they say.'

'I'm here now,' he says, realising that he probably hasn't spent as long with Lily on her own in one go since he used to take her to feed the ducks by The Swan and then to warm up in the arcade, since she was a toddler, still drinking from a bottle, still in nappies.

'Yeah, well, it's a bit late, isn't it?' she says, retrieving a long cigarette butt from the crumpled packet. 'Why have you come to see me anyway?'

'To see how you are,' he says, relieved to watch her light the charred butt with the slim, gold-plated lighter he gave her, thinking that at least she's using this present, that at least she's kept it, and that surely it means she values and respects him to some degree. If she was really fed up with him, and totally blamed him for messing up her life, for giving her low self-esteem, for making her want to harm herself, surely she would have thrown it away, or perhaps sold it – like he sold the fancy watch Lawrence gave him all those years ago.

'You could have phoned,' she says, inhaling deeply.

Noticing, as she removes the butt from her lips, that her hand is shaking violently, he says, 'Yeah, well, I wanted it to be a surprise.'

'Why would you want to surprise me? You don't care about me. You don't know me. Even my mum doesn't want to know me any more, getting me sent off to that loony bin up the road. You know why she did it? So if I kill myself she doesn't have to clear up the mess. People do themselves in all the time there. Like once a week. It's famous for it.'

'Lil,' Mark says quietly, aware a group of lads have entered the room, while sadly, perhaps resignedly, beginning to wonder whether he'll ever be able to convince Lily of his true convictions, 'You know I care for you – how many times do I have to tell you? You know I love you. You're my daughter, for Christ's sake.'

'What's that bruise doing on your head, then? I bet you had a fight with Nicole and she chucked you out for being a jerk – it takes one to know one, all right – and because you were feeling sorry for yourself you thought you'd come and pester me. The one person left who you imagined was stupid enough to go along with your shit. That's it, isn't it? Poor Lil, who nobody else wants. You thought I'd come running.'

'No, no,' he says, reaching for his lager, feeling slightly less conspicuous behind the pint glass while he's drinking, though he takes a much larger sip than he intended and some of it goes down the wrong way, making him cough and splutter, only helping, he's sure, to make himself appear guilty. When he has cleared his throat and can breathe properly, he says, though sounding hoarse, 'I don't know what you are talking about.'

'My mum says you were always attacking her,' Lily says, 'and were like this big control freak who never let her out of your sight. She says you were paranoid mad and blamed everything on your mum for marrying some swanky idiot, and your dad for taking your brother off with him to America or wherever, and not you.'

Lily's shouting now, and Mark can feel they are being closely observed by the group of lads who are just a few steps away. He wants to get out of the pub. He wants the conversation to end, though he wants to prove to his daughter that she's wrong – that Kim was lying to her (and all the others) and that Nicole hasn't chucked him out, and that he's not paranoid mad, as she put it, and blames everything on his mum for marrying Lawrence and his dad for taking Robbie off to Canada and leaving him behind – his dad for always favouring Robbie who happened to look just like him, everyone said so – but most of all that he does love her, his little Lil, his funny features, his beautiful teenage daughter, the love of his life. 'None of that's true,' he says. 'You've got it all wrong. I'll tell you what happened between your mum and me, I'll tell you everything. But not now, not here in this pub. Besides

Nicole hasn't chucked me out. She hasn't. No way. How can I prove all this?'

Then it comes to him. Finally, it comes to him with a force that makes him feel slightly dizzy and not quite himself. It comes in a flash, a massive surge of electricity, soldering every circuit in his brain, providing instant, glaring clarity. He's had similar feelings before but this time he's certain it's a message from outside, from another being, from God, who he's never believed in, who he's never really thought about, but so what, he's prepared to admit he's been wrong in the past. He'll take Lily back home with him, this minute (where else was he ever going to take her?) and show her that he does still have a wife – a wife who'll never say nasty things about her stepdaughter behind her back again, he'll make sure of that – and a young kid, and is therefore capable of holding together a secure, loving family. That'll be his vindication. His proof. What's more, he'll bring Lily home with him for good.

Nicole will come round to the idea, of course she will, because she is rational and sensitive and understanding, and does ultimately love him, regardless of the fact that he gets so jealous – what man wouldn't, he thinks, if they were married to a woman like her, with her super-athletic figure, her shapely legs and tasty trim fuzz? – and isn't afraid to use his hands, to become physical if necessary. She won't have changed the locks, as she suggested she would do last night. She won't bar him from entering his home. She won't do that. Not if he's with Lil. There's no way she'll just leave them out on the pavement to freeze to death. Besides, he can't possibly take Lily back to Berkshire House, where she'll only slash her wrists, or take an overdose, or set fire to herself, from what she's led him to believe.

'I've got it,' he says, grabbing her arm, ready to guide her out of the flickering, stinking room, ready to escort her to his car, and to the beginning of the rest of her life – pleased that at last he's the one who's being decisive, at very least – 'come back home with me,' he says, tightening the grip on her arm, starting to pull her out of the room, 'and see for yourself. Come and live with us. I'll make sure you're made welcome and that no one says nasty things about you when you're not in the room. Nicole has been under a lot of pressure at work recently but now she's been promoted she's fine.

She's as happy as ever. She never means what she says anyway, Lil. Come back with me, love.'

He can see how it will all work quite happily, with Nicole earning this massive salary, and with him staying at home to look after the kids, cooking their tea for when they get back from school – complicated, nutritious, free-range dishes too – making sure Lily gets to bed early, as well as Gemma, being every bit one of these sensitive, domesticated, modern males.

'It'll be all right,' he says. 'I promise you. I'm not like your mum. I'll never get sick of you and send you off to some nuthouse. I'll always be there for you. Come on, Lil, love, make my day.'

She's moving with him, though hesitantly, dragging her platforms on the dull, patterned carpet, letting her hands, her arms snag on anything solid. Mark's acutely aware of these lads watching everything and for a moment he wonders whether Lily's doing it for their benefit, so they can think he's some pervert, dragging this drunk-looking young girl with a bare midriff, with acres of exposed flesh, flesh that is soft and baggy, and flushed and pierced, outside to be done in. 'What can I do to persuade you?' he says, knowing that if she says yes everything will work out, knowing that she has to say yes because it's a message from God. Knowing that he can't afford to lose her again, that he can never let her out of his sight for even a second. That without her everything is lost. 'What can I give you? What can buy you?'

'Another Dooleys,' Lily says. 'Get me another Dooleys and a packet of fags, then I'll see.'

13

You know, he thinks to himself, breathless and driving on automatic – letting the patchy road whip under him and the shadowy, near-colourless verge quickly sink into deep night, so in a way it's like he's driving in a dimly lit bubble, a cocoon, with the whole cocoon shifting along the M3 at seventy, or maybe it's more like a spaceship, a half-baked extra-slow-moving spaceship (he's not going to be pulled over for speeding) – there was a particular moment when he realised he couldn't live with Kim any more. When he knew she had finally gone too far – and only he knows quite how much torment he had to put up with.

But what was peculiar about this moment was that they hadn't been fighting beforehand. They hadn't even been arguing. They had been having sex. Not violent or rushed sex – as was normal – but quiet, cosy sex. With both of them tightly gripping on to each other, with their arms, their legs, almost afraid to let go. When they had finished and separated and with probably both of them feeling embarrassed at the calm intensity of what they had just done – given that they had barely been communicating with each other for weeks – Kim said, and she hadn't said anything throughout the whole act, certainly none of her usually smutty, scary come-ons, none of her 'fuck me harder', and 'throttle me', comments, she said, 'Does your brother really exist, Mark? I mean, are you sure you haven't just made him up, and this whole scenario about him going off with your dad? And how poor little you were left behind with your wicked mum who promptly married some chinless wimp and had you move into his swanky executive house with her, which you then tried to burn down?' Rolling away from him she continued, 'You know what I think? I think you've invented it, most of it, anyway – I mean, it's not exactly a normal family break-up, is it? I don't know any men who'd have taken even one kid with them – in the hope that people will feel sorry for you, because you've got nothing else going for you, have you? You've got nothing except your self-pity.'

Somehow remaining calm, perhaps because most of what she said hadn't yet penetrated deeply enough his consciousness, his feelings, he tried to explain to Kim what it felt like to have members of your immediate family, to have people who are a part of you, just walk out of your life one day. He tried to explain what it felt like, in these strange few minutes of unusual calm, what it felt like to be betrayed by your dad and your mum and your kid brother also. To be unloved by them.

She said, 'You won't get anywhere in this life unless you let that stuff just brush off you, as easy as dried dirt. What the hell do you think I've put up with in my life? Do I go on and on about never having a dad, about how my uncle used to stick his finger up my fanny when I was six? Do I ever complain about that stuff? No. Do I let it eat away at me? No. I get on with the next thing. I move on. When the shit gets too heavy I move on and forget about the past. I block it out. I say, that's it, it's over. Never again. It's all you can do.'

'You're inhuman,' Mark said, knowing she would never understand him. Knowing his very existence, everything that had shaped him, was being doubted by this woman. His very being. Who he was and where he came from. The life he'd striven to make for himself. Because he was not capable of so casually dismissing the past, his chequered history – strongly believing, being ever the traditionalist, the conservative, in the importance of maintaining roots, of building on family ties, of laying down the seeds, the foundations for future generations. Of trying to belong.

Merging on to the M25 clockwise, and finding the four lanes surprisingly devoid of traffic, seeing this virtually clear super-highway stretching to the very parameter of the Astra's full-beam light field, he says, staring ahead, his focus absorbed by the edge of this light field, where the light suddenly tips into blackness, this vast wall of blackness, this endlessly oncoming blackness, this black hole of blackness, he says, thinking of Lily, and with no sense of bitterness seemingly left inside him, not a shred, exhausted, sated, he says, 'I'll tell you what happened between your mum and me. It's simple, really. People are made differently, very differently, and they don't always get on. Just as families don't always stay together. Sometimes it's better for people to split up and start afresh – a long way away from each other. Completely out of contact. But that doesn't mean I didn't always have a special place for you in my heart. This soft spot.' He laughs, he laughs to himself, he laughs out loud. A soft spot. A fucking soft spot. Continuing clockwise, towards the M11 turn-off (Why shouldn't he still go home? Where the hell else is he meant to go?) in the odd emptiness of an early Saturday evening in March, Mark can see what Lily's inherited from him all right. A need to feel wanted, to feel loved, to feel that you belong, and the capacity to lie and be dishonest to achieve that small ambition, that small, and not at all unusual, he thinks, necessity. 'Haven't you, Lil?' he says, looking over at her slumped in the passenger seat, with her head having flopped forward and lolling slightly with the motion of the car, with the lights from the dash playing quietly on her now near-luminous skin and those stainless-steel studs. He knows she hasn't been listening to a word he's said, and said coherently, lucidly for once, just as he never listened to his dad when he tried to tell him why he was splitting up with his mum – did he? When his dad burst in on him while he was watching Abba on *Top of the Pops*, mesmerised by the blonde one's bum.

Having looked over, he can't stop glancing in her direction, feeling he should do something to make her more comfortable. To check, as he used to do when she first came home from hospital – a six-and-a-half-pound baby girl with tufts of scaly orange hair – that she is breathing normally. That her airways are clear. When Kim wasn't looking he was forever walking over to her crib and putting his ear to her face, her chest. Though who is he still trying to kid? Of course he knows she's not breathing normally. That only a short while ago he deliberately blocked her fourteen-year-old airways. Crushing her windpipe. Snapping a couple of small vertebrae in her neck.

14

He can't believe how easy it was. That she barely struggled. That indeed it was in him.

That having eventually left the pub, after Lily had tricked another three Dooleys out of him – and then still insisted he take her back to Berkshire House – he found himself motoring along quiet country lanes, somehow having taken a wrong turning, somehow completely accidentally but thankfully having done that, with Lily clearly beginning to doze off in the passenger seat beside him. And soon bursting for a pee, his cock throbbing and solid because of the urge, as it often is first thing in the morning, he pulled over by a small, deserted electricity terminal plant, being careful to drive the Astra gently over the deeply rutted track. But instead of leaping out and finding some tree to piss behind he shifted in his seat so he could more easily observe his daughter. By now she had totally zonked and was breathing slowly and heavily as her chest, her distinctly womanly, Kim-like chest, and smooth bare belly steadily rose and fell. He has no idea how long he sat watching her, this hypnotic rising and falling, this mesmerising, living, breathing female body – with the windows steaming up, with his shocking erection. His cock was hurting him badly, being blocked inside his tight jeans, with him sat at that odd angle so as to face

Lil. But he didn't want to get out of the car, he didn't in any way want to disturb his girl. His dozing princess, his sleeping beauty, with her oddly large bust, her pushed-up, Kim-like tits. Her almost Gail-proportioned breasts.

Unable to breathe as softly, as calmly as Lily, unable to regulate his breathing to anything like hers – in the way he and Kim and later he and Nicole used to try to do going to sleep (he used to think you couldn't get closer to anyone than that) – he tried to ease the pressure in his crotch by changing his position, knowing he'd drunk too many lager tops and still thinking of Gail, and of giving Gail one in Chapel Field Gardens when he was fourteen, and then of having sex with Kim for the first time in the toilet of Henry's, at least getting a blow job off her – the sheer sense of achievement, of acceptance, of release those encounters induced.

However, he didn't stop hurting, even as he stretched himself across the middle of the car and was practically on top of Lily, where he thought he'd remain a while, and love her, closely, tightly, before he had to take her back to Berkshire House. Before he lost her for ever.

However, he wasn't going to let that happen – was he? He wasn't going to lose his child, his baby again. Oh, no way. Meaning to kiss her, to brush his lips across her forehead, her cheeks, a corner of her mouth perhaps just so he might be able to taste her, her sweet, Dooleys-flavoured saliva – meaning to just steady himself while he was kissing and loving her (this daughter of his and Kim's, of Kim's especially at that very moment, with her inflated tits and alcoholic breath, and the lazy way her legs seemed to have swung apart – what was she doing to him?), he slipped his fingers around her throat, just as he used to slip his fingers around Kim's throat when they were having sex (at her insistence, of course, entirely at her insistence) and slowly squeezed.

With Lily going in and out of focus as his eyes watered and his body throbbed and burned, with the rising and falling of her chest notably ceasing, with her breathing being replaced by a low, nasally sucking sound, Mark realised that this was the only way he could protect her, from herself, her rapidly ripening, teenage self, and from her classmates – her fellow inmates – and from Kim as well, of course, and all the other dangers out there – the dirty uncles and disgusting hippy New Age travellers, the pimps and perverts, and misguided social workers who so ill-treat disturbed young girls like Lily – and keep her with him for ever. Keep her by his side, loving him, respecting him, taking him seriously. As he would never have abused her himself. He would never have let himself soil his daughter, his own flesh and blood.

Squeezing harder, sensing his hands, his thumbs particularly pushing into a strange empty space in her neck, pushing and stretching her skin into this space with them, and hearing the sucking sound increase in noise but become intermittent too and perhaps a little gurgly, really short bursts of this terrible, dying sound, he was aware of Lily's face becoming wet with his tears, with his tears falling on her unlined forehead and soft, childish cheeks, and a tear even hitting that stupid nose stud, and a growing wetness on his own face and hands, on his legs somehow, this hot wetness all over his thighs and middle, and then her big, black platform boots began to pound the floor while her knees banged into the glove compartment, which made him only squeeze harder still, much harder, as instinctively part of him didn't want her wrecking the interior of the Astra, or his sweater, though her arms remained strangely by her sides, as if she were never really aware of what was happening, as if all the Dooleys, on top of the drugs she was taking to stop her being skitzy, had finished her already. Or maybe he never knew how strong, how effective his hands could be, despite the long years of carpentry, despite all his past battles. Despite having been stuck for words before. Because while he was squeezing something gave in her neck, some piece of cartilage, or bone, both maybe, and her struggling, her stamping and banging, her appalling gurgly sucking for air, immediately stopped and her head, her lovely, soft face – bearing his nose and eyes and angular bone structure, bearing so many of his features – fell forward like a baby's. Like a tiny baby's.

He wishes her head wasn't still flopped forward quite like that, thinking she looks so uncomfortable and that he might have to stop at a services to rearrange her. However, he's pleased she's by his side, that he didn't leave her on the rutted track by the lonely pylon, or bury her in some field. Of course he kept her with him. She's where she was always meant to be. Besides she's his proof that she does love him and want to be with him – more than Kim. That she can't do without him, her dad. He's going to show Nicole and Gemma this, that he is capable of caring and loving, that he is capable of being a proper, grown-up human being, worthy of a family, a smart car and a comfy home. He'll show everyone who's ever doubted him this very simple but essential fact. He'll show them, because even if he were able to explain himself they were never going to listen to him anyway. He'll show them what he's capable of, what hands are really for. How life is going to be from now on. When he gets home.